"You must lock away your heart at all costs."

Falling in love was the darkest moment of Garrett Wollstonecraft's privileged youth, even as he and Abigail Hughes shared a blissful summer of passionate promise. Sworn to keep Abigail safe from the curse plaguing generations of Wollstonecraft men, Garrett sacrificed his future happiness. Now, fourteen years after he lost his heart, Abigail reenters his life. But the woman who arrives unannounced at his ancestral manor is very different from the sheltered girl Garrett once knew.

The widow of a country doctor, Abigail can't forgive Garrett for his cruel rejection. Yet she can no longer keep the truth from him—a secret that could have resulted in her ruin. But as the embers of desire reignite, and Abigail and Garrett slowly rebuild trust, a malicious enemy plots against them. Is their love strong enough to break free from the sins of the past— and to end the tragic cycle that consigns Garrett to a life of loneliness?

Visit us at www.kensingtonbooks.com

Books by Karyn Gerrard

The Hornsby Brothers
The Vicar's Frozen Heart
Bold Seduction

The Ravenswood Chronicles
Beloved Beast
Beloved Monster

The Men Of Wollstonecraft Hall
Marriage With A Proper Stranger
Scandal With A Sinful Scot

Published by Kensington Publishing Corporation

Scandal With A Sinful Scot

The Men Of Wollstonecraft Hall

Karyn Gerrard

LYRICAL PRESS
Kensington Publishing Corp.
www.kensingtonbooks.com

Lyrical Press books are published by
Kensington Publishing Corp. 119 West 40th Street New York, NY 10018

All Kensington titles, imprints, and distributed lines are available at special quantity discounts for bulk purchases for sales promotion, premiums, fundraising, and educational or institutional use.

To the extent that the image or images on the cover of this book depict a person or persons, such person or persons are merely models, and are not intended to portray any character or characters featured in the book.

Special book excerpts or customized printings can also be created to fit specific needs. For details, write or phone the office of the Kensington Special Sales Manager:
Kensington Publishing Corp.
119 West 40th Street
New York, NY 10018
Attn. Special Sales Department. Phone: 1-800-221-2647.

First Electronic Edition: June 2018
eISBN-13: 978-1-5161-0547-2
eISBN-10: 1-5161-0547-8

First Print Edition: June 2018
ISBN-13: 978-1-5161-0550-2
ISBN-10: 1-5161-0550-8

Printed in the United States of America

To my husband, who always finds the time to critique and beta read my stories. Love you.

Acknowledgments

Many thanks to Martin Biro, editor, at Kensington Publishing, my editor, Amanda Siemen, and my agent, Elaine Spencer from The Knight Agency. What a support you all are!

Prologue

Insolvent Debtor's Court
Lincoln Inns Fields, London
Early January, 1845

Garrett Wollstonecraft, and his nephew, Riordan, sat in the gallery of Insolvent Debtor's Court, awaiting the hearing of Riordan's father-in-law, Baron Thomas Durning. Four imperious-looking judges in robes and white wigs sat before a long table high above everyone. Directly below, the barristers sat to their right, the debtors to their left. The room was crowded, the air stale, the lighting as inadequate as the heat on this frigid winter day. Due to the dimness, an aura of gloom hung over the proceedings.

Riordan's bride, Sabrina, decided not to attend her father's hearing, which was completely understandable since the loathsome man had tried to sell her on three different occasions, most recently to the equally loathsome Marquess of Sutherhorne. It was by sheer luck that the Wollstonecrafts managed to locate Sabrina before she'd been hidden away. Despite his despicable behavior, Garrett gave the baron a reluctant nod for not fleeing to France to escape his debts, as many peers before him had done. Durning had stood his ground, facing his fate head-on. Let justice be done.

"The blasted man deserves a worse fate than debtor's prison," Riordan whispered fiercely to Garrett. "We all agreed to keep the incident quiet to protect Sabrina, but he deserves to be sent to Newgate Prison to rot. Surely kidnapping and selling another human for profit would be adequate enough for a conviction."

"For a common man, it would. It's a miscarriage of justice when peers are protected above all others," Garrett solemnly replied. "This was the only solution, especially since you wished for Sabrina to be protected from speculative gossip, which I wholeheartedly agree with."

"Yet Sutherhorne walks free," Riordan replied in a low voice. "A miscarriage of justice indeed."

Garrett couldn't agree more. "We will remain vigilant. I don't trust the marquess. He is a soulless cretin who will seek revenge. Mark my words." He no sooner spoke when the marquess strode into court, causing a buzz of excitement. A lumbering brute of a man followed directly behind him and took a seat next to him in the front row of the gallery.

The marquess turned and stared at them, his expression dark and chilly. Once they had rescued Sabrina from her father and Sutherhorne's clutches, the marquess had threatened: *This is far from over. I will never forget the humiliation.* Judging by the way Sutherhorne glared at them menacingly, Garrett believed this *was* far from over. He was ready. It would be his distinct pleasure to break the thin, putrid old marquess like a brittle stick.

"Hear ye, hear ye! Court is in session."

Sutherhorne turned his attention toward the judges. The baron tried to catch the marquess's attention. Was he hoping for a last-minute intervention? A payment of the debt? But Sutherhorne patently ignored the desperate man. He had come to watch his downfall, not assist him. Garrett's original assessment held true: the marquess was malevolence personified.

As the court proceeded, people from all walks of life were hauled before the judges, their sentences rendered in swift fashion. At last, the baron stood before the austere justices. "With the sale of Durning House and all its possessions, the sum is inadequate to meet all creditors," a barrister intoned.

"How much of the debt is outstanding?" a judge asked.

"Twenty-six hundred and twenty-two pounds, my lord," the barrister answered, reading from an officious paper. "And thirteen shillings and seven pence."

"My lord. Here are thirteen shillings and seven pence. I will at least cover that much," Sutherhorne sniffed, holding up a handful of coins. The court broke out in raucous laughter, and Durning flushed with embarrassment. So the marquess was not only here to observe the baron's disgrace, but to humiliate him as well. Garrett couldn't keep the contempt from his expression as he glared at Sutherhorne.

"Order!" One of the judges banged the gavel. "The bench acknowledges the Marquess of Sutherhorne. Even though you meant it as a jest, we *will* take the coin tendered." The judge ordered the bailiff to gather up the offering. "Baron Durning, are you able to pay the outstanding amount?" "No...my lord," he muttered, looking down at his shoes.

"It is the judgment of this court that you be taken to Queen's Prison in Southwark immediately, and remain there until such time you can meet your debt in full. Next case."

"Debtor's prison, as we surmised. Well, some justice at any rate. We should take our leave," Garrett suggested.

They headed for the exit, but were blocked by the marquess placing his silver cane across the doorjamb. "Satisfied by the verdict?" he sniffed. "Had to see for yourself the man's downfall?"

God, this man made Garrett's blood boil. "As did you. And no, we are *not* satisfied. *You* are still free from the guilty verdict you so richly deserve," he growled. "Remove your cane or I will..."

"What? Assault me once again? Here, in a room full of witnesses, including judges? Knowing of your animal urges it would not take much to provoke you to a response. Your temperamental Scottish blood will lead to your ruin." Sutherhorne gave him a slimy smile of contempt.

Garrett's fury bubbled to the surface, but he fought showing it outright. Be damned if he would allow this sorry excuse of a peer to goad him. "Remove the cane, or I will snap it in two, and do the same to you, as I promised. Remember?" Garrett's voice was low, the tone deadly.

"Ah, a decided threat. Did you hear him, Delaney?" he said to his brute. Delaney, an indifferent expression on his face, replied with a brisk nod. They were attracting attention. Sutherhorne, at last, moved his cane. "We will meet again, and then we will see who snaps whom in two. Good day, gentlemen."

Garrett pushed his way through the door, and Riordan followed until they stood outside on the cobbles. Hell, Sutherhorne could rile him. The family had made a true enemy of the marquess.

"You're correct, Garrett. He's a soulless cretin. I detected the hate in his eyes—and the desire for revenge." Riordan blew out a cleansing breath. "Shall we head for Wollstonecraft Hall?"

"I have further business. Since you have to take up your schoolmaster position once again in Carrbury, head home to Sabrina. Tell Da I'll return by the end of the week."

"Very well." His nephew hesitated, then met his gaze. "Thank you for all that you've done, not only in assisting me these past several months, but our entire lives. You are the rugged stone on which our family's foundation is built. The mortar that holds us together. We all feel this way. I wish more than anything for you to find love and happiness as I have. If anyone deserves it, it is you."

After the men went their separate ways, Garrett relaxed in the inn's common room, sipping a tumbler of scotch. Riordan's generous and heartfelt words still reverberated in his mind. It humbled him to know that his family thought well of him.

Strange lot, the Wollstonecraft men. Once touched by tragedy, they did not give their hearts easily. Happiness? Love? Garrett decided early on to lock his heart and toss the key. It had only been engaged once. So long ago it was if it had happened in a dream. Her name formed on his lips, begging to be spoken aloud, but it remained a quiet whisper. *Abbie.*

Never again. Frowning briefly, he pushed the memories away, as he often did.

He was better off alone.

Chapter 1

Two days later
Whitechapel, London

A curse could be a damnable weight to carry, but Garrett reasoned he had shoulders broad enough to handle the burden. How does a curse come about? Did a medieval witch cast it on the ancient Wollstonecrafts for an imagined slight, or was the sixteenth century Earl of Carnstone born under a black moon, passing the curse down through the generations?

Every man born through this particular bloodline of Wollstonecrafts suffered incredible tragedies. Women in the family, either born or wedded into it, did not live long. Didn't matter how many times the man remarried.

Why such darkness hung over his family remained a complete conundrum. After all, they had dedicated their lives to progressive causes and the plight of the poor, especially his father and brother in parliament. It should count for something. Yet sitting here in Edwin Seward's office in Whitechapel, Garrett wondered if the curse moved beyond romantic attachments to include other aspects of the Wollstonecraft men's lives. There was no better example than his brother Julian's oldest, Aidan.

His nephew had been missing for close to four months, as if he'd fallen off the edge of the earth. Since he was only six years older than his paternal twin nephews, Aidan and Riordan, they all were more like brothers. They shared a close bond, as did all the men in the family, but none like the one he shared with the twins.

Riordan was happily settled, and though Garrett had tried to make him see sense regarding the curse, he would have none of it. He was deeply in love. No talk of an ancient curse had deterred him from Sabrina. Well, it was his decision. Garrett could only wish them the best.

He turned his attention back to Aidan, the main reason he'd remained in London. The reason he hadn't had a decent night's sleep in weeks. For more than a year, Aidan had been wallowing in the seamy underbellies of London and Bath by sinking into even darker, more debauched depths. Despite his vices, he'd kept in touch. Returned home every month without fail. Well, until last September, that was. Shortly thereafter, the contact ended.

Garrett had hired an ex-Bow Street Runner, Edwin Seward, and finally the investigation bore fruit. Garrett decided to keep the information to himself until he had a chance to probe into the particulars.

At that moment, Edwin strode into the room, a thick folder clutched in his beefy hand. The man was nearly as tall as Garrett's own imposing six-foot-five frame. An aura of danger followed Seward, and the jagged scar running down the left side of his face added to the implied menace.

"Edwin."

"Garrett." He sat with a huff, slamming the folder in front of him. "Where would you like me to start?"

"Where is Aidan?"

Edwin opened the folder. "As of last night, he is living in a rookery in St. Giles, a doss-house on Petticoat Lane."

"Jesus." St. Giles was one of the worst slums in London. Even the coppers loathed to enter it because of its maze of hovels and alleyways. Overcrowding, squalor, and the resultant stench, along with a generous helping of disease, completed the bleak picture.

"We're friends, correct?" Edwin asked.

They'd known each other for years, originally met in Scotland one summer. Both were half Scottish and visiting relatives, so they gravitated toward each other and kept up a correspondence through the years. When Garrett ventured to London, they would meet and share a pint. "Absolutely."

"Why are you taking this burden on yourself? Why haven't you told your brother, Julian? Your father, the earl? Or Aidan's brother, Riordan? Wasn't he here in London with you? If I've overstepped the bounds, tell me."

A fair question. "No, not overstepping. Guilt perhaps? Aidan's decline was slow, over a period of years, and instead of reaching out and trying to discover why he behaved in such a manner, I became disgusted and ignored him. We all did. I turned away when he needed me most, and because of it, didn't hear his cry for help under all the arrogance." Garrett exhaled a shaky breath. "I also want to protect Julian and the rest from the worst of this."

"I just met your brother a couple of months ago, but I have the distinct feeling he will be livid when he finds out that you didn't inform him of his son's discovery right away," Edwin said.

"No doubt, but one drama at a time. Aidan means the world to me, both the twins do. They are much like brothers instead of nephews, and when we were younger, they often followed me about like eager puppies." He paused, as speaking of this caused a lump of emotion to lodge in his throat. "I love them. Aidan especially. Though always in one type of trouble or another, he possessed a good-natured charm, which meant that I couldn't stay annoyed at him for long. There is goodness in him. He's worth rescuing. I aim to be the one to do it."

"Fair enough. I'll do all I can to assist you in your quest."

"I appreciate it, Edwin."

"To continue. As your brother suggested, we've been watching your family's bank for close to two months. Last week, a man approached the building, hesitating, as if deciding whether to proceed inside. He fit the description, and resembled the small portrait that you gave us, so we instigated a surveillance. I thought it best not to contact Julian until we were sure of his identity." Edwin flipped a page over. "The subject did not enter the bank, and my man followed him to the aforementioned doss-house on Petticoat Lane. He's not alone. There are at least four or five others, with many more coming and going at all hours of the day and night."

After clearing his throat, Edwin continued. "I had my man blend in with the great unwashed, and he got close enough to observe that the place is used for deviant pursuits. Opium. Orgies. From what my man reported, financed by thievery and prostitution. There are two women in there with the men. Probably prostitutes."

Garrett rubbed the bridge of his nose. Aidan had hit rock bottom, sunk to the lowest depths. Hearing this, he was glad that he'd decided to keep the discovery from Julian. "They're living in total filth," Edwin stated. "I'm not sure if you have ever been to St. Giles..."

Garrett stood. "Let us head there with all due haste. Extract him immediately."

Edwin shook his head, motioning Garrett to take his seat. "One does not casually wander into St. Giles. This will take planning and a number of men, more than I employ. Also, when we snatch him up, what do we do with him?"

Garrett arched an eyebrow. "What is your meaning?"

"Aidan is in no fit state to return home. Let me read you this: 'Aidan Wollstonecraft is emaciated, wearing dirty, ragged clothes, hair long and unwashed. Appears glassy-eyed, stumbling when he walks. When he speaks, his words are slurred. The subject is suffering from acute addiction.'" Edwin looked up and caught Garrett's worried gaze.

"Your nephew will need medical attention, long-term care for his withdrawal. I have taken the liberty of contacting a private sanatorium. It is north of here, in Hertfordshire, outside the village of Standon. It is run by a Welsh physician and the cost is expensive. But he has done miraculous work with those addicted to opium. It's becoming a rising problem in all classes. The place is confidential and clean; I have inspected it myself."

"Aidan is in such poor condition, then?" Garrett whispered.

"Aye. He's extremely ill, physically and otherwise. I'm sorry it has taken us this long to track him, but apparently the group of hooligans that he's running with move about often. We may have never found him. It's only by chance we spotted him when he approached the bank." Edwin paused. "If he continues down the path he is on, Aidan will be dead in a matter of months. When the dragon gets its claws in you...well, it's a sorry state indeed."

Shaking his head, Garrett said sadly, "I never would have believed Aidan to be weak of character and sink to such depths."

"Society sees opium and its derivatives as merely a bad habit. Dr. Bevan and his predecessor, Dr. Hughes, see it as an addiction of which certain people are more susceptible than others. Not by weak character, but by a brain disorder. His treatment is humane, not like at the asylums. There Aidan could be diagnosed with moral insanity and never see the light of day again. You do *not* want your nephew to go to one of those places."

No. He didn't. Garrett had heard the stories. People were locked up in no better than a prison cell. Mechanical restraints were used, as well as inhumane treatments that involved dousing with water hoses and hours of endless prayer. "What is your strategy?"

"We head in at the break of dawn. There will be ten men all told. We seize your nephew, and the three of us will head straight to Standon. We will need a private carriage. Fresh water. A bucket in case he starts to vomit before we arrive. The journey will take several hours, and he'll begin to go through withdrawal, which includes nausea, vomiting, aches, cramps, body tremors. His bowels could let go."

Garrett grimaced. "You know a good deal about this, Edwin."

"Aye," he replied softly. "More than I care to. Dr. Bevan set me on the path of recovery. He'll do the same for your nephew."

Edwin? Succumbing to an addiction? The man stood for all that is tough and unyielding. If addiction could fell him, what chance did Aidan have?

"Then we shall make plans." How in hell could he explain all this to his father and brother? What will Riordan do? The twins were close, or had been up until Aidan disappeared. He rubbed his forehead, as a sharp ache had taken root.

No matter. Aidan was family, and Garrett would do anything to protect him. If cloistering him away in a small village clinic would assist in his recovery, then he would do it. The Wollstonecraft men stuck together. History had given them a hard hand, and their allegiance was the one constant they had, other than the curse.

* * * *

The early dawn sun cast a disturbing illumination over the slums of St. Giles, where raw sewage ran in rivulets down the broken cobblestone streets. Gin cellars and distillers packed the overcrowded courts and narrow lanes, while men and women addled by gin staggered about or lay unconscious in filthy alleyways. As the group of formidable men crossed into Petticoat Lane, Garrett saw a prostitute being rutted against a brick wall in the alley, her tattered skirt pulled up to her waist showing a dirty leg covered with sores.

Bile rose in Garrett's throat, but he swallowed it down. The clash of rank odors was enough to bring up one's breakfast. Sweat, human waste, and rotting garbage in overflowing rubbish bins. Dead animal carcasses—could be dogs and cats, hard to tell—lay in some of the alleys. The building that they were heading toward had broken and boarded-up windows and a decaying foundation. Gloom and despair were clearly present in this section of London. It was worse than he could have ever imagined.

Garrett carried a club, as did many of the men. Edwin held a pistol, and kept it in plain sight to show that they were not to be approached.

"We'll have to make this quick, for our presence has no doubt been reported. The criminal in charge of this section of the rookery will send his men along sharpish," Edwin said.

One of Edwin's burly group kicked the door in with little effort, as the wood was rotten and splintered apart. Edwin ran up the dark, narrow stairway to the third floor, with Garrett right on his heels. The building was not quiet; shouting, swearing, and crying voices drifted in from all directions. Due to the boarded-up windows, the dour place lay in darkness. Luckily, one of the men carried a lighted lantern.

"In here?" Edwin indicated to one of his men.

"Aye."

Edwin gave the door a shove with his shoulder and it gave way. At least there was some light, as the one window had a tattered piece of sheer material hanging over it. Garrett scanned the room. Dirty mattresses and wooden pallets filled the floor space with unconscious people of both sexes sprawled across them in various states of undress.

The stink was enough to gag a horse. Rubbish lay across the floor, rotting food, empty gin bottles, dried vomit, and buckets overflowing with piss and worse. There had to be close to twenty people crammed into the crowded area.

"Do you see him?" Edwin yelled.

His eyes lit on a familiar form. Aidan lay on a mattress, wearing nothing but frayed trousers, with a young man curled up to one side of him and an older woman curled up on the other. The young man stroked the front of Aidan's trousers, as the woman trailed her tongue across Aidan's nipple. An opium pipe lay on his nephew's chest. Aidan looked ghastly, hollow-cheeked, haggard, and near death's call from months of debauchery.

"Here," Garrett called out. Edwin rushed to his side, and together they brought Aidan to his feet. He mumbled incoherently, limp in their grasp.

"Move out," Edwin bellowed. They hurried toward the door, dragging Aidan, as he was semiconscious and not able to place one foot in front of the other. The stench of him made Garrett's nose twitch and his stomach roil.

The older woman screamed, "They're takin' our luverly Aidan! Stop 'em!"

Some of the people on the pallets stirred, but the men were out of the room and down the stairs before any of them could take action.

"Head to the carriage," Edwin commanded. Two men stepped in their path, as if to halt them, but Edwin's men felled them with clubs before Garrett could even blink. Thank God Edwin could navigate the twisting lanes. They made it to New Oxford Street, the main thoroughfare that ran through the middle of the rookery. Since it was under construction, confusion reigned, making escape easier to achieve. Here they parted, with Edwin and Garrett bundling a moaning Aidan into the carriage while the other men splintered off, running in different directions.

Edwin thumped the roof of the carriage. "Move!" he shouted. With a snap of the reins, the conveyance lurched forward.

Aidan lay across Garrett's lap, limp, with eyes closed.

Edwin grabbed a blanket. "We'd best wrap him in this; he no doubt has fleas and worse. Plus the cold chills will start soon enough."

"I hardly recognize him," Garrett whispered worriedly. "He's lost too much weight."

"Opium will do that. It leeches the good right out of you." Edwin sighed. "I'll not sugarcoat this: he's in a bad way."

Garrett nodded as he assisted in covering Aidan in the woolen blanket. "I've sent word to Dr. Gethin Bevan, the physician that I told you about. I informed him to expect us later today. If we keep up a brisk pace, we should arrive just before the sun sets. He's offered us a room for the night. I gave the name Aidan Black. You said your other nephew used Black when he accepted the schoolmaster position?"

"Yes. It's their mother's maiden name. Smart to use an alias, wish I'd thought of it." He pulled Aidan close, and Garrett's eyes glazed with unshed tears. Damn it all, they should have found him sooner. Never should have allowed him to descend into the darkness alone. The family should have locked him in the attic until this wave of destructive behavior passed.

He could only hope that this Welsh doctor could work miracles.

Chapter 2

As Abigail Wharton Hughes gathered her cloak, bonnet, and gloves, she mulled over her plans for the day. Very little happened in Standon, Hertfordshire, and she reveled in the serene quiet of the small country village. Living here the past fourteen years had brought contentment to Abbie.

She'd been a widow for more than two years, and seeing as her late husband, Dr. Elwyn Hughes, had been the local physician, she held a position of respect. Living in her tidy brick and wood bungalow on the outskirts of the village gave her the quiet privacy she needed. Since Elwyn had died, she spent her days toiling in her garden or volunteering at her late husband's clinic.

Mrs. Jones would be by later to clean the house, so she must return by four o'clock. It gave her ample opportunity to shop at the small bakery. Well, it was not much of a bakery; a woman sold goods out of her front parlor. Then Abbie would stop in to the medical clinic and assist Dr. Gethin Bevan and his daughter, Cristyn.

Gethin Bevan, a colleague of her late husband, was a friend but nothing more. Although he'd hinted more than once that they could marry, seeing as he was a widower and she a widow. At thirty-two, Abbie was young enough to find another husband, only she did not want one. She was not looking for companionship or a lover. Living a quiet, contented life meant she could avoid any messy dramas that often accompanied most relationships. She'd never find another amiable partner like Elwyn—they were all too rare.

Stepping outside, she inhaled the crisp January air. A dusting of snow clung to the ground, but the temperature was not too cold for a brisk walk. The semi-frozen soil crunched under her boots as she headed to the village proper.

Once she'd purchased fresh rolls and a currant cake, Abbie made her way to the clinic, or as Gethin wished it to be called, the Standon Sanatorium. Being alone most of the week suited Abbie fine, though she was looking forward to her daughter Megan's visit Friday afternoon. Megan attended Miss Bartley's School for Young Ladies in nearby Little Hadham. Megan was not Elwyn's, but he'd accepted and loved her as if she were.

Abbie smiled softly as she thought of her late husband. A kind and gentle man close to twenty years her senior, she grew to adore him, if not exactly love him. He had assisted her out of a tight spot, and because of it, she would be eternally grateful and cherish his memory.

At the tender age of eighteen, she found herself in a frightening predicament: unwed, alone, and pregnant. Until a friend of her father's, the kindly Dr. Hughes, came to her rescue. It was another reason to esteem her late husband. Her heart ached that she could not love him as he deserved, but he often said he would take what she had to offer and be glad of it.

Striding along the lane, the sound of thundering horses' hooves filled her hearing. A black carriage whizzed by her at a rapid pace, nearly spinning her like a child's toy top and running over a couple of sheep grazing lazily on bits of grass visible on the snow-covered ground. *What on earth?*

Curious, Abbie hurried along the lane until the sanatorium came into view. Three men emerged from the carriage. Two of them were assisting another, who looked to be unconscious or close to it. Her blood stilled, and she dropped her basket. No. It couldn't be *him*. Not here in this tiny village. Not after all these years.

But there was no mistaking the breadth and height, or the shoulder-length hair the shade of a fire blazing in the hearth. He seemed bigger than life, larger than she remembered. But then they were both barely eighteen when last they spoke. Curling an arm about her stomach to stem the nausea, she shook her head as if to convince herself that it was *not* Garrett Wollstonecraft heading into Gethin's medical facility. They stood near the door, and the large man turned slightly.

Dear Lord, it *was* him. There was no mistaking the handsome perfection. She stumbled, her vision turning hazy as if she'd been pulled into a heavy mist. The memories she'd buried broke free and roared to the surface. Along with it came the intense emotions, whether she wanted them or not. For years she'd packed them neatly away, to the point she wondered if what had transpired between her and Garrett that summer had been merely a dream.

A younger version of Garrett stepped into the mist of her mind, tall, leaner, handsome beyond measuring. She'd first encountered him in the woods riding a large stallion. When he pulled up on the reins and smiled warmly at her, time stood still.

As it did now. Blood thundered in her ears, her heart racing. More memories flickered through her dizzying brain, of stolen kisses and fumbling in the hayloft and weeks of heated, clandestine meetings where they had taught each other about love and passion. The glorious moment when he had first entered her. A doleful sob escaped her throat with the remembrances.

It had all started with a summer visit to Alberta Eaton's uncle's small estate in Kent. The holiday had changed her life. Her future. She and Alberta were dear friends, and they had kept in contact through the years. Alberta and her brother-in-law, Jonas, had visited her in Standon twice. They exchanged long, gossipy letters, so Abbie was aware of Uncle Keenan's death and Alberta's inheriting the small manor house. But during those visits and letters one truth held firm: the name Garrett Wollstonecraft was never to be mentioned.

It was as if it had all happened yesterday, not more than fourteen years past. The emotions were still powerful and passionate. Prickles of searing electricity tore along Abbie's spine as she gazed at him. Through the years, she'd often wondered what she would do if she'd ever encountered Garrett. Considering that he had broken her heart, would she rail and scream, pound his massive chest and curse him to the depths of hell? Or would she weaken and throw herself into his strong, warm embrace and sob uncontrollably?

Well, she would do none of it here. This was not the time nor place. Bending, she almost fell forward as her shaking legs buckled. Taking a deep breath, Abbie gathered up her basket, then broke into a run.

In the opposite direction.

The dam had burst. The unruly water rushing out of control. There would be no gathering all the memories and emotions and hiding them away ever again. First, she must write to Alberta and find out all she could about Garrett. Then she must decide if the past should be confronted at long last.

* * * *

"Damn it, this is nothing more than a barn. Where have you brought my nephew?" Garrett hissed through clenched teeth as they carried Aidan into the exam room.

"It's a converted barn, actually," Dr. Bevan replied. "All paid for from treatment fees. You may lay Mr. Black there."

A young woman came to stand beside the doctor. Garrett cast a sidelong glance at her and made note of her beauty. Petite, dark haired, and fair skinned, with eyes the shade of a field of violets.

"Gentlemen, this is my daughter, Cristyn. She is training under me as a nurse, and is my trusted assistant." The doctor turned to her. "My dear, burn the blanket. The clothes will be next." Glancing up, he said to Edwin and Garrett, "If you will wait outside. There is usually someone here from the village to see to you, but she is late. Cristyn will be out directly to fetch you something to eat and drink while I perform my exam. Opium, you say?"

"And gin. God knows what else," Garrett muttered.

Aidan stirred and started to thrash about. "I'm sorry...so...so sorry."

Garrett clasped his hand and squeezed it tight. "It's all right, Nephew. I'm here."

"I take it your name is Black as well?" the doctor questioned.

Hesitating, Garrett nodded. It would be best to keep the name Wollstonecraft out of this tragic situation. At least initially.

"Then, Mr. Black, I will have a more inclusive picture to discuss shortly."

Reluctantly, Garrett released Aidan, who didn't even seem aware of his presence.

Edwin clapped a hand on his shoulder. "Come. Dr. Bevan knows what he's about."

He followed Edwin out into the hallway. Before he sat, he took a moment to inspect the premises. The large barn structure had been cordoned off into a long hallway with numerous rooms on either side. It was clean, bright, and not at all what he'd expected when they had first arrived. His initial thought was Edwin had brought him to a place out of the medieval era. The ancient stones and wood timbers that made up the bulk of the facade proved his theory.

He'd never been to Hertfordshire. Unlike Julian, who had travelled extensively, Garrett had not been north of London. Except for Scotland. He never believed he would find a sanatorium here in the middle of farm country. Exhausted, he plunked down on the large chair in the hallway. They sat in silence for God knows how long, and while they did, Garrett tried to think of a way to break this to the family. However he framed the narrative, it would be a jarring shock.

The trip to Standon had been harrowing. As Edwin had predicted, Aidan's symptoms of withdrawal began about halfway through the journey. The chills and vomiting were the first to appear. Garrett glanced down at his shirt. A good thing he'd brought his valise, for he needed a wash and a change of clothes.

Cristyn stepped into the hall. "If you gentlemen will follow me. I hope you don't mind sharing a room. It's at the end of this hall. You can freshen up, and I will bring you a bite to eat. Slices of *bara brith* and tea."

Garrett stood and fell in step beside Miss Bevan. "I am very much obliged. What is *bara brith?*"

She smiled. "It's Welsh for speckled bread. It is a tea loaf, with currants, spices, and fruit peel." Her gaze roamed over Garrett. "Are you Scottish?"

He nodded, not bothering to state he was only half. He was well aware that he looked as if he'd stepped directly out of the Highlands.

"Then you will like the bread." Cristyn opened the door and held out her arm. "Make yourselves comfortable. And please, don't worry; your nephew is in good hands." She closed the door softly behind her.

"As soon as I have my tea and cake, I should see if the carriage driver and the horses are settled in. The coachman is taking a room at the George Inn." Edwin strode to the basin, picked up the pitcher, and poured water into it.

"Thank you for making all the arrangements," Garrett said solemnly.

Edwin splashed water on his face, then reached for the small towel. "It won't be cheap. My fees, hiring the men for St. Giles, the carriage, accommodations, not to mention the costs for treatment. You do realize your nephew may be here several months?"

Garrett leaned against the wall and crossed his arms. "How long were you here?"

Once he dried his face, Edwin laid the towel on the table. "A little over three months, and I was not in the shocking condition Aidan is." He turned to face Garrett. "Prepare yourself for possible dreadful news. There could be any number of complications. Considering the orgies, syphilis may be a possibility, or any other poxes one catches from excessive and indiscriminate sex. He may even have sold himself or others for money. Those chasing the dragon will stoop to low levels to obtain the euphoric highs of opium."

Garrett shook his head sadly. "Then let us hope that he escapes such a fate." He paused. "What is 'chasing the dragon,' by the by?"

"Chinese slang, for inhaling the vapor from smoking opium." A knock sounded at the door. "Ah, our tea and cake. Try to relax, Garrett."

Only he couldn't relax or stop his mind from racing. He tried not to wallow in guilt over not intervening sooner. Instead, he puzzled over why Aidan would live such a desolate, dissipated life. Hell, the lad had everything going for him. Why toss it all away on an opium pipe? But now was not the time to judge his behavior; Aidan needed empathy and support. Garrett would be standing by, ready to offer it.

His nephew looked horrible, filthy, a shocking change from the carefree lad he'd been previously. Aidan had often invited him on his erotic adventures, but Garrett soon grew weary of the meaningless sex and declined further romps to London or Bath. He'd found more gratification staying at Wollstonecraft Hall raising and breeding his horses. His father used to employ a steward, but about five years past, Garrett took charge of running of the estate and seeing to the tenants. The position gave him purpose.

Aidan obviously had no purpose in his life. No responsibilities. Society called him a 'notorious rake.' The nom de guerre fit. Perhaps he and the entire family should have taken Aidan to task. But since his oldest nephew was the heir apparent, sowing wild oats was expected, and, sadly, accepted. Only Aidan went too far—right off the cliff into complete darkness.

After they consumed the food and drink, Edwin headed for the village, leaving Garrett alone with the doctor. Bevan's face was grave as he took a seat in his office. "Aidan is malnourished and dehydrated. I would guess he's lost close to two stone."

Jesus. Garrett recalled the last family meeting Aidan had attended in September. The lad had looked thin. But everyone was caught up in their lives and causes and didn't think to question him on his gaunt appearance— or his behavior. He'd stumbled in drunk in the middle of the night on more than one occasion. While there was enough blame to go around, the focus must be on Aidan's recovery.

"His body shows signed of abuse," Bevan continued.

Garrett froze, thinking of Edwin's dire warning. "Tell me, Doctor. I want to know it all."

"There are indications of beatings, with various old bruises and scars. Someone held a lit cigar to his back, making a circle. The scars have healed, for the most part. But the most grievous is the indication of recent... violation. You know of what I speak?"

Garrett's stomach turned as his blood ran cold. He had no words, and merely nodded in response.

"The injuries are inconclusive; there is no way to know if Aidan was a willing participant or not. Again, he will heal, and we can only hope that your nephew has no memory of the incident." Dr. Bevan paused and clasped his hands on his desk. "I have seen this in others. The further one sinks into opiate-fueled oblivion, the more they no longer care about anyone or anything. Or what is done to them. Only procuring the drug matters, and the elation it brings."

"Does…does he show signs of any pox or syphilis?" Garrett whispered.

"Not that I've observed. There are no open sores as such. But most symptoms occur two to twelve weeks after infection. Rest assured we will monitor the situation. Aidan is sick, running a fever, and has rat and flea bites on his hands and torso. Then there is the withdrawal. It will be extremely rough going."

"I will stay here with him," Garrett stated firmly.

Dr. Bevan shook his head. "There's no need," he said in a gentle tone. "He won't recognize you, especially during the next two weeks as he goes through the worst of it. After that? Once he becomes lucid again, the guilt and shame will overtake him. I have found having family members around only exacerbates the feeling of low self-esteem in the patient. My advice is to leave tomorrow with Edwin. I will send detailed updates."

Garrett didn't like the sound of this. Leave Aidan here with strangers? What if Edwin was wrong about this man? Yes, he and Edwin were friends. The man upheld the law, first as a Bow Street Runner and now as an investigator. Hell, he *did* trust him. If Edwin said this Dr. Bevan could be trusted, what choice did he have but to believe it? Aidan needed help most desperately. "You may send the reports in the care of Garrett Black, postal office in Sevenoaks, Kent. And what of the payment?"

"Ah. My fee is a monthly charge, regardless if the patient stays the entire thirty days. Shall we say two hundred pounds a month to start? The fee may seem excessive to most, but it funds this sanatorium and allows me to take on patients who could not otherwise afford to stay here."

Well, he had to admire the doctor's honesty. Edwin said it would be expensive. "My family is progressive, Doctor. We have our causes. It seems that I have just found mine. I can think of no better cause than assisting those suffering from addiction, especially those who cannot afford it. Money is no object. I wish to make a donation above and beyond the monthly fees. Shall three thousand pounds be sufficient?"

Bevan's eyes widened in surprise. "More than sufficient, Mr. Black, and most welcome. Be assured Aidan will receive the best of care. We will bring him out of this dark abyss, never fear."

Garrett reached in his coat pocket, pulled out a roll of pound notes, and placed them on the desk. "There is five hundred pounds, enough to pay for a couple of months of Aidan's stay. You have a solicitor?" The doctor nodded. "Excellent. Give me his name before I depart tomorrow and we will set up a payment schedule for the fees and the donation. I will warn you, Doctor, once our family takes on a worthy cause, we are all in."

"If I may ask in what way, Mr. Black?"

"We like to be involved in all aspects, such as planning for the future. Perhaps I can fund a scheme for expansion. More doctors, new clinics. I will contact you when I have it worked out. Now, I wish to see Aidan. I understand that he won't recognize me, but I *must* see him, for I have to report all this to the family. To his father."

Dr. Bevan clasped the roll of notes and placed them in his coat pocket. "Then come with me, sir."

He followed the doctor to a room farther down the hall. Dr. Bevan opened it and bade Garrett to step in first. Aidan lay in what looked to be a comfortable bed, the blankets pulled up to his mid-chest. The doctor's daughter stood by, wiping Aidan's brow with a cloth.

She gave Garrett a slight smile. "He is sleeping, though fitfully. Mr. Black has been bathed and put in a clean gown. The garments that he wore when he arrived have been burned. I will try and coax him to take a little broth later."

A lump formed in Garrett's throat as he gazed at the napping Aidan. There was no denying he was deathly ill. "I will send along some of his clothes and personal articles as soon as possible." He clasped his nephew's thin hand. It was cold and clammy to the touch. Leaning down, he kissed him on the forehead. "Get well. I love you."

Never did Garrett feel so utterly helpless.

Chapter 3

Abbie had spent the rest of the afternoon penning a lengthy and honest letter to Alberta. It had helped to calm her turbulent mind. She revealed her shock over Garrett's appearance, and the complicated and powerful emotions that had reignited at the mere sight of him. Since Abbie had a standing invitation, she informed Alberta that she would visit as soon as she could arrange it. At four pages, the newsy letter was thick when folded and would require extra postage.

When Mrs. Jones arrived to do the housekeeping, Abbie slipped a shilling in her hand and sent her along to the post, then to Gethin's to relay that she was unwell and would not be able to attend to her volunteer duties today. Once the woman departed, Abbie took to her room and curled up on her bed, burrowing under her quilt. Confronting Garrett today was not feasible, not while she remained in this current mood of uncertainty and turmoil. Abbie had to be in complete control when she faced him. Also, she needed to decide whether to mention Megan or not.

One glance at the fourteen-year-old girl, with her tall, slender form, reddish-blond hair, and profusion of freckles, made it clear Garrett was the father. When Megan was first born, she and Elwyn had decided they would tell her about her real father when she turned sixteen, an age when she would be mature enough to absorb the news. Does she tell Megan now, or wait as she and Elwyn had originally planned? For Megan believed Elwyn her father. To tell her otherwise would be upsetting indeed. For more years than Abbie cared to count, she'd been hurt and angry over Garrett. When at last it had dissipated enough for her to think rationally, she had struggled with the decision of letting him know that he had a daughter.

But she had respected her husband too much to bring the whirlwind that was Garrett into their lives.

For her own self-preservation and fearing her response, Abbie had not wanted to face him. If today was any indication, she had been wise to avoid Garrett in the past, because—damn it all!—she still desired him, and she would have never allowed Elwyn to see it, for it would have hurt him.

Besides, Elwyn had been Megan's father in every way that counted. He brought her up, loved her unconditionally. The years flew by, and Garrett had slowly disappeared into the haze of memories. Why upend their quiet, content lives?

And what would be the impact on Megan? She was at an emotionally tender age; how would she take the news? Not well. Abbie had gone back and forth the past two years arguing with herself over what to do and how to proceed. Now, with Garrett's appearance, the decision had been made on its own accord.

After a fitful sleep, Abbie rose the next morning determined to see Garrett and at least renew their acquaintance. She could not put it off any longer, regardless of her trepidations. Perhaps he wouldn't care to see her again one way or the other. No doubt he'd moved beyond their brief, intense encounter; he could even be married. Though Alberta had mentioned in one of her recent letters that Garrett's nephew, Riordan, had taken a bride, the rest of the occupants of Wollstonecraft Hall remained unattached. It was best to meet with him before bringing Megan into the picture.

Once she managed to eat a late breakfast, Abbie donned her heavy wool cloak and her hat and gloves and made her way toward the village. Steeling her spine, she entered the sanatorium. The carriage was nowhere in sight, but the driver could be staying in the village proper.

Cristyn stepped out of a patient's room and closed the door. "Feeling much recovered today, Abbie?"

Not really, but she gave Gethin's pretty daughter a polite smile. "Yes, thank you. A new patient?"

She nodded. "Mr. Aidan Black. His uncle brought him in yesterday. Opium addiction."

Aidan? She remembered the twins; they were twelve that summer, following behind Garrett like a pair of adoring devotees, especially Aidan. He often had to put the run to them so that she and Garrett could be alone. Heavens, they would be twenty-six now. *Opium? How horrible.* Abbie removed her cloak and bonnet and hung them on the hook. "How can I assist?"

Abbie followed Cristyn to the kitchen area to the left of the entrance. "I will need your help in encouraging him to take some broth. Last night he knocked it out of my hand. I fetched Dad to help and we managed to coax him to take a few spoonfuls, but Aidan promptly brought it back up."

Volunteering here the past fourteen months had given Abbie an eyewitness account of what a person suffering from addiction goes through. Elwyn had often spoken of it in detail through the years, but to see it firsthand was shocking indeed. "A rough night, I take it?"

Cristyn nodded. "We had to tie his hands to the bed rails, as he thrashed about constantly. We took turns sitting with him." Her expression took on a sad look. "Between the bouts of cursing, then crying, and the tremors and vomiting, it was quite an ordeal."

Once they gathered the broth and fresh water, they headed to the room. Abbie opened the door. In the bed lay a shirtless young man, emaciated, sweating, his hands tied and his eyes unseeing.

"He is not wearing a nightshirt for the time being. He ruined two yesterday from sickness and perspiration," Cristyn said.

Underneath the horror of opium withdrawal was a handsome face with light blue eyes and black hair. She could see the resemblance from the gangly twelve-year-old of years past. This *was* Garrett's nephew. Her heart ached at the sight of him.

Obviously they were using a false name, and Abbie would not reveal their secret. Would he recognize her? It would be fifteen years this summer since they had last laid eyes on each other. Aidan pulled at the restraints, grunting and snarling like a wild animal. Perhaps not, for he was glassy-eyed and not aware of his surroundings. As soon as Cristyn approached and wiped his fevered bow, he quieted. "There, *cariad,*" Cristyn whispered. "Be at peace."

My goodness. There had been a development during the past twenty-four hours. Abbie had not witnessed Cristyn being quite this familiar with previous young male patients. Calling Aidan "love"? Yes, it was often used as a general term, as in "Hello, love. How are you?" but the way she gazed at him led Abbie to believe that there were more emotions at play. How interesting.

Sitting the tray on the table near the bed, Abbie asked, "What of his uncle, is he still about?"

"No, Dad insisted he return home to Kent. There was nothing he could do here. Mr. Black left this morning with his friend, Mr. Seward."

Blast it. Now she would have to travel to Kent and confront Garrett there. Or should she? Writing him a letter informing him that he had a daughter was rather impersonal and craven on her part. Did she really wish to stir up this hornet's nest of emotions? It was too late on her end, for the hornets were already buzzing about, stinging her with heated memories and giving her no relief. Abbie understood that she would not find respite until she met with Garrett in person.

But first she would have to speak to Megan. Tell her the truth. And ask if she even wanted to meet Garrett. Regardless, he would be told of their daughter. What Abbie needed to hear more than anything? An apology. She also wanted Garrett to admit that he'd been wrong when he cruelly turned her away, for whatever reason. Surely it couldn't be because of that family curse he had told her about.

Regardless, it became rather important that she heard those words from him.

* * * *

Oliver Wollstonecraft, the Earl of Carnstone, had not been looking forward to saying goodbye to Riordan. He'd enjoyed having his grandson at the hall the past six weeks. As much as he had enjoyed it, and becoming acquainted with Riordan's bride, Sabrina, it was Mary Tuttle, former lady's maid, who had held his full attention at this moment.

Since she'd discarded her servant title and the plain outfits, a mature attractiveness had emerged. She wore colorful day dresses and styled her chestnut brown hair differently. She also had a well-rounded and luscious figure. But it wasn't her looks or figure that made him give her a second look. Mary Tuttle was honest and humorous, with no counterfeit emotions or sly machinations. She had a ready smile and a full-throated laugh that made his insides heat. They were of a like age, and had much in common.

Now they must say goodbye, at least temporarily. Riordan and Sabrina had already said their goodbyes and were outside, seeing to the new carriage and horses that Riordan had bought and making sure the trunks were well secured before their imminent departure.

Oliver only had Mary alone for a few minutes. She gazed at him, unblinking, waiting for him to speak. Damn it all, tongue-tied at sixty-four.

"My lord—"

He clasped her gloved hand. "I've asked you to call me Oliver when we're alone. Carnstone when we're not. You agreed." He smiled.

"Yes, I did agree. It feels strange to use your first name. I must be still thinking with my servant's mind...Oliver."

His eyelids lowered briefly, savoring the way her voice deepened when she said his name. "I will miss you, Mary." He opened his eyes and caught her gaze. Let her see the heat simmering in them.

"As I will miss you," she replied, her voice soft.

"Then will you allow me to start a correspondence with you, until we meet again in June?" he asked hopefully.

Mary pulled her hand out of his. "To what purpose? I'm merely the daughter of a sailor. Not fit for the proper company for an earl."

"I believe that is for me to decide. Besides, you said that your father was a sailing master on a sixty-gun frigate. An important position. You were *not* poor."

She scoffed. "Until he died at sea and left us with nothing and I had no choice but to head into service." Mary smoothed her skirt. "At age fifty-five, I've seen plenty. Though I have not been intimate with a man in decades, I recognize...I..." Mary stammered. "Oh, blast. I've tried to hide how flustered I am when I'm with you, but it's to no avail."

Oliver stepped closer. "Only flustered?"

Mary smiled. "No, blast your beautiful blue eyes. Much more than that."

He pulled her into his arms and kissed her soundly. Mary froze, but for only a moment. Then, as if remembering what to do, she met his kiss with decided enthusiasm. Oliver deepened it, plunging his tongue into her sweet, hot mouth and taking complete possession.

A soft moan escaped the corner of her mouth as the exploration continued. Mary rubbed against him, turning up the heat sizzling between them. Slowly and reluctantly, Oliver ended it. She had to leave. Someone could walk in on them. He cradled her cheeks with his hands, gazing into her eyes. "We are too far along in years to play games. I want you, but I can be patient. We will write each other. Deepen the friendship that already exists...you agree one exists?"

She nodded, her eyes glistening with emotion.

"Come June, the school term ends and you will all return here. By then we should be certain of what we both want." He stepped back. "Goodbye, Mary."

She blinked, her lower lip trembling. "Goodbye...Oliver."

With a swish of her skirts she was gone, leaving an alluring scent of vanilla lingering in the air. Like a lovesick schoolboy, he moved to the large window and watched as the footman assisted Mary into the carriage. Before she entered it, she paused, looked up, and caught his gaze. Her warm smile made his heart stutter in his chest as it hadn't done since he first met the love of his life, his second wife and Garrett's mother, Moira, so long ago.

Once the door closed, the driver gave a command and the horses whickered in response. The carriage was off. Oliver stood at the window and watched until, at the bottom of the long drive, the carriage made its turn and disappeared.

He'd made his peace with the fact that he would never have deep feelings toward a woman again. Never imagined that he would experience it at this late stage of his life. He had no right to pursue the lovely Miss Tuttle. He already had three wives and a baby daughter buried in the family cemetery. Why place another woman in harm's way? The curse had played a huge part in his life—how could it not? Caution would be needed. Even though Riordan had decided love would triumph over all, Oliver knew it had not been enough to save *his* true love.

Well, he had the next several months to decide how to proceed with Miss Mary Tuttle. Taking a seat by the fire, he stretched out his long legs and started to nod off. *Forgive me, Moira.*

"Da, wake up."

Oliver woke with a start. God, he'd fallen asleep. Rubbing his eyes, he looked up. "Garrett. I did not expect you for at least a couple of days. What is it?"

His younger son had spent a large segment of his life tucking away outward emotions, but they often broke free when least expected. Or they blazed in his hazel-green eyes, as they did now. Oliver knew how to read his son's often shuttered expressions.

"I've sent Gordon along to collect Julian. I have news on Aidan. Did I miss Riordan?"

Oliver glanced at the mantel clock. Three hours had passed. Well, he did not get much sleep the previous night. No wonder he was exhausted. "He left hours ago; he must be close to home." Oliver stood and stretched his back. "What about Aidan?"

"Damn," Garrett said softly. "I should've returned sooner." He shook his head. "Let us head to the main library. I instructed Martin to pour us generous tumblers of whiskey."

"That bad?"

"Yes. Come. Julian is no doubt awaiting us."

As they headed to the library, Oliver found it strange that the footman, Gordon, was not standing in his usual place. Was he still looking for Julian?

Yet when they stepped in the room Julian was already seated, whiskey in hand. Martin, their venerable butler, efficiently served their drinks, stirred the fire to life, then left them alone. Oliver had a terrible feeling of foreboding. Glancing at Julian, he could see his oldest son felt the same.

"Edwin Seward contacted me, stating he'd located Aidan. It is why I journeyed to London," Garrett said. "Well, that and Durning's court hearing."

Julian's face turned thunderous. "And you thought not to inform us? He's *my* son."

"Hold in your anger and hear me out," Garrett replied. "Edwin suggested that we not descend on Aidan. Once I arrived and found where he had been holed up for the past several months, I agreed with Edwin's assessment."

Garrett, not one for long, drawn-out conversation, proceeded to paint a horror-filled narrative of invading a St. Giles rookery in the early morning and finding Aidan with a group of thieves, prostitutes, and other deviants in a filthy doss-house. How, along with Edwin's men and a few hired toughs, they had snatched him up and made their escape.

To Hertfordshire, of all places. As he described the clinic and the Welsh doctor who ran it, Julian's face crumbled and all anger vanished. "Opium? Gin? How...how did he look?"

"Ghastly." Garrett answered in a quiet voice. "He's lost weight; the doctor claimed that it could be two stone or more. His skin is an unhealthy gray shade. He's malnourished, dehydrated, and sick to his very core."

Oliver's insides twisted at the news, but in shrewdly watching Garrett he had the feeling that there was more to Aidan's injuries than his younger son let on.

"It will take months for him to recover, weeks to come out of the worst of the withdrawal. And before you demand that we head to Hertfordshire, Dr. Bevan recommended we all stay well clear until Aidan wishes to see us. The doctor said that his recovery will move ahead at a more rapid pace if family is not around to add to his guilt and shame."

"I would never admonish Aidan, not in this condition. He's ill," Julian said, his voice shaking.

"Yes, precisely. He *is* ill. The doctor suggested that we not blame ourselves for how low Aidan has sunk," Garrett replied.

"And how does this damned doctor propose we do it?" Julian snapped. "All I did was reprimand and lecture him. It never even crossed my mind that his behavior was a call for help."

Oliver stood and laid a hand on his oldest son's shoulder. "None of us recognized the signs. Why would we? He was always a little wild. Never liked being told what to do. Bucking us at every turn. I thought him merely rebellious, as many young heirs are. I believed that he would grow out of it. There is enough blame to go around, but I agree that it is best we avoid such self-indulgence."

Julian glanced at Garrett. "I am his father. You should have told me. I should have been there when you extracted him. I will not forget this."

"Julian," Oliver said. "Enough. I know you are upset..."

"Upset? Try devastated. I have failed my son. Failed as a parent," Julian barked.

"You are not thinking clearly," Oliver replied, his voice gentle. "Garrett did as Edwin instructed, and hearing the circumstances, it was for the best. Think how distressed Aidan would have been if you had seen him in such a condition. It would not help his recovery. I truly believe this." He squeezed Julian's shoulder. "We wait for word. The doctor will be keeping us apprised?"

Garrett nodded. "Regular updates. He promised."

"Julian, you are the farthest thing from a failure as a parent. When Fiona died, when the twins were four years old, I observed how you bravely hid your grief from them and focused all your attention and love on them. Instilled in them a sense of honor, of service to one's fellow man, and deep down, I believe Aidan embodies all that and more. He will prove it to you someday soon; I know it in my heart." Oliver gave his son's shoulder another affectionate squeeze.

Because of the many tragedies in their lives, the Wollstonecraft men shared an unshakeable and solid bond. Much like soldiers in a field of battle. They were trusted allies, confidants, brothers-in-arms, bound by the curse but more importantly by blood and mutual respect. They were close friends, and they supported each other no matter the crisis. More than anything, however, love cemented the connection. Enriched it. Enhanced it. Hearing of Aidan's fate and witnessing Julian's anguish reminded Oliver of how devoted they were to each other.

Julian buried his face in his hands, his shoulders heaving. Good God, he was crying. Oliver's heart twisted with pain at seeing his son's desolate grief. Oliver was about to comfort him when Gordon, the footman, appeared at the door.

"Master Garrett, Mrs. Eaton has arrived."

Alberta Eaton stepped into the room, her gaze falling to Julian. "Tensbridge." Without hesitating, she ran to his side, fell to her knees, and embraced him. Julian held her close, his face buried in her neck. She smoothed his hair, whispering what Oliver supposed was words of comfort, though he could not make them out.

Garrett took Oliver's elbow and they both left them alone. Gordon closed the door and resumed his position in the hallway.

"Very shrewd, Garrett. For a man who claims women are nothing but a complication in a man's life, you've showed acute instincts. Well done," Oliver said, proud of the way his younger son handled this difficult situation.

They strolled toward Oliver's study. "It's obvious he has a tendre for her. And since I've been helping with her renovations, I've come to know her. I believe that she is what Julian needs at this moment."

Oliver arched an eyebrow. "And the curse?"

"Oh, I still believe in it, and Julian would be wise to avoid anything long term."

A short bark of laughter left Oliver's throat. "By God, you are as stubborn as your mother ever was. Have you even entertained the possibility that you are wrong about it all?"

Garrett shook his head. "Never. The proof is clear, as well you know, Da."

Oliver frowned. He didn't like being reminded that he had suffered more losses than any man in the family. But a part of him still hoped there was a way to end the blasted curse.

"Riordan wouldn't listen, and if Julian wants to take another chance at possible tragedy, that's his decision," Garrett continued. "I plan on staying clear of any emotional or romantic attachments."

Oliver nearly snorted aloud in disbelief. Yes, his son was obstinate and unmovable on this subject. This was not the life that he had wished for Garrett, or for any of them for that matter. His youngest son had lots of love to give, like his late mother. What a complete shame to waste it. Only an extraordinary woman would be able to pull down the persistent and protective wall Garrett had constructed around his heart.

Chapter 4

Ten days later

"Megan, don't sulk. It doesn't become you," Abbie admonished gently.

Her daughter's lips pursed further. "How else am I to feel considering what you've told me? I should have stayed at school. Never should have agreed to this trip."

Megan had been furious for days, the atmosphere between them chilly and fractious. Abbie would have to endure hours of watching her daughter pout. But she could hardly blame the girl considering the shocking news that she'd relayed to her.

The carriage lurched in a deep rut on the road, sending them reeling across the bench seats. Abbie sat up straight and adjusted her bonnet. She'd taken the extravagance of hiring a private coach. Granted, it wasn't exactly lush and comfortable, but at least they were alone for the journey. It would take several hours to reach Kent, a change in horses, a meal at an inn.

Megan crossed her arms defiantly and gazed out the carriage window. A frown replaced her pout. "I will not call this man 'Father.' I utterly refuse. I had a papa, and he died."

"Elwyn was your papa in every sense. He loved you as if you were his own," Abbie said gently.

"You have ruined my life," Megan accused as her lower lip quivered. "Why tell me at all? And don't say because you and Papa agreed to wait until I was older. You could have kept this horrible secret once he passed and I never would have been the wiser. Please turn the carriage about and head home."

"No, Megan."

"You *want* to see this man again, and you are using me to reopen the acquaintance," she snapped irritably.

This lay close to the truth. Too close. But it wasn't the entire truth. "Yes, I want to see him again. I've had sufficient time to move past most of my anger. But more importantly, what your father told me more than once in years past holds true: Garrett Wollstonecraft deserves to know."

"He truly doesn't know about me?"

Abbie shook her head. "We had already gone our separate ways when I found I was with child. Our parting was not under the best of circumstances." *A decided understatement.*

Megan glared at her. "Why didn't you tell him then? If he was any kind of gentleman he would have married you. You said that he's the son of an earl."

"My dear, we were both eighteen years old. Barely four years older than you are now. We were children, and we fought before we parted. Hurtful words cutting deep on both sides. I never even told my parents who the father was." Abbie gave her daughter a shaky smile. "I was scared, angry, and, yes, immature. I came to understand that I should have returned to Kent and informed him of my condition. You see, we had no business doing...what we did. We were too young and naïve to understand the consequences."

"And I am the consequence." Megan frowned. "Did you love him at all? Or was the encounter nothing but a scandalous affair?"

Abbie moved to the opposite bench and slipped her arm about Megan's shoulder. "You were not a consequence, but a miracle. The happiest day of my life is when they placed you in my arms." Megan's eyes glistened with unshed tears. "I did love him, most desperately. Never think that you were not conceived in love, for you were. It was not cheap and tawdry. Ill-advised, perhaps, even scandalous, but the emotions were real." *At least on my end.*

"I cried all night when you told me this. Papa, who I still love dearly and miss fiercely, is not my real father. Do you understand how devastating it was to hear? I feel like a part of me has been ripped away. How could you do this to me?" Megan pulled away from her. "I wish you had never told me. I also wish I hadn't agreed to this. I don't want to meet him. I've changed my mind. Please, *please*, can we turn about and go home?"

Abbie could hear the anger and hurt in Megan's voice, and her heart tightened in empathy. Who wouldn't be affected by such a revelation? The secret was indeed shocking. "No, Megan. We are already more than halfway there. Meet him, at least. If you choose, you never have to see him again. The decision will be yours. I promise."

"I will hold you to your vow." Megan gazed out the window for several minutes. "What does he look like? Is it because of him that I have all this red hair?" she asked. "I often wondered why I had red hair and you and Papa did not." Her lower lip quivered. "I look nothing like Papa. I see it now." At least the question showed she was a little curious about Garrett, though her tone displayed her annoyance. It also revealed her deep sadness at not being Elwyn's biological daughter.

"Yes. Garrett is half Scottish on his mother's side. What does he look like?" Abbie sighed. "He was formidable at eighteen, well over six feet in height then, with broad shoulders and the most glorious head of silky red hair. Handsome beyond measure. I became smitten immediately."

Telling Megan that she had seen Garrett in the village last week would not be prudent. It had opened an old wound, and as a result all her passionate emotions had escaped. Abbie believed she had conquered them and buried them deep. The sad truth is that she had never stopped yearning for Garrett. Not even when she lay in her husband's arms. A lone tear slipped down her cheek, and she quickly dashed it away before Megan saw it. She'd adored Elwyn and tried her damnedest to fall in love with him, but her heart belonged to one man only. The man who had broken it.

Abbie would not be able to move on with her life if she did not face Garrett one last time. Tell the truth about Megan. Find out once and for all if his cruel words were true. Or had he used them to distance himself from her, all because of his so-called family curse? "We will have a nice visit with Alberta and Jonas, and while we are there you will meet Garrett Wollstonecraft."

Megan nodded, her expression still stony. "Very well, Mama. I will meet him. But I do not have to like him or accept him." She paused, then said. "The only thing I *am* looking forward to is seeing Jonas. Truly, he is why I agreed to this. He's the most beautiful boy that I have ever seen. Can a boy be beautiful?"

"Well, Jonas is twenty-four now, hardly a boy."

Megan tapped her temple with her gloved finger. "He is a boy in here, a very sweet boy."

"He always will be, Megan. And if a man could be categorized as beautiful, Jonas would fit, with his perfect features and golden-blond hair." She sighed. "Do not become too attached, my dear. Nothing can come from it."

Megan remained silent for several moments, as if digesting what Abbie said. "But he is a man; he would have all those desires men experience, would he not?"

Abbie sat up straight and stared at her daughter incredulously. "What are they teaching you at that school?" A frisson of alarm tolled in Abbie's head. Five years past, when Alberta and Jonas had last visited, Megan had formed an attachment to Jonas that Abbie had found endearing, but with Megan on the cusp of womanhood? Already she was a well-developed girl for her age and too bold by half. Perhaps this trip was a mistake on more than one level.

"Love can happen at a young age. It did in *Romeo and Juliet*," Megan declared.

"It's a tragedy."

Megan shrugged. "Not all love has to be tragic. Or turn out as terrible as yours."

Well. A direct hit. "We are not speaking about me. You're still young, with years ahead of you and many young men to meet before you decide about love." She patted Megan's gloved hand. "In the meantime, this will be a difficult enough visit. Thinking of Jonas as only a friend would be wise."

Megan turned to stare out the window again, not replying. Oh, good heavens, did she harbor a tendre for Jonas? There lay heartache. First loves could cut to the very soul—especially when they go wrong. Abbie knew this more than anyone.

The carriage arrived at the Eatons' shortly past the dinner hour, and with the happy greetings out of the way, everyone had been ushered into the parlor and trays of food brought in.

When they had first stepped into the room Jonas happily hugged them both, though Megan had held on to him longer than was decent. The young man looked as dazzling as ever. Goodness, should she allow them to be alone at all?

Once they were seated in the parlor, Alberta smiled and poured the tea. "I am glad the new furniture arrived last week, or we would have been hard pressed for seating. I should have waited until the room was completely renovated, but the state of my uncle's furnishings was shocking indeed." She smiled amusedly. "Can you imagine, we found a nest of swallows when we first moved in. In one of the fireplaces upstairs."

"I took them outside and cared for them, and after two weeks they flew away. Bert says they headed south for the winter," Jonas enthused. The young man had always been interested in all sorts of animals and birds through the years, taking many in as pets, including a llama and an array of hedgehogs.

Abbie gave him a warm smile, then took the cup and saucer offered. "The manor house certainly has deteriorated since I was here last. But you are slowly making it your home. How wonderful."

Megan stood. "I would like to go to my room, if I may. I am very tired." Her voice was flat, her annoyance still present and obvious for all to see. Abbie fought her growing irritation. Her daughter was not going to make this easy.

"Of course, my dear. Jonas, please show Megan to her guest room. The blue room. Then you may retire as well." Alberta smiled.

Abbie watched the young man closely. He was dressed in an immaculate brown suit; his manners while they ate had been impeccable, though he did not offer much in conversation except about the swallows. Truly, he was beautiful, as Megan had stated. But the fact remained he was ten years older and...somewhat simple. How else could she describe him?

"All right, Bert. Come with me, Meg." Jonas wiped his mouth on the napkin and stood, allowing Megan to leave the room first.

Once they departed, Alberta sighed and passed Abbie a plate of sandwiches. "He is a joy to have about, but takes a good deal of supervision."

"He is quite handsome...it is...how to say this?" Abbie began.

"A sin he is an idiot?" Alberta replied crossly. Then she shook her head. "I am sorry. I should not have said that, and in such an angry tone. I heard him being spoken of as such in town today while I shopped at the grocer and I'm *still* furious. I left immediately, before I made a scene." Alberta sipped her tea. "Jonas is *not* an idiot. The doctor who examined him last year claims that he has the intelligence of a twelve-year-old, and unfortunately, the emotional development of one as well. It will always be thus." She smiled sadly. "Jonas had been slow to develop, didn't speak until the age of four. Yet for a while, my husband, Reese, thought that he might be 'normal'—for lack of a better word. But he hit a plateau and stayed there. Many doctors have examined him over the years, and most agree that the stunting of his intellectual and emotional growth may have occurred during his difficult birth. The doctor who had been in attendance revealed that it took several minutes to get Jonas to take a breath. The lack of oxygen...it is hard to know. No one knows for sure."

"You've never spoken of this before," Abbie whispered.

"It makes me sad, in one way. But in another he has been a great comfort, especially when Reese passed. Before he died, I promised Reese I would look after Jonas and not allow him to be sent to one of those awful asylums. I've grown to love him as a dear brother." Alberta laughed softly. "Tensbridge described him as a man-child. The narrative fits."

"Garrett's older brother? There was no mention of him in your recent letter."

Alberta's cheeks flushed. "I believe that there is something developing between us."

"How fascinating, and worthy of a lengthy discussion. But regarding Jonas. Megan is infatuated with him. I do not want to make an issue out of it, as there will be enough drama involved with this visit," Abbie said.

"We will keep an eye on them. You don't have to worry, as Jonas has shown no inclination toward romantic pursuits. Now, speaking of drama, have you thought of a way to approach Garrett?"

Abbie bit into her egg and ham sandwich and chewed thoughtfully. Invite him over here and surprise him by causally walking into the parlor? Call at Wollstonecraft Hall? "I have no idea how to proceed. I know nothing about him, not then and certainly not now. Have no idea what sort of man he became. If our parting is any indication, he no doubt is an arrogant, selfish arse." She gave Alberta a shaky smile. "Who knows how many women came after me… Lord, I am envious of nameless women. I cannot believe how violently my insides are churning." Abbie laid a hand across her middle.

Alberta sipped her tea, then placed the cup and saucer on the tray. "Though Uncle was a recluse, we did keep up a correspondence. He stated that through Garrett's mid-twenties, for a period of about two years, he had cut quite a swath through London. He and the younger Aidan especially. Then the sojourns to London ended, though not for his nephew. If anyone in the family has a scandalous reputation, it is Aidan. Notorious, even."

Why did the news that Garrett had sought female company hurt so blasted much? She couldn't expect him to live as a monk, alone in a dark room, pining away for her. Abbie had certainly found comfort elsewhere. With Elwyn.

"But regardless of his temporary wild streak," Alberta continued, "Garrett is well thought of by his tenants and neighbors. He is honest and forthright in his dealings. Why, he is assisting me with renovations…" A knock sounded at the door. "Gracious, who could that be? It's past eight o'clock." Alberta stood and smoothed her skirt. "One moment."

Abbie set aside the sandwiches. The parlor was directly located off the front entrance, making listening to conversations easy to achieve.

"Alberta, I am sorry to arrive unannounced and at an inconvenient hour."

There was no mistaking that deep, masculine voice. Her heart stuttered in her chest. *Garrett.* God, what to do? Run for her room? Hide behind the curtains? Crouch behind the settee?

"Er...come in." From the tone of her voice, Alberta was obviously flustered. The door was closed—he must be standing in the front hall.

"I can stay but a moment. I neglected to inform you there will be a delivery of lumber tomorrow, for the repairs in the kitchen area. With all that has been going on, it slipped my mind. I also wanted to thank you for coming to the hall last week. For Julian."

"How is he? I haven't seen or heard from him since," Alberta asked, concern in her voice.

Abbie stood; her hands shook. It was now or never. If she didn't see him now, she would be awake all night in nervous agitation.

"The news about Aidan has struck him hard, and he has been keeping to himself..." Garrett's voice trailed off with her appearance.

With wobbly legs, she moved forward to stand beside Alberta. The gas lamp on the wall illuminated his face, the shadows accentuating his high cheekbones. They were more pronounced than she remembered. Lord, he was even more handsome than she recalled. Maturity had enhanced his near-perfect features, and his imposing, fine form filled the doorway. So tall. Such shoulders. Seeing him up close—face-to-face—seized her breath. He'd always been a virile, vibrant presence. Positively shimmering with masculinity. Yes, age had improved every aspect of his good looks. As she had observed in Standon, his hair now hung to his shoulders, the colors more effervescent than ever. He met her gaze and his eyes widened, then his full lips parted in shock.

Megan was upstairs. Pray she did not come down. Not yet. Especially considering her current mood. Abbie needed to reveal this slowly. "Good evening, Garrett. It's been a long time."

* * * *

The hallway spun. Slow at first, then increasing in speed. Abigail Wharton. *Abbie.* It was as if a load of bricks had been dumped on his head. Or he'd been kicked in the chest by a horse. Yes, that was the sensation, for his heart had ceased to beat. A buzzing sounded in his ears, growing louder as each second ticked by. Then it faded and disappeared altogether.

Gradually, and in small increments, he came back to life, his heartbeat sluggish, his breathing shallow. The shock of seeing her caused his insides to plummet. *Jesus, she is beautiful.* Still, after all these years. More beautiful than memory served. He'd so carefully cut her from his life. From his very soul. Considering his response, the extraction had been a complete failure.

Garrett could not stop his gaze from sweeping over her form. More mature, rounded, more sweetly curved. Her raven-black hair was styled simply, piled and pinned on top of her head; loose tendrils framed her face. Her flawless, creamy skin shone in the muted light. Her dark brown eyes glistened, her look hopeful but guarded. *God, get control. Say something.*

But the words would not come. Instead, a long-buried memory took form in his mind: the two of them writhing in the hayloft. They were clutching each other desperately as he thrust in and out of her while she moaned and dug her nails into his back, scoring and marking him... He closed his eyes briefly in order to dismiss the erotic image, but it merely made it all the more vivid. His eyes snapped open.

"Well, this is...awkward," Abbie said, her voice soft.

"Perhaps the two of you should head to the parlor. I'll give you the privacy you need," Alberta offered kindly.

Did someone speak? Garrett could not keep up with the conversation. It was as if all moved in slow motion.

Mutely, he followed Abbie to the parlor, mesmerized by her swaying hips. He was fully and painfully hard. The desire heating his blood was as real and heartbreaking as it had been fourteen years before. He buttoned his greatcoat. Be damned if he would show how she still affected him. Alberta closed the door and left them alone.

Garrett had the sudden urge to push Abigail Wharton against the wall and kiss her senseless. Tunnel his hand under her skirt until he found her heated core. Fumble with the fall of his trousers; pull out his erect cock and—

"Do you believe in fate, Garrett? A silly question, since you believe in curses. Of course you believe in fate. I did not. Until ten days ago." Neither of them had taken a seat, but they kept a wary distance. "I saw you in Standon, of all places, a small village in the middle of nowhere. Big as life as always. There was no mistaking you. The moment that you stepped from the carriage, all my carefully packed away feelings and memories were torn asunder to haunt me once again."

"What do you want me say?" He kept his voice as devoid of emotion as he could.

Abbie whirled about to face him. "Say? I want you to admit that *you've* been haunted by the memories. That perhaps *you* have regrets for the way you acted and the cruel, heartless words that you flung at me like daggers."

Garrett defiantly crossed his arms. "Still bitter? I don't have any regrets."

She shook her head sadly. "Ah. You never loved me after all. I truly was young and foolish. Why am I not surprised that you have no regrets, considering our contentious parting?"

Garrett stepped closer. His arms dropped to his sides; his hands clenched into fists to keep them from pulling her into his arms. "I never said I didn't love you, Abbie."

Her eyes blinked rapidly. "Of all the arrogant... I asked if you loved me at our last meeting, and you gave a very emphatic 'no.' Forgot about all of our secret encounters, I see. It had meant nothing to you." Anger sliced through her cool tone. "Well, I remember everything. Especially your cruel statement: 'I will think of you now and then, but otherwise, not at all.' It turns out that the callous statement was true. Of all the young men I could have chosen, why did it have to be a heartless bastard?"

Their affair *had* meant everything. The women who came after—and if he were to do a tally, it wasn't as many as the gossips claimed—none of them came close to stirring his emotions like Abbie had. It was the reason he'd said those spiteful, pitiless words. To make her leave. He didn't mean them, and he hated himself for a long while afterward but remained convinced it was the only way to avoid tragedy and heartache. He glanced at her hand. A wedding ring. Another solid blow to his aching heart.

"Why are you here? Seeking a carnal adventure away from your husband?" He'd no right to be hurt at the fact she was married. *Selfish beast.* And cruel, for his tone was a mocking one.

Abbie lifted her chin into the air. "A carnal adventure with you? Ha! Don't flatter yourself. I am a widow, and have been for close to two years. I am content to be alone."

That she no longer had a husband made his heart soar, but he tamped down the inapt response. "You waited for the appropriate mourning period to pass. Decided that life in a quiet country village no longer suited."

"Oh, it suited me fine. *You* are the one who invaded my world and pushed it off its axis," she snapped.

Garrett took another step closer. She stood her ground, as he remembered. "So you decided to return the favor, come here and stir up a painful episode for both of us." His tone no longer mocked; he could hear the pain in his voice. *Bugger it. Let her hear it as well.*

Her eyebrow arched. "Are you in pain?"

"Bloody hell, yes." *And in more ways than one.*

At such a confession, he expected her to give him a look of smug satisfaction. Instead her expression softened, but only for a moment. "We have much to discuss. But not tonight." She rubbed the bridge of her nose.

"I've had a long journey and am utterly exhausted. Perhaps we can meet at Wollstonecraft Hall?"

Not tonight? She's dismissing me. Perhaps it was for the best, considering his overwrought reaction to her presence. How tempting to state that there was nothing to discuss, but he should hear her out. *Pathetic.* He wanted to see her again. Talk to her, be near her. Inhale her evocative scent. Still the wildflower combination he remembered. God, he could hardly think straight. Blood roared in his ears...and in his still-stiff prick. He couldn't carry on a rational conversation if he tried.

"If you wish. Three o'clock." He turned on his heel, flung open the parlor door, and stomped down the hall. Didn't even say good night. All he knew was he had to get away from her. Once Garrett opened the front door, he broke into a run. If he had any damned sense he would keep running and never see or talk to her again. His heart pounded furiously in his chest. The cold perspiration that had collected at his hairline trickled down his cheeks.

Abbie: the only woman he'd ever loved. And damn it all, despite his determination to never think of her...he loved her still.

He was in a world of trouble.

Chapter 5

Garrett sat alone in his dark room, sipping a tumbler of scotch. The alcohol spread through him and he savored the flavor of it. He needed the comfort and warmth of the ritual, for the events of fourteen years past were as vivid and real as if they had happened last night.

Abbie ran to his arms. "It's my last night here in Kent. I return home tomorrow." The thought of her leaving tore him to pieces. But he had to remain strong in the face of temptation. Garrett pulled her close, reveling in her soft curves and heat. She was tall for a young woman, perhaps seven inches over five feet, but ideal for him. Her head fit under his chin perfectly.

The past six weeks had brought about such heights of ecstasy, but never leaving him was the fact that this could not last. The curse could not continue. When he was ten years of age he may not have cared much for his stepmother, but watching her die a horrible death after giving birth to a daughter made a decided impact on Garrett. Not fair. He didn't dislike her. Lady Gwendolyn was polite if distant. Even kind now and then. Just not exactly...motherly.

The baby girl was named Sarah, and just when Garrett was growing attached to the tiny, mewling infant she died of a lung ailment and was buried with her mother, who'd passed away three weeks before. Standing in the family cemetery with his father and brother, gazing at the rows of tombstones, most of them women who had dared to love Wollstonecraft men or had the bad luck to be born into the family, Garrett made a life-altering decision.

He would not do as his father and brother had done. He would never love or marry. A bold declaration for a ten-year-old lad, but he'd meant the words.

Enough of the past. He was still determined never to fall in love. Not even the glorious girl in his arms would shift him from his firm belief. He kissed Abbie. Their tongues tangled as he took the kiss deeper. Already he was hard and aching. To think that when they'd first met he was still a virgin. Oh, he had a few playful tumbles in the hay with a farm girl or two, but it never culminated in actual sex. Now, after six weeks of daily, clandestine couplings, they had both grown more confident. More ardent. God help him…more loving. The most difficult thing that he would ever do would be to say goodbye to Abbie.

Breaking the kiss, he took her hand and they scrambled into a clean, empty stall. One of the horses whickered at their proximity. The groom and the stable hands were having dinner in the servants' quarters. They didn't have long. Garrett closed the gate as Abbie laughed and laid on top of the straw.

There would be no time for the exploration of past encounters. No slow removal of clothes, caressing bare skin, kissing her in the sweetest of places. Instead they desperately tore at the fall of his trousers while rucking up her skirt. Garrett slipped his hand between her legs. So ready for him. Such a passionate lass. Gripping his stiff shaft, he entered her with a powerful thrust, causing her back to arch as a husky moan escaped her lips. "Shh, love. We'll spook the horses and bring out MacAdam and the lads. We would be quite the discovery."

She laughed throatily as she lifted her hips to meet him. For a brief, joyous moment, he imagined the two of them doing this for the rest of their lives, until they were too old and feeble. But this joining had a tinge of sadness, for it would be the last. Abbie cried out, and he quieted her by kissing her. Then his climax peaked. Garrett shook, shuddered, and held her close to his heart as they rode the wave of passion together.

After they calmed, they set their clothes to right. "When can I tell my father you will be by to see him? I know Brighton is a bit of a journey, but we have plenty of room for you and your father. The earl will accompany you, will he not? Our fathers should meet. I was thinking of a Christmas wedding. I always wanted one. To wear a white fur-trimmed cape decorated with lace and silk snowflakes." She stared off dreamily. "Though my father is only a knight, he can well afford a decent wedding. Oh, Garrett. I cannot wait!"

He froze. Wedding? Jesus, they were only eighteen. When this began, he had honestly believed they could part as friends. Yet his feelings for her had deepened into love. It didn't bear thinking about. He would not allow it. Not with the curse. Garrett could never reveal his true feelings, *or reveal the fact he had already placed her at risk. He must protect her at all costs, even if it meant breaking their hearts in the process. It was best this way.* "There will be no wedding." *He stood, fastening the last buttons on his trousers.*

Abbie stared up at him incredulously. "But there must be. After what we've done..."

He shrugged. "No one else knows about us. And if you tell your father, I will deny it."

Her shocked expression turned to hurt and it cut him deep. He was not cruel; he was brought up to be the opposite. "How could you?" *she exclaimed.*

"This was a summer dalliance, nothing more. We will never see each other again. Besides, there are many women out in the world to enjoy. You were merely one in what I imagine will be a long line. I will think of you now and then, but otherwise, not at all." *He paused.* "You should thank me. The next man to get between your thighs will find you well broken in."

Abbie jumped to her feet and slapped his face. Her hurt had turned to anger. Good. *He wanted her to be furious enough to walk away.* "I told you last night that I loved you; I laid my heart bare." *She searched his eyes as if looking for any sign of a decent human being.* "Do you love me?"

With the question posed before him, he knew deep in his soul that he did love her, most desperately. Hurting her like this was destroying him, as if part of his soul had blackened and broke away. He rubbed his cheek, for she packed quite the wallop. But he would never marry, and after this would never allow any woman close enough to capture his heart. "No." *The denial stabbed deep and would no doubt leave a permanent scar. Garrett deserved to be damaged from this, for he never should have allowed their love affair to progress this far.*

"I don't believe you," *she said fiercely.* "Not after the way you held me, loved me. Kissed me. You lie. Pushing me away will not lessen our feelings."

"In time you will forget," *he replied dismissively. Inside, his gut was twisting into knots.*

"You are a miserable beast." *She poked him in the chest; fire came alive in her lovely brown eyes.* "It is because of this stupid curse you told me about, isn't it?"

"The reason hardly matters. I do not love you. That is reason enough." *He stepped away from her.* "The curse is not stupid—it is as real as you or I."

Fury danced in her eyes. "One day you will be sorry you lied and pushed me away. You will regret denying the love that exists between us. I pity you. And I hate you."

He *had* been a miserable beast. God, how magnificent she'd been, standing up to him, toe-to-toe, poking him in the chest, calling him on his lies. And he more than deserved that slap in the face.

They *were* lies, all of them. Garrett detested lies and liars, yet he had easily deceived Abbie; it sickened him to have done it. Moreover, he was so damned weary of lying.

He'd hurt for a good while after she'd departed for Brighton. But as with most tragic events, time had lessened the pain and made the memories fade into the haze of past regrets. He remained determined to forget her, and thought that he'd succeeded for the most part. What a fool.

The mantel clock chimed twice. *Two in the morning.* He couldn't bloody well sleep. Why in hell had she appeared in his life again? She never gave him an adequate answer. To torture him? He could act as he had all those years ago: as an arrogant ninny denying what existed between them. Truthfully, he didn't have the strength to deny his feelings. God, would he have to act out this scenario again?

Perhaps he could convince her that too much time had passed; they had changed, and were not the same green adolescents they once were. He should try to convince her to leave him in peace. But now that he'd seen her, how could he ever be at peace again?

It had crossed his mind briefly, when Alberta Eaton took possession of her late uncle's home, that Abbie may turn up at some point. He had no idea if the women had been in contact and had no desire to inquire about it. Abbie's appearance answered that particular question.

She had seen him in Standon? What were the odds? Could it be fate? Abbie saw it as a sign; was it possible? How could he dismiss it? For she was correct: if he believed in the curse, he surely believed in fate. Damn it all, the curse. He must remain true to his convictions and make it clear that there cannot be anything between them.

If she even came here looking to reignite their brief but intense passion. How arrogant. Perhaps she'd arrived to visit Alberta and nothing more. It would be a solid blow to his ego, but it would also be a relief.

Regardless, there would be no tranquil sleep tonight. She wished to talk. *Lots to discuss.* Garrett should hear her out; it was the least that he could do. He owed her that much, and more besides. Damn her for upending his quiet life. For causing his heart to beat. For making him feel. Garrett threw back the rest of his scotch, stood, and poured himself another.

It would be a long night.

Early the next morning, Garrett readied himself for a walk, hoping it would clear his head. He'd managed a couple hours of restless sleep, but it was full of heated memories and reliving over and over the horrible way in which he'd ended the most passionate episode of his life. He had no idea how to proceed here. Logic stated that he push her away a second time. But he couldn't bring himself to be so blatantly cruel. Or could he? Somehow, he hadn't the strength to deny his feelings, for they were as real and raw as they were all those years ago. How strange, for he'd believed he'd placed all these wayward and intense emotions in a dark corner, never to be thought of again. He absently rubbed his chest. His heart ached, yet pounded against his ribcage at the prospect of holding Abbie in his arms again. To follow down that particular path would be a mistake of epic proportions.

He still hadn't the faintest idea as to why she came here. Garrett had the distinct impression that she was keeping something from him. Later this afternoon when they met, he would demand answers.

Inhaling the crisp January air, he was pleased that it was milder today than it had been in past weeks. They would be able to put some of the horses through their paces outside instead of the indoor exercise paddock. As he exited the wooded area between the Eaton's property and the hall, Garrett stopped short. Sitting on a large rock was a young woman, completely absorbed in the book she was reading. She wore a heavy wool cloak with matching fur-trimmed hood. Part of her face was obscured, but he could tell she was younger than he first thought.

Even in a sitting position she was a tall, willowy creature with an abundance of freckles. As he observed the young lady absently stroking her chin as she read, an amused smile quirked at the corner of his mouth, for it was a gesture that he often used. Who was she? Did she come from a nearby house? He knew all his surrounding neighbors; none had a daughter or sister of this age. Perhaps she was a visitor. The girl kept reading, oblivious to his presence. There was something familiar about her. He shook his head and continued on his walk.

Garrett's thoughts turned to Abbie. He must remain detached. Protect his heart. Protect…her. Which meant that he must continue to lie. The oath he had taken all those years ago must remain in place. Because of the curse, his love was a death sentence to any woman, and he cared for Abbie too much to allow anything to happen to her. Better to hurt. Better to lie. Better to let her go. He snorted. Right. *Good luck with that, mate.*

* * * *

As Abbie marched across the field and through the thin line of alder, beech, and juniper trees separating the two properties, the sprawling Wollstonecraft Hall came into view. The estate was as eclectic as she remembered. Garrett had told her that the front entrance and hall was from the original Tudor style of centuries past, while the Georgian and Gothic wings were more recent additions.

She had only been inside the place once, during an informal dinner party hosted by Garrett's father, the Earl of Carnstone. Of course Sir Walter had declined, but he'd bid her and Alberta to attend with a chaperone, Sir Walter's venerable housekeeper, Mrs. Claxton. Abbie had been overwhelmed by the opulence and the size of the estate, and it had struck her that Garrett was far out of her sphere. The son of an earl? Granted, he was a second son, but it became crystalline clear that the daughter of a man who had recently been knighted for his bravery as a soldier might not be an adequate companion to such a formidable family.

Abbie sidestepped an icy puddle. What would she discuss with Garrett? The past? The present? A possible future? Megan? What did she want from him? An apology would be a good place to start. It would allow her to bury most of her hurt and bitterness; at least, she hoped it would. Gazing at Garrett last night, she had the overwhelming urge to embrace him *and* slap his face, which showed how jumbled her emotions were about the infuriatingly handsome man.

Placing a light to the powder keg of emotions and memories they'd shared may not be prudent. Considering that she had no interest in taking a lover or remarrying, Abbie had acted impulsively in following him to Kent. What if Garrett were to suggest that they indulge in an affair? Would she be strong enough to say no? If the past was any indication, she would throw all caution to the wind. How troubling. She should have thought this through more thoroughly before she had come here. *Too late.*

As she continued to tread along the path, she caught a glimpse of the stables. Abbie wagered that she would find Garrett there, as it wasn't quite three o'clock. With a half smile, she headed toward the building. Sure enough, she found him brushing down a magnificent brown stallion. "Garrett."

He looked up and raised an eyebrow. "Am I late?"

"No. I imagined I would find you here. Are horses still the center of your life, raising and breeding them? You did claim that they would be your future."

He gave the stallion an affectionate pat, then motioned to one of the stable boys. "Place Patriot in his stall. See there is fresh hay, and give him his special mixture of oats."

The youth touched his forelock. "Aye, sir. Right away."

Garrett didn't answer her question. Abbie sighed and glanced about the familiar structure. How many surreptitious meetings had taken place here? She inhaled. It smelled the same, but she had never minded the scents of a barn or a man around horses. It possessed an earthy element. Masculine. Real. "I suppose the Wollstonecraft horses fetch a pretty penny?"

Garrett gathered up the brushes and curry comb. "It has become a lucrative business. We charge several thousand pounds, as our horses are of sturdy stock with impeccable lines. Well-bred. Beautiful even."

Abbie smiled. "Much like the Wollstonecraft men." He turned and stared at her. "Oh, come on, Garrett. Fourteen years ago you would have laughed at my teasing."

He tossed the grooming tools into a nearby bucket. "I'm not the same man."

"Fair enough. I'm not the same woman."

He removed his coat from the hook and slipped it on. "Do you mind if we take a walk? I think it best I not take you to the house today. There would be too many questions. Julian and my father are in residence. And before you become indignant, I'm not ashamed of our past association."

Abbie fell into step with him as they exited the stables. "Truly? For your parting words relayed the complete opposite." He frowned and did not answer. *Infuriating man.* "Last night as I lay awake well into the early hours of the morning, I recalled your recent statement: 'I never said I didn't love you.' But you *did* say it. Allow me to remind you again that you said the actual words."

Garrett blew out an exasperated breath. "I lied about a number of things when we parted that summer." He paused. "I didn't sleep much last night either. And if I recall, all those years ago, your parting shot was, 'I hate you.' We both said things we didn't mean, unless you *did* mean it."

The fact that he admitted he'd lied angered her afresh, but she had known it all along. "I did mean it. I hated you for a long time after we had separated. You hurt me. Very deeply. A permanent scar," she replied angrily. Abbie stopped walking and briefly laid her hand on his arm. Muscles clenched under her touch. "Oh, Garrett. Why would you lie?" she whispered.

He turned to face her. "To be blunt, I wanted you out of my life. You were a distraction that I did not want or need. You were a threat to my future. To my plans." He shook his head. "Believe it or not, I am sorry I hurt you. I could have cut it clean between us in a more compassionate manner."

Abbie did not expect this honesty, and her expression softened as she stared into his beautiful hazel-green eyes. "Thank you for apologizing."

Grasping her elbow, he steered her toward the rear of the hall. "We can talk privately in the orangery." He pulled a small ring of keys from his coat pocket and unlocked the door. Heat from the wood stoves hit her immediately, along with the scent of various citrus plants and trees. Garrett closed the door. "Why are you here?" he asked pointedly. "Why, Abbie? Tell me."

"I would have happily continued on with my quiet life. I had effectively packed away all memories and emotions as far as you are concerned..."

"Obviously, since you married. How soon after we parted?" His tone was rough with emotion, his gaze penetrating.

Abbie glared at him. "You have no right to sound indignant. You tossed me away. Remember?"

Garrett stepped closer and his masculine scent made her dizzy. "How. Soon."

"Two months after I returned home." She'd had no choice. It was either marry Elwyn or shame her family with her scandalous affair and be turned out into the streets. "An arranged marriage."

His thick eyebrows shot up. "Arranged? So you were miserable then."

"No," she answered softly. "I adored him."

Garrett flinched as if she'd struck him, but quickly regained his cool composure. "Did you have children?"

Here would be the perfect opportunity to bring up Megan's existence, but she wanted to introduce Garrett to her first. Or would the shock be too great? Perhaps she should tell him. No, they had much to sort out first. She carefully crafted her reply so that it would not be a complete lie. "I had no children with my husband."

"You saw me in Standon. Why didn't you approach me at the sanatorium?"

Abbie clasped her gloved hands. "By the time I recovered from the shock of seeing you, you had already departed. My late husband was a doctor; he started the clinic. His friend, Dr. Bevan, took over after he passed." She met his gaze once again. Garrett's eyes danced with green fire, his freckled cheeks flushed with emotion. She understood his reaction, for it took all her inner strength to make certain her voice did not tremble as she spoke. "Allow me to offer my sympathies regarding your nephew. I volunteer at the clinic, and I assisted with his care before I departed to come here."

With two quick strides, Garrett grasped her upper arms. "Tell me about Aidan. Tell me everything. How bad is it?"

Worry and concern were clear in his eyes. Abbie would tell him the truth. "Bad. He was going through the worst of the withdrawal before I left the village. I offered to stay, but Gethin and Cristyn thought it best that they be the ones to be the main caregivers. I fetched fresh water, cloths, broth, whatever they asked, but I was not in the room after the first few days." She sighed. "I heard the screams. Tormented dreams, Cristyn said. Pain. It is a terrible thing to come off such poison. Gethin was right to send you home. You would not have wanted to witness it."

Garrett released her and started to pace about. He always did it when agitated. Nothing had changed there. "You've seen others in this condition? Did they recover?"

"Yes. The vast majority have stayed off the opium. I have great hopes for Aidan. He is a Wollstonecraft, after all. He will come through this, I'm certain."

He stopped walking. "Could you tell Julian this before you leave? He's taking it rather hard."

"Your brother?" She remembered him from the dinner. He was thirteen years older than Garrett. Had a different mother. Abbie had found him imperious and standoffish all those years ago, yet Alberta held him in high regard. "Of course, if you wish it."

"How long *are* you staying?"

"It hasn't been decided yet."

Garrett started pacing again. "Nothing has changed. Regardless of past regrets and past lies, I still believe in the curse and still believe it best to stay clear of any romantic entanglements. I've managed to achieve it thus far. If you came here to see if there is still something between us, you've made a wasted trip."

Blast this inflexible man! She should have known he still held to the curse. Stubborn as ever. "Alberta informed me that Riordan was married at the hall mere weeks ago. Apparently he is not as committed as you are to an old family tale of woe."

He halted and scowled. "Woe? Try death. Generations of women. Rows and rows of tombstones. Shall I take you to the cemetery?"

"You've already taken me there, more than once if I recall." Abbie stepped before him, removed her glove, and cupped his whiskered cheek with her bare hand. A roll of warmth moved through her. Garrett closed his eyes, rubbing against her palm as if savoring her touch. "Enough about death and curses, at least for today. Kiss me, Garrett. See if the spark is still there. If it is, come by Alberta's tomorrow afternoon at one o'clock and I will prove you wrong about your curse." He started to speak, but she shook her head. "No reply. Just kiss me."

He was so blasted tall that he had to lean down. But he captured her mouth with his and the room, with all its trees and plants and their exotic scents, faded away. All that existed was them. The contact seared, and Garrett groaned and pulled her close, deepening the kiss.

Hungry. Desperate. On both their parts. Abbie grabbed fistfuls of his long ginger hair. As soft and silky as she remembered. His probing tongue swirled about every inch of her mouth. She gave the same in return as she slid her hands up and down his muscled arms. He was much broader and more solid than she remembered.

His large hands grasped the sides of her head, holding her still while he plunged deeper. Abbie could not stop the husky moan from leaving her throat. This was even more intense than when they were young. Garrett slid his hands down her sides, then reached behind to clutch her rear, bringing her in tight against his prominent erection. Tears shimmered in her eyes. He still wanted her. After all these years. Probably as much as she wanted him.

Garrett broke the kiss and stepped away from her, stumbling as he did. "Tomorrow, one o'clock. You can show yourself out." With a sweep of his greatcoat, he left the orangery.

Abbie was numb, stunned into shocked silence. She wasn't done speaking to him. *Typical.* The room slowly righted itself, but her heart would never recover. How bold to demand he kiss her. But she'd always been far too bold in his presence. Garrett still cast a spell over her. Still affected her. Abbie could not allow this to happen. *He's pulling me back in.*

God help her, she loved him still.

Chapter 6

Garrett couldn't continue this pattern of sporadic sleep and restless, erotic dreams. It was all because of Abbie. His well-ordered life had been upended. His emotions were a tangled mess, his heart aching with regret, but also with a stark yearning. All because of Abbie.

He admonished himself for his spineless exit from the orangery yesterday afternoon. The kiss had torn him in two, and because of it, he never got a chance to ask more questions. To find that the passage of time had not dampened his attraction for her was a harsh admission. Though Garrett had made it clear he was not interested in anything romantic between them, the kiss had proved he lied to himself. Again. He wanted her like he wanted to take his next breath. What in hell was he to do next?

Snow flurries swirled about him as he marched toward the Eatons' residence. The cold wind whipped about his face and he pulled his wool muffler tighter about his neck to keep the stinging cold from penetrating his exposed skin. Garrett didn't bother with a hat in most situations, but he wished he had today, since his long hair kept blowing across his line of vision.

A small gatehouse sat at the end of the small drive leading to the Eatons' modest manor house. Along with the rest of the property, it was in a shocking state of disrepair. Garrett mentally added it to his calendar for the spring. He didn't mind helping his neighbors, either with supplies or labor when required.

Since the sky was overcast, a beam of light reflecting through the small window of the gatehouse caught his attention. He halted. *Voices.* How strange. Thieves perhaps? He listened, and was shocked to hear a young woman speaking.

"One day soon we will marry, Jonas. You do know what it means?"

What in the hell? Garrett was tempted to barrel into the gatehouse, but curiosity got the better of him. Didn't hold much with eavesdropping, but he wanted to see where this conversation was going before he responded.

"Yes. Bert was married to my brother," Jonas replied.

"Were they happy?"

"Happy enough."

"So will we be, I promise." There was a pause. Then the young woman continued, her voice shaking with emotion, her tone earnest. "You are *not* simpleminded, Jonas. Don't let anyone tell you different."

"But in town—"

"I don't care what they say, all that matters is what you and I think. You do love me?"

"Yes, I do, Meg. You're pretty and nice to me."

"Pretty? Hardly. I'm too gangly and tall."

"Not to me. I think you are perfect."

A smile quirked at the corner of Garrett's mouth. *Jonas, you sly flatterer.* For a young man with many emotional and intellectual limitations, he handled himself well. Confident. Sure. But who was the young woman?

"I want you to kiss me, Jonas. Not like a sister, but how a man kisses a woman. You *are* a full-grown man. Kiss me."

Right. That was more than enough. It was time to put a stop to this clandestine encounter. Garrett jiggled the handle. *Locked.* The audacity of the young woman! She had lured poor, unsuspecting Jonas, who was too handsome for his own good, to this private spot to seduce him. Lifting his leg, Garrett gave the door a solid kick and the rusty hinges gave way. Pushing the door aside, he stepped across the threshold and found the lass sitting on Jonas's lap, kissing him enthusiastically. Jonas, for his part, returned the kiss with equal ardor. They broke apart at Garrett's appearance and Jonas stood, causing the girl to slump to the dirty floor. Her bonnet went askew and a ringlet of fiery red hair tumbled across her cheek.

Good God, it was the young chit that he'd seen yesterday sitting on the rock reading a book. *The brazen seductress.*

"Oh, sorry. Here, Meg." Jonas grabbed her arm, hauling her to her feet while she sputtered and brushed the dust from her cloak.

The young woman was more of a girl, or somewhere between a girl and a woman. And, in Garrett's book, she was far too young to be kissing a twenty-four-year-old man. "Who are you?" he demanded.

The lass straightened her bonnet and met his gaze. Her eyes widened and her mouth opened as if in shock. A look of fright spread across her features. What did the girl think he was going to do, harm them in some way? When she didn't reply, Jonas said, "Garrett, this is Meg. She's staying with Bert and me."

Garrett's eyebrows knotted in puzzlement. *What?* No one said anything about... He looked at the flustered girl more closely. The red hair, the hazel-green eyes. *Jesus. No.* His stomach dropped clear to his toes at the insane direction his mind wandered. "Your name?" he barked.

"You'd best speak to my mother, Mr. Wollstonecraft," she murmured. The girl blinked and looked away, turning toward Jonas as if for comfort. In response, he placed his arm about her shoulder. And her mother had to be...*Abbie*. Bile rose in his throat and his head spun.

"Both of you, leave this gatehouse. At once." He turned and ran toward the residence, his heart pounding frantically. The girl knew who he was. Damn it all, was she *his?* Garrett's confused brain scrambled to do the math. If so, she'd be around fourteen, close to fifteen—far too young to be kissing a man ten years older. Red fury clouded his vision as he pounded on the front door. The housekeeper, Mrs. Claxton, opened it, but he pushed right past her. "Abbie!" he yelled, his deep voice reverberating through the hallway. "Abbie!"

She emerged from the parlor, a puzzled look on her face. "Garrett, what's wrong—"

He clasped her elbow and dragged her back into the room, slamming the door shut with his boot. "Is. She. Mine?" His voice dripped with fury.

Abbie paled. "You've seen her?"

"Yes. I ask again: Is. She. Mine?" he hissed through gritted teeth.

Tears shone in Abbie's eyes. "Yes. Megan is your daughter."

He moaned and covered his face with his hands. My God, he had a daughter. *A daughter.* All these years... He'd had no idea. No inkling. His insides churned like a ship caught in a vicious storm. Megan. What a beautiful name.

"I...did not want you to find out like this. I wanted to reveal it gradually," Abbie stuttered.

His emotions ran the gambit from agonized shock to raw anger. "How could you not tell me?" he roared.

Abbie frowned. "After the way we parted? You sent me away. Said you never wanted to see me again. I hated you. Why would I tell you? I never even told my parents who the father was. I refused. There were a lot of tears and recriminations. Our relationship to this day is strained. I haven't seen them in years." Abbie gulped deeply. "They made it plain they were ashamed of me. Called me a harlot and accused me of being immoral for indulging in a scandal with a sinful man. They arranged a marriage with a family acquaintance." Her words came out in a heated, emotional rush. A tear trickled down her cheek and she dashed it away. "It was either marry Dr. Elwyn Hughes or be turned into the streets. They would have done it, as my parents are exceedingly pious."

Garrett could not stop himself from grasping her upper arms and giving her a shake. "You should have come to me. I would have married you. Do you hear me? I would have done the right thing." His voice rose with each word, not necessarily with anger, but with an aching pain that cut straight to his heart.

"After all you said about the curse? Not wanting anything to do with me or any woman? I had been humiliated and hurt enough. Be damned if I would show up on your doorstep only to be rejected again. I had too much pride. I still do. Yet here I am. I couldn't stay away." Her eyes flashed with a mixture of resentment and sadness.

Garrett learned his forehead against hers. "Damn you," he whispered fiercely. "For upending my life. Damn you for not telling me."

"The complete arrogance. *You* upended mine. Thank God Elwyn was a decent man who loved Megan as if she were his own. We decided that we would tell her about you when she turned sixteen. But then Elwyn died of a heart ailment. I thought perhaps I would never tell her. What purpose would it serve? Then *you* appeared in Standon." Abbie exhaled a shaky breath. "Fate. It is fate. I knew then that you *must* be told. Despite the way we parted, you deserved to know."

He pushed her away, sick to his core. "I deserved to know the moment you discovered you'd conceived. Talk about arrogance. How could you do this to us? You did not have to go through this alone."

"I did *not* go through it alone. I had Elwyn. He stood by me. Besides, you made your feelings perfectly clear. The truth is that I didn't want you in my life, nor did I wish you to be Megan's father. Think about it: we were no more than children. We acted recklessly. Not once did we take precautions or even discuss that there could be consequences. Never did you say the words: 'If you become pregnant, contact me.' Not. Once. So to hell with you."

He stared at her, surprised at how deeply the words sliced at his heart. "But you tell me now? I am to be a prisoner of your whims? To hell with *you*."

Flame crackled to life in her brown eyes. She marched toward him until they were merely inches apart. Her redolent wildflower scent surrounded him, making him dizzier than he felt already. "How dare you." She poked him in the chest as she had many years ago. "It was my body, my decision. I decided what was best for me and my unborn child. Do I marry a kind, generous, older man who promised to give a good home to me and my baby, or do I choose a stubborn, cruel, young man who cannot even acknowledge his feelings? Who clings to an ancient curse in order to keep his emotions at bay?" Her voice rose with each sentence. No doubt the entire household could hear them. "Your daughter lives. I am alive and well. No curse has taken us. *We* are the proof that the curse does not exist. Chew on that salient bit of truth."

Could she be right? Damn it all, he couldn't think straight. *Clings to an ancient curse in order to keep his emotions at bay.* Surely he wasn't that much of a cruel jackass. The emotions swirling between them were suffocating. He pushed her away once again. "Stop bloody poking me. I didn't like it then; I like it even less now."

"It's either that or I kick your stubborn arse," she yelled.

The anger between them boiled with intensity. All the poisonous thoughts that they'd kept bottled up the past several years rushed out in a furious wave. "Why not slap my arrogant face as you did before? Do I not deserve it? Besides coming here to reveal the truth about my daughter, you came here to yell and rail at me. And to punish me for turning you away. To rub my face in what I've missed these past years." Garrett took a step closer. "In what *you* have denied me."

She crossed her arms and her frown deepened. "You think me so petty that I would come all this way to exact revenge? You do not know me at all."

No, he didn't know her. They had spent most of their secret meetings making love, not talking and becoming acquainted. "And you don't know *me* if you believe that I would not have taken responsibility for our actions. I would have. In a heartbeat." Christ, his eyes welled with tears. Be damned if he would shed them. "I would have loved my daughter as I loved you. I was not even given the chance."

Abbie turned away. The anger rushed out of the room with an audible *whoosh.* Exhaustion took its place. It felt as if he'd been put through a wringer. No doubt Abbie experienced the same, going by the slump of her shoulders.

"Where did you see her?" Abbie asked, her voice subdued.

"I caught her and Jonas in the gatehouse, kissing. Very ardently, I may add. In actuality, I found Megan…your…*our* fourteen-year-old daughter— she is fourteen?" Abbie turned to face him and nodded. "I found her sitting on Jonas's lap, kissing him far more enthusiastically than she should. He is twenty-four, and, from what I observed, reacted physically, as a young man would to a passionate kiss. It was plain to see, as he had removed his coat." Abbie's hands flew to her cheeks. "Oh, no."

"I heard the conversation. She said she loves him, that in a few years they will be married. She can't be around him. Can't be anywhere near him. Surely you must agree."

A knock. The door opened and Megan peered in. She had removed her bonnet and her long red hair fell to her shoulders. Garrett stepped away from Abbie. *God, his daughter.* The resemblance in their physicality was stark indeed, including the eye color and abundance of freckles. But he could see Abbie there as well, in the shape of the face, the jawline, the contour of her mouth. His heart tumbled at the sight of her. "I heard yelling. Is he upsetting you, Mama?" Megan glared at him accusingly.

"The conversation became a little...emotional. I am fine. Come in, Megan. Come meet your father."

The girl glowered at him, a mulish expression on her face. No doubt as stubborn as both her parents. She stepped into the room, closing the door behind her. "My father died close to two years ago." Yes. Stubborn. Already he adored her. "I am sorry, sir, but I will not call you Father."

Garrett nodded. "I understand." He did, but her matter-of-fact statement hurt nonetheless. "Your mother told me Dr. Hughes was a good man. I'm heartily glad he was in your life, and thankful he was your da. I certainly don't wish to take his place, but I would like us to get to know each other." He removed his glove and held out his hand. "I am Garrett Wollstonecraft. It is nice to meet you, Megan Hughes."

Unshed tears glittered in Abbie's eyes as she watched the exchange. Hell, he felt like crying as well. Megan took tentative steps toward him. He did have an imposing physical presence, and he certainly didn't want the lass to be afraid of him. She slipped her slender hand in his. "Hello, Mr. Wollstonecraft." Her tone was cool, but polite. Perhaps it was the best that he could hope for under the circumstances.

Garrett clasped her hand with both of his. "When you are comfortable, call me Garrett. Will you?"

She shrugged, clearly flustered. The awkwardness between them was noticeable. And because of it, it was best he made his exit. He released Megan's hand and slipped his glove on. "I should make for home. I need to inform the family of these developments."

"Yes, of course," Abbie murmured.

"If you will allow, I would like to return tomorrow morning in order for us to continue our conversation." Abbie nodded. "Then I will see you about nine o'clock." He bowed slightly, then exited the room, though his legs trembled with each step he took.

A daughter. He had a *daughter.* Elation mixed with trepidation. He still could not accept the fact that Abbie never told him. Perhaps her reasons were sound. Maybe they would make sense once he wrangled control of his wayward emotions. They *had* parted all those years ago on a sour and bitter note. They *were* far too young and irresponsible. But they both were going on thirty-three years of age. Far past time to admit wrongs, and perhaps time to examine everything he had ever believed in.

Once he returned to the hall, Garrett located Julian sitting alone in his darkened room. He swiftly strode across the carpeted floor and flung open the curtains. "Enough damned brooding, Brother. You've been in here feeling sorry for yourself for days. Shouldn't you have returned to parliament by now?"

"We are awaiting Peel's decision on when to reconvene, which could be later in February," Julian muttered.

"I need you. Come to the library immediately," Garrett demanded.

Julian blinked rapidly, adjusting to the light flooding through the window. "What is it?"

"Only the fact that our lives are going to change from this moment forward. Well, mine more than any other. I need all hands on deck. Where is our father?" Garrett didn't wait for an answer. He stepped into the hall and bellowed, "Gordon, Peter, Thomas...one of you, come at once!"

The youngest footman, Thomas, appeared. "Yes, Master Garrett?"

"Where is the earl?"

"Napping in his room, sir."

"Then rouse him at once and inform him that I wish to see him in the main library, right away, lad. Go."

Julian stood. "Now I'm starting to worry. Tell me this has nothing to do with Aidan. I cannot take any more dreadful news."

"No, not Aidan. I should have clarified at the beginning. I beg your pardon."

Julian blew out a relieved breath. "You are right about one thing: I've brooded long enough. I wanted to ask if you would come with me to see Riordan. I started to write I don't know how many letters, but I've come to the conclusion that I should tell him about Aidan in person."

Damn. "I don't believe I should. The reason will become clear as soon as I explain."

"Of course," Julian replied.

They both headed to the main library and found their father rubbing his eyes. "What is it?" he asked sleepily. Julian and the earl took a seat; Garrett remained standing.

"Oh, hell. He's pacing," Julian muttered.

"I have a daughter. Her name is Megan," Garrett blurted. Both his father and his brother stared at him as if he had sprouted a second head. "I had no idea of her existence. She is fourteen, soon to be fifteen, I imagine, and is with her mother at Alberta Eaton's residence."

His father rubbed his forehead. "Good God. Fourteen? That would make you about eighteen when she was conceived. Explain."

Garrett removed his greatcoat and tossed it onto the settee. "It happened the summer Sir Walter had his niece and her younger friend for a visit. The friend was Abigail Wharton and..."

"Wait. I remember. The young ladies attended a dinner," his father said. "Good God."

Exasperated, Garrett ran his hands through his long hair. "Yes. They did. Abigail and I met nearly every day. We fell in love." There. He admitted it aloud. The pain in his heart grew more acute the more he revealed to his father and brother. He held nothing back and did not paint himself in a good light. "In conclusion, I thought it best to push her away. The curse. I had vowed never to become involved or fall in love. Ever."

Julian arched an eyebrow. "But you *did* become involved. Very much so. If you say you loved her, why—"

"Besides being an arrogant fool, I was young and irresponsible. Completely out of control. Stupid." Garrett paced some more. "In essence, I broke both our hearts."

His father shook his head sadly. "You should have come to me, Garrett. My God, why didn't the young woman seek you out when she found herself with child?"

Garrett explained in a few short sentences about her arranged marriage and subsequent widowhood. "On the way home, I decided that I will bring them here for two nights—if they agree, as I have yet to ask them—not only for them to meet you, but a situation has arisen." He explained about Jonas and Megan in the gatehouse.

"Well, that is certainly an unexpected development. And what will happen going forward?" Julian asked. "Regarding your daughter and her mother?"

"I have no bloody idea." And he didn't. "The curse is still at the forefront of my mind, and has a firm hold on my soul. Were Abbie and Megan spared because I had not been with them all these years?" Garrett began pacing once again. His father and brother exchanged dubious looks.

His father replied, "It is a distinct possibility. Or perhaps the curse is broken."

Was the curse indeed broken? Finding true love was the supposed caveat. Was it true love that they had shared? It had certainly felt like it. Nothing he'd experienced since came close. Bloody hell, his life would never be the same.

One thing became apparent: the kiss in the orangery had proved that passion still sparked between them—and that could only prove to make this situation more complicated.

Chapter 7

As promised, Garrett arrived promptly at nine. Emotionally drained to the point of prostration, Abbie was not up for another angry encounter this morning. Last night she took her dinner on a tray in her room, then promptly fell asleep, not awaking until dawn.

Mrs. Claxton showed Garrett into the parlor. His wild hair was ruffled from the breeze and the disheveled look made him more attractive. He must have walked, for his freckled cheeks were ruddy from the winter wind. The housekeeper offered to take his coat, but Garrett waved her off. "Thank you, but I am not staying long." Mrs. Claxon curtseyed, then left the room, closing the door behind her.

"I am not up for another confrontation," Abbie said. Her voice sounded weary. She certainly felt it.

He removed his gloves. "Neither am I. Pack your things."

She blinked. "What?"

"You and Megan are coming with me to Wollstonecraft Hall."

Her eyes narrowed. "Do not think you can order me about—"

"Easy. Allow me to phrase it more tactfully: Will you and Megan do me the honor of coming for a short visit? Father and Julian are eager to meet you both."

Abbie gave him a dubious look. "You've told them about us?"

"I've told them everything. We tend to share secrets in our family, at least eventually. Come for a visit; I think it prudent that we place a little distance between Megan and Jonas. Even if it is only for a couple of days."

Well, he spoke sense there. "I don't want to hurt Alberta's feelings, or Jonas's."

Garrett clasped his hands behind his back. "I'm sure that Alberta will abide by our decision once you tell her of the details. Their relationship is inappropriate. Bad enough he is ten years older, Jonas is...has...emotional and intellectual development problems. You do agree?" Abbie nodded, though reluctantly. "And beyond such, she deserves to meet her family. Her grandfather, uncle, and, ultimately, her cousins."

Abbie clasped her hands, wringing them agitatedly. "This is happening far too quickly."

"Let us say that you both stay at the hall for two nights only. Give what passed between Megan and Jonas a chance to cool. It will give us a chance to talk to her, and Alberta the chance to speak to Jonas." Garrett placed two fingers under her chin and forced her to meet his gaze. "Besides, I want to come to know our daughter. To begin an acquaintance. You may stay longer at the hall if you wish, or return here, but I *will* come to know her."

Abbie exhaled. "I suppose two nights wouldn't hurt. But I should warn you: Megan is still angry and annoyed at both of us."

Garrett stroked her cheek with the tip of his finger, leaving a trail of heated flame in its wake. "Understandable. I do not expect her to embrace me warmly. I will not demand her affection." His finger trailed across her bottom lip. "I also wish to know you better. Let us put aside bitter thoughts and memories, at least for the next two days. Agreed?"

How could she think straight while he touched her? Megan should meet the earl and viscount. How her daughter would feel about it was another matter. "Agreed."

"I'll return after dinner with the carriage. It will give you sufficient time to explain, especially to Alberta." Garrett dropped his hand and slipped on his gloves. He stared at her, his gaze dropping to her mouth. Was he going to kiss her? He seemed to consider it. Her insides fluttered at the prospect. Then he gave her a slight bow and exited the room.

* * * *

The afternoon passed in a whirlwind of drama. Abbie explained to Megan about staying the two nights at Wollstonecraft Hall and she proceeded to indulge in a fit of temper, which proved to Abbie that her daughter was still far too young to cope with certain emotional issues. When she broached the subject of Jonas and their kiss, Megan ran to her room in tears.

Furthermore, fetching her dear friend Alberta to the parlor to discuss this gatehouse kiss proved to be as difficult. They were unlikely friends, considering Alberta was close to seven years older. But Alberta's uncle, the late Sir Walter Keenan, and Abbie's father were friends, had served together in the Peninsular War decades ago. Before Alberta's uncle became a complete hermit, there had been many visits exchanged. The two girls, regardless of the age difference, had become fast friends.

The visit to Sir Walter's manor house fourteen summers past was the last time Abbie had been in this area. Shortly thereafter, Abbie married Elwyn, and Alberta married the barrister, Reese Eaton, and lived outside of London for close to ten years. They had visited sporadically throughout the decade, but their letter correspondence never abated, nor did the affection and high regard that they held for each other. Today it was being put to the test.

Alberta sat, stunned, as Abbie relayed what Garrett had told her about Jonas and Megan in the gatehouse. "Oh, Lord. And here I said with such confidence that Jonas had never shown any romantic inclinations."

Abbie passed her dear friend a fresh cup of tea. "He is a man, after all. With a young man's yearnings, even if he is not sure what it all means."

Alberta's hand shook as she clasped the saucer. "I have been dreading this conversation. How to even broach it with Jonas?"

"Perhaps Garrett could speak to him."

"A fine idea. I will ask Tensbridge to attend as well. He and Jonas have grown close the past couple of months. Jonas looks up to him. I know this is an imposition, but could you deliver a note for me tonight when you go to the hall?"

"Yes, of course."

Alberta sighed wistfully. "And what do we do about Megan and Jonas? Keep them apart indefinitely? Seems cruel."

"We will have to set boundaries. Certain rules of engagement. Perhaps Megan will grow out of this; perhaps it is only a girlish infatuation." Abbie hesitated, taking a small bite from her biscuit and chewing thoughtfully. "Or perhaps she truly loves him, just the way he is. A young girl's heart can be fickle, but mine never was. Perhaps my daughter is the same."

"Goodness, are you suggesting they could marry one day?" Alberta's tone was dubious.

Abbie smiled. "As my daughter pointed out to me not an hour past, she can marry. It is legal. Any girl can at her age, though most rarely do."

Shocked, Alberta took another sip of tea. "Good heavens, what are they teaching her at that school?"

"The law of the land, I suppose, and, shockingly, twelve is the legal age of consent. Most young women wait to marry until they are eighteen. Do we impose such a restriction? Four years is a long time. However, it may be long enough to see if their love is constant and real." Abbie reached for another biscuit. "And to see if Megan grows up a little. As it stands today, she is far too immature."

"Yes, and if she wishes to marry Jonas, she will have to understand and accept his limitations. She would have to be fully able to handle it... and him. Truly, she will have to be the mature one in their relationship, if there is to be one. Oh, what a quandary. On one hand, I would be thrilled at such a union. Alas..." Alberta's eyebrows knotted with worry.

Alas indeed. What a jumbled mess. Abbie should have stayed in her tidy little bungalow and forgot she ever saw Garrett Wollstonecraft at the sanatorium. It had been impulsive of her to come here—usually not her nature—but their entire past relationship had been impulsive.

Abbie closed her eyes briefly, reliving the kiss in the orangery. The desire between them still subsisted, pulsing with life. She came here to see if the intense love she'd felt for him years past still lingered. It did. She could choose to ignore it, allow it to return to a dormant state. Two days hence, she could hire another coach, return to Standon, and not look back.

But Garrett would never leave her in peace, whether he was physically in the vicinity or not. He'd stormed back into her life with the force of one of those new steam train engines. The only way she could move on was to confront the past and accept the present.

If there could be nothing further between them, better to face it head-on then continue always to wonder what if. It would take an infinite degree of courage. This time she would fight for what she believed in and follow where ever it leads—but remain wary. For she would not survive having her heart broken... again.

* * * *

Garrett arrived promptly at eight o'clock, driving a brougham, no doubt one of many carriages the affluent family owned. He assisted Abbie and Megan into the conveyance; he sat above in the box seat. Taking the reins, he clicked his tongue and the fine black gelding whickered and moved forward at a slow canter. Megan gazed sadly out the window at the Eatons' residence as it disappeared from view.

"It's only two nights. We will return to Alberta's, I promise. Now, will you behave civilly and act as a proper young lady while we stay at the Wollstonecrafts? No pouting or sulking. If you wish me to consider a possible union between you and Jonas, you must discontinue acting like a spoiled young girl. Do you understand?" Abbie kept her tone polite, but firm.

Megan met her gaze, an incredulous look on her flushed face. "Consider? Truly?"

"There is much to discuss, and Garrett Wollstonecraft will be involved in those discussions, but you must prove that you are capable of acting in a grown-up fashion."

Megan's eyes glistened. "I will, I promise. I love Jonas to distraction. My feelings will never waver."

"Well, that remains to be seen. Threatening to marry him without my permission is not the way to go about this."

Megan lowered her head. "I am sorry, Mama. The thought of never seeing him again upset me so."

Abbie shook her head. "How dramatic. No one threatened you with never seeing Jonas."

Frowning, Megan pointed to the front of the brougham, where Garrett sat outside on the bench seat. "He will. You did not see his face when he broke the door down at the gatehouse. Mama, he is scary."

Abbie bit her lower lip to keep from smiling. "Anyone would have been shocked at your brazen behavior. He does have a temper, but I've found his anger often vanishes as quickly as it appears. I imagine that he's the same as I remember." She paused. Megan should know what kind of man her father is. "Allow me to tell you about Garrett. He is praiseworthy and generous. Do you know he's been coordinating the renovations at Alberta and Jonas's home? Even donated building supplies and labor. From what Alberta tells me, he has done it for many of the Wollstonecraft neighbors and tenants if they fell on hardships because of failed crops and the like." She took her daughter's hand. "He is a good man. Give him a chance. Give the family a chance."

Megan sniffled. "All right, Mama. I will try."

Perhaps she should heed her own words.

Moments later they arrived at the hall. As the sprawling residence came into view, Megan gasped. "What a magnificent house!"

It never failed to impress Abbie. Such a stark difference in style, but for some reason the eclectic divergence worked. Much like the men in the family. Heavens, butterflies formed in her stomach. She was eighteen all over again, coming to the hall for the first time.

The brougham came to a stop and a number of tall, handsome footmen rushed forward to help them from the carriage and take charge of their small cases. Martin, the butler, stood by the entrance and bowed. "Welcome to Wollstonecraft Hall, Mrs. Hughes, Miss Hughes."

"Thank you," Abbie replied.

Garrett came up behind her and laid his hand gently on her back. A roll of heat moved up and down her spine at his touch. "Father and Julian are in the Georgian parlor; it's the wing that you will be staying in. We've set up a small tea as a welcome: sugar biscuits, frosted cakes, and assorted treats. Are you hungry, Megan?"

She whirled about to face Garrett, as she'd been completely caught up in inspecting the ornate Tudor hall. "I adore frosted cakes," she replied politely. *Good girl.* Abbie smiled. *Make an effort.*

Garrett escorted them to the parlor. When they entered the two men stood, and Abbie was struck by how little both had changed in fourteen years. Garrett's father, the earl, still stood straight, a fine figure of a man who must be well into his sixties. More white hair than she remembered, a few more lines, but it only enhanced his classic handsomeness. His gaze softened as it landed on Megan. "Moira," he whispered. His large blue eyes shimmered with emotion. The sadness in his eyes touched Abbie's heart. He stepped forward. "Forgive me. Miss Hughes reminds me of my late wife, Garrett's mother."

"Megan, this is my father, the Earl of Carnstone," Garrett said.

Megan gave a perfect curtsey. "My lord." *Well, the school turned out to be good for something,* Abbie mused.

"Ah. Lovely." The earl nodded his approval. He stepped toward Abbie and clasped her hand. "I do remember when you were here for the dinner all those years ago. I never would have guessed that there was anything between you and Garrett. You both hid it well." He winked, and Abbie flushed in response. He bent over her hand, then released it.

"This is my older brother, Julian Wollstonecraft, Viscount Tensbridge," Garrett said.

Besides threads of gray at his temples and those attractive little lines fanning out from his eyes, he hardly looked to be a man in his forties. He was certainly as self-contained as she remembered. The viscount bowed. "Mrs. Hughes, Miss Hughes."

Abbie reached into her reticule and pulled out the note, then held it toward Garrett's brother. "Alberta asked me to deliver this to you, my lord."

He took it, and warmth flared in his eyes. *Oh, my.* No cool standoffishness there at all. Alberta had placed her name on the outside of the note, and he reacted at seeing it. Alberta was indeed correct in surmising that there was something between them. What a development. He met her gaze. "Thank you." Tensbridge opened the note and scanned it with them still standing there. A small smile formed at the corner of his mouth as he folded the note and tucked it in his jacket pocket.

They entered the parlor, and Abbie was struck by its coziness. A fire blazed in the large stone fireplace; the furniture was modern, as were the colors. Instead of the usual burgundy or dark green, this room was done in creams and different shades of blue, from the walls to the large rug. A blue floral settee sat at the front of the room, a marble-top table in front of it. Surrounding the table was a circle of plush, blue bergère chairs, ideal for conversing. On the table sat a huge silver serving tray, complete with a three-tier stand loaded with all manner of sweets. Also on the tray were a silver teapot, china cups and saucers, small plates, and linen napkins. The butler and a young footman stepped forward to take the ladies' coats, hats, and gloves.

"Would you do us the honor of pouring, Mrs. Hughes?" the earl asked.

"Of course," she murmured, not used to being in such august company. Hopefully her hand would not shake. Once seated, she commenced pouring while the men loaded their plates with various treats.

"Go ahead, Megan. Take what you want. May I call you Megan?" the earl asked.

She nodded, then tentatively reached for a plate and laid four small frosted cakes on it. "My lord, are you related to the authoress of *Frankenstein,* Mary Wollstonecraft Shelley?"

Abbie was shocked that Megan had started the conversation. She took a quick glance at Garrett, and he met her gaze and held it, heat simmering in his eyes. Then he slid his gaze to his daughter and he smiled, pride clearly reflecting in his handsome face.

"As a matter of fact we are, albeit distantly," the earl replied. "She is my fourth cousin; her mother, Mary Wollstonecraft, was my third. Alas, the branches of the family are not close. However, she did send me signed copies when it was first published. Have you read it?"

Megan smiled and nodded. "At school, my lord. I liked it."

"What did you like about it?" Tensbridge asked.

Megan paused, as if forming her answer. Abbie could not be more proud that she was holding her own with an earl and a viscount. "The science at the core of the story. It makes sense, using an electrical current. It makes it believable and all the more shocking. I know it is thought of as a gothic horror, but I found it to be a tragedy. I felt sorry for the monster. He only wanted to be loved."

"Well said." Julian nodded.

"Yes, a good description of the book. Would you like a signed copy of your very own?" the earl asked.

Megan turned toward her on the sofa. "Could I, Mama?"

"Yes, you may."

Megan looked at the earl. "Thank you very much, my lord."

"Excellent. We will locate one tomorrow morning; I'm not sure what library it is in."

Megan's eyes widened. "You have more than one library?"

"We do," Garrett replied. "I can give you and your mother a tour of the hall, including the libraries, after tomorrow's breakfast."

Megan glanced at Garrett, then looked away. "Thank you, sir."

To give Garrett credit, he didn't let the conversation end there. "Do you ride, Megan?"

Abbie could tell Megan was all nerves talking to her...father, more so than with the earl or the viscount. Her daughter nodded while shoving a piece of chocolate frosted cake into her mouth. She swallowed, then said, "My father owned a couple of horses. He bought me a mare for my twelfth birthday. I ride her when I can, when I am not away at school."

At the words "my father" a pained expression flashed across Garrett's face and regret— and perhaps guilt—stabbed Abbie's heart. She had denied Garrett of being the one to gift her with a horse. *Yes, but with good reason.* Under the dire circumstances, Abbie made the only decision that she could. An unmarried young woman who found herself with child had few options.

Garrett cleared his throat. "We have the finest stables in Kent. In fact, I breed horses. There is a particular sweet mare who would like to make your acquaintance. Perhaps tomorrow afternoon?"

Megan looked to her, and Abbie nodded encouragingly. *Make an effort, Megan. Please.*

"Thank you, Mr. Wollstonecraft. I would like to ride." Again, a cool response. It would have to do.

Polite conversation broke out, the earl questioning Megan about her home and school and Julian asking her about Standon and Hertfordshire in general. Through it all, Abbie felt Garrett's intense gaze on her. She dared not meet it, for every emotion churning inside her would be clearly visible if she did.

"There is a portrait of your grandmother, Moira, in my study. I will show it to you tomorrow," the earl said to Megan.

"Oh, may I see it now, my lord?" Megan said, her eyes alight.

The earl stood. "Of course. Come with me."

The viscount stood as well. "I have a note to reply to. I'll see you all in the morning." He bowed and followed the earl and Megan out of the room.

They were alone. Abbie was flustered and shakily placed her empty cup and saucer on the table.

Garrett rose and sat next to her on the sofa. "Think of the years we have wasted."

All the compassionate emotions she'd been feeling dissipated. "And that is my fault, I suppose?" she snapped.

He clasped her hand, his thumb brushing across her knuckles. Her insides tumbled at his touch. "I say again: You should have come to me." She bristled, about to retort, when he said, "But would I have handled the situation in a mature manner? At eighteen I was impulsive, wild, not in control of my emotions. My father would have insisted on a marriage had you shown up at our door. I would have agreed. But would I have grown to resent you? Would I have even allowed myself to love you and Megan, or would the specter of the curse have destroyed it all?"

"Hasn't it destroyed it all anyway? You keep yourself hidden away in the stables, avoiding life. Avoiding love. To what end? To die alone?" she cried.

"You sound like my blasted father," Garrett barked. "It is my choice to be alone, just as it was yours to marry a stranger. I don't regret my decision."

Abbie pulled her hand from his, sick to her core. So much for placing bitter thoughts aside. *Damn him and his stupid curse!* "And I don't regret my decision. Did I think of you while my husband made love to me? Not once. I had completely erased you from my mind." Abbie did not like the spiteful turn this conversation was taking. Hurt obviously still lurked on both sides.

Garrett frowned. "You lie."

She did, a little. At first she'd thought of Garrett, but time had dissolved him into mist and memory. "With all the many women that came after me, I will guess you did not think of me once. Why would you? I was merely the first in a long line of willing women succumbing to your charms." How petulant of her, but she did not care.

He shook his head. "There haven't been as many as you imagine, but the ones I have been with paled in comparison to you. None of them came close. You were always there, haunting me with every thrust, every kiss. You haunt me still."

Her eyes filled with tears. "Oh, Garrett." She did not know what else to say, although the thought of him with other women, however few, cut deep.

"Do you truly believe that I did not think of you out there, somewhere in the world, lying in another man's arms? Moaning softly as you did with me? Urging him deeper, faster, as you did with me? Scoring his back with your nails as you cried out?" He clasped her arms and brought her closer. Their mouths were inches apart. "You said that you adored him, this man you married. Did you love him as you did me? Tell me the truth. Did you find the idyllic ecstasy we found in each others' arms? Tell me."

Abbie trembled. She couldn't lie. Not about this. "I did not love him. I wanted to so very much—if any man lived who deserved to be loved, it was him." A gulping sob left her throat. "Elwyn knew about you; I told him everything. He was well aware that I still loved you, but he told me he was grateful for the affection that I did show him. He was wonderful and kind and I couldn't love him." Tears trickled down her cheeks. "I enjoyed his lovemaking; we had a steady physical relationship up until he became sick, a year before he died. Elwyn was affectionate and giving. No, I did not find the ecstasy that we had shared, but I found something else. Constancy. A generous soul, a man who loved me unconditionally, accepted me, flaws and all, and did—"

Garrett covered his mouth with hers. The kiss was demanding, fierce, and desperate. He ran his tongue along the seam of her lips and she opened for him. With a ragged groan he took possession, exploring every inch of her mouth. The kiss was tender, then wild. Everything she remembered, only heightened. The flame that had simmered on low flared to life as he deepened the kiss. One of his hands grasped her breast, and she groaned in response as his stroking thumb made her hardened nipple ache. "I want you, Abbie. I never stopped. Never."

The sound of voices approaching broke them apart. Good Lord, they were both flushed, with swollen lips, and... Garrett stood abruptly and faced the window. There was no mistaking his erection. Quickly brushing the few tears from her cheeks and smoothing the front of her dress, she then reached for a biscuit and nervously began to nibble on it.

A moment later, the earl and Megan entered the room. The earl's eyebrows shot up and Abbie's cheeks flushed further, because by the expression on his face, he had no doubt guessed what had passed between her and Garrett, as the air crackled with sensual energy.

"Oh, Mama. I must show you the portrait tomorrow when we have the tour. I look very much like the countess, though she is much more beautiful."

"Not necessarily, my dear," the earl said. "You have a little more growing to do. In the next couple of years, your beauty will shine all the more."

Megan gave the earl a warm smile. Already they had formed a bond— how surprising. But then, Megan had never had a grandfather in her life before. Abbie stood. "It has been a long day, my lord. If we may be shown to our rooms?"

"Yes, at once. There will be a buffet-style brunch at about ten in the morning. Hope you brought your appetites, as breakfast is our favorite meal here at Wollstonecraft Hall. I have a maid who will see to your needs. She did such for Riordan's wife, Sabrina, over the past several weeks." The earl moved to the door and a footman entered. "Show Mrs. Hughes and her daughter to their rooms. Good night, ladies."

Garrett turned his head slightly. "Goodnight, Abbie, Megan."

* * * *

"All right, Son. The ladies have departed. What is going on?"

Garrett remained facing the window. His damned erection was still at half-mast. "Not sure what you mean, Da."

Oliver laughed. "Come and sit."

With an exasperated sigh, Garrett did, but growled when he observed the amused expression on his father's face.

His father reached for a raisin biscuit. "You were kissing her, weren't you? Quite vigorously, I would guess. The passion still exists between you. What do you plan to do about it?"

"Do? What can be done, with the curse—?"

"Hang the damned curse for the moment. The woman you loved—and no doubt still love—and your daughter stand before you hale and hearty. No tragedy has befallen them."

"Did you ever stop to think they are 'hale and hearty' because I have been apart from them all this time? Now that we are in the same vicinity, the curse will return in full fashion..." The earl laughed, and Garrett's quick temper sparked. "Do not laugh at me. You more than anyone know what havoc the curse can wreak. I watched Lady Gwendolyn rot away from childbirth infection. I watched baby Sarah gasp for every breath. I watched Fiona slowly die of a heart ailment. Factor in my mother's death? Yes, it made a damned impression."

His father ceased laughing. "No child should be exposed to such tragedies. But you cannot let it rule your entire life."

Garrett snorted. "You haven't remarried, neither has Julian. Deep down, you believe it exists. Admit it."

"I married three times. I did not allow the curse to deter me or rule my life, not to the extent you are doing. As far as Julian is concerned, did you see the expression on his face when he was given the note from Alberta Eaton? I will be starting a correspondence with Miss Tuttle. If we both believed in the curse as fervently as you, wouldn't we have pushed these lovely women aside?" His father crossed his arms. "Perhaps nothing will come from these attractions, or perhaps we will fall in love for the last time in our lives. I am willing to find out where this will lead. Are you? Or will you toss that beautiful woman away once again? I've seen the way you gaze at each other. The love is there, ready to be rekindled. Do not be hasty and dismiss it."

Garrett grabbed handfuls of his long hair in frustration. "I honestly have no idea how to proceed."

"Follow your nephew's lead. Curse be damned—marry the woman you love. Riordan has shown more courage than any of us."

Garrett glanced up at his father. "And if something should happen to his bride, what then?"

"We face it together, as a family. As we've always done. And, Garrett: Megan and Abigail should be a part of this family. Deep down you *know* it."

"We've both changed, Da."

"Suggest that she extend her visit. I have selfish reasons, for I wish to know my granddaughter better. Already I find her to be a delight. See where this leads. You've been alone long enough."

Well, his family had never shied away from discussing difficult subjects or emotions. The man spoke sense as always. "All right, Da. I will ask them to stay longer, but it is up to Abbie."

He hoped to hell that he was not making a mistake. The last thing he wished was to place Abbie and his daughter—or his lonely heart—in jeopardy.

Chapter 8

Since the air held a determined chill, Garrett decided that their ride would encompass the perimeter of Wollstonecraft Hall, but no farther. While he rode Patriot, Megan sat on Jade, the gentlest mare in the stables, and Abbie rode a chocolate brown gelding, Ivanhoe.

The conversation was sparse but pleasant. Megan still acted uncomfortable in his presence; he couldn't blame the lass. She answered him when he directed conversation toward her, but did not initiate any toward him. He wasn't sure how to bring her out from behind her protective wall other than to be himself.

"I forgot how impressive the property is," Abbie stated.

"It is even more so when all is in bloom, if you recall, especially the roses and hydrangeas. Remember the afternoon we spent picking cherries?" Garrett replied.

Abbie flushed prettily. "I do remember that you ate them all before we had a chance to deliver them to the kitchen."

Actually, Garrett recalled feeding them to each other in the hayloft. It had soon turned sensual, with Abbie slowly sucking on the succulent fruit while he held it out for her. It led to a particularly vigorous bout of sex. Garrett shifted in his saddle at the heated memory.

"Do you have other animals or pets, Mr. Wollstonecraft?" Megan asked, pulling him from his erotic and inappropriate thoughts. My God, she had asked him a question. His heart swelled with joy.

"Not as such; this is not a working farm. My late grandfather, the old earl, had chickens, but Da did not like the odor enough to keep them. We are strictly a horse breeding operation, although we do have two goats that live with some of the horses as companions." Garrett pulled on the reins to slow Patriot. "Beyond the stables there, is the breeding shed." Garrett pointed toward a cluster of buildings. "And the large building with the conical roof is our indoor paddock, where we train and exercise. As for pets, we did have a number of housecats through the years. When I was younger my Scottish grandfather gifted me with a beautiful Scotch collie during one of my summer visits. The dog passed about six years ago, and I meant to travel to Scotland to procure another, but have yet to do so."

Though he and his grandfather corresponded on a regular basis, Garrett had not visited the Mackinnon side of his family since taking on the combined duties of estate manager and land steward.

"Is it like a sheepdog?" Megan asked.

"Both are herders, but a Scotch collie is somewhat different from a sheepdog, in that they are little larger and have thicker, longer hair. Collies are intelligent, and extremely loyal."

"You should get another," Megan stated.

"Perhaps I shall. Very soon."

"What was her name?" Megan asked.

An actual conversation with his daughter, the first one ever. Although there was barely a trace of warmth in her tone, at least she was speaking to him openly. His heart squeezed with emotions he could not name. "'He' actually. I called him Laddie. Appropriate, considering his birthplace." Garrett sighed wistfully. "I miss him still. He went with me everywhere. As I said, loyal to a fault." And good company when loneliness crowded in, especially after he'd sent Abbie away.

"I remember Laddie. A beautiful dog, with multicolored sable fur." Abbie smiled. "He had a sunny disposition, and he was completely devoted to you."

"He was," Garrett replied.

"Is Scotland beautiful?" Megan asked. Garrett glanced at Abbie and she smiled encouragingly.

"My family—our family—lives outside of Edinburgh, and are involved in the making of spirits. The family is descended from Clan Mackinnon; our ancestors lived on the Isle of Skye and were fierce warriors in all number of battles, including the Jacobite Uprisings." Garrett gazed across the bleak winter landscape. "Rolling, lush hills, yet the land possesses a stark ruggedness, especially when storm clouds form overhead. Beautiful? It is one of the most breathtaking places that I've ever seen."

"When were you last there?" Abbie asked.

"Many years, close to five. I became steward of this estate… and along with the horses, I'm far too busy for traveling." How he wished that he could show Abbie and Megan his mother's homeland. Hell, when had he become a romantic, waxing poetic about Scotland? "We should head home. I've ordered pots of hot chocolate and frosted cakes for our tea this afternoon."

"Mama, may I canter ahead?"

"Yes, but stay in our sight."

Megan snapped the reins and headed in the direction of the stables. Abbie and Garrett stayed behind, side by side.

"Your family has been very welcoming, considering the circumstances," Abbie said.

"What circumstances?"

Abbie arched an eyebrow at him. "The fact that I kept the pregnancy secret, and that Megan was conceived outside of wedlock."

"There is still hurt and resentment on both sides, Abbie. Something that we need to come to terms with. The edge in your voice proves my point."

She sighed. "Yes, you're right. You've apologized for the way that you treated me, the things you've said. Allow me to do the same. I should have told you that I was with child..."

"You had sound reasons not to contact me. I understand them, but as I said, hurt and resentment lingers."

"You blasted, stubborn man, can you at least allow me to finish? Everything that happened between us was because of your obstinate nature and your unnatural belief in your family's curse," she snapped irritably.

"Me, stubborn? Good God, lass, look in a mirror. You refused to tell your parents who the father was. And you refused to contact me."

"You're making me cross, and I don't wish to be. We were both at fault—too young, too stubborn, and far too emotional." Abbie gave him a stern look. "And we are picking up right where we left off."

Garrett grabbed her reins. "I ask you once again: Why are you here? What do you want? For us to pretend the past fourteen years did not happen? To pretend we did not do and say things that cut so deeply we both carry scars to this day?" He pulled her closer, until the horses were barely inches apart. Patriot shook his head and whinnied. "Do you want us to continue where we left off, indulging in a passion so fierce it scorched us both?" The last words were whispered in her ear, his voice husky and his emotions raw.

Abbie blinked, her eyes glistening. "Yes. No. I don't know."

"I don't accept your irresolute reply. You came to me. You want me. Say it." He pulled on the reins. "Because it can't be half as much as I want you."

"Garrett..."

"Mama, are you coming?" Megan called out.

Hell. He released the reins and turned Patriot about. As Abbie had stated, this was far too emotional. He'd better get a handle on things, or this situation would spin out of control. Blast it, it had already.

* * * *

The Marquess of Sutherhorne watched the affecting encounter through his opera glasses with a good deal of amusement. The Scottish beast acting emotional in a woman's presence: what a delight to the imagination. The marquess was far enough away, hidden in a cluster of oak and beech trees to ensure he could not be seen. "Delaney, who is the lady?"

His hired man sat upon a horse next to him. "Not sure, my lord. Do you wish me to find out?"

He lowered the glasses. "Yes. Find out her name and where she comes from, and the flame-haired chit with them. It might prove to be useful in my scheming."

"What about the schoolmaster?" Delaney asked. "Any plans for retribution there?"

Sutherhorne glanced at him. He had recently employed Delaney after observing him as a participant in a brutal bare-knuckle fight, and later performing sexually with another man at a brothel. Both acts were illegal, but Sutherhorne saw Delaney as a man after his own heart. He liked to inflict pain on other men as much as Sutherhorne enjoyed watching it. A particular personality quirk he'd discovered during his youth at Eton.

He'd also hired him for protection. No man would ever lay a hand on him again with Delaney hovering nearby. The boxer stood nearly as tall as the Scottish beast. If Wollstonecraft ever threatened him again, he would unleash his own animal, and enjoy watching the spectacle. What had Delaney asked? Ah yes, the schoolmaster.

"I am not concerned with Riordan Wollstonecraft at the moment," Sutherhorne stated. "He threatened me verbally, but the loutish uncle?" He pointed toward Garrett Wollstonecraft. "He had the audacity to manhandle me, and he must answer for it. I haven't decided how yet. I will head to London in my carriage. You stay. Discover what you can and join me afterward."

He paused, watching Wollstonecraft and the woman head toward the stables. "If needs must, we will return in a timely fashion. Meanwhile, stay out of sight. Wollstonecraft saw you at the Debtor's Court; he knows you are connected to me."

"As you say, my lord."

They turned and headed toward Sevenoaks. It was not as if Sutherhorne believed in cold-blooded murder—that particular response would be exaggerated for the insult he'd endured. But he would come up with something adequate to satisfy his lust for revenge.

Sutherhorne's eyes narrowed as he stared across the horizon. The entire family had to be taught a lesson. How dare they interfere in his plans of obtaining the woman he'd desired for the past eleven years? It still galled him that Sabrina Durning Lakeside threw him over for a lowly schoolmaster. Him, a marquess and a close advisor to Prince Albert. Granted, the schoolmaster turned out to be the grandson of an earl, but the insult stood nonetheless.

Now Sabrina was married to the beast's nephew. Sutherhorne smiled cruelly, as he'd already found satisfaction in exacting a certain sort of retribution by proxy, and because of it, may not even bother with the schoolmaster and his bitch bride. Yes, he'd managed to soothe his ache for revenge on that score.

His thoughts drifted to the party he and had Delaney attended in London last month. A truly wicked and corrupt affair, with vices of all sorts available for consumption. When a rather motley crew announced they had an earl's heir to sell, Sutherhorne could not resist. He started when the cockeyed, disheveled young man stepped forward. The schoolmaster!

Then he took a second look and recalled that Carnstone had paternal twin grandsons. *Ah yes. The black sheep.* The look was similar, but not the same. No names were offered, but it hardly mattered. The wraith-like wreck wore the stamp of a Wollstonecraft, with his dark hair and startling light blue eyes.

This would be part of his vengeance on the smug, arrogant family. *Destroy the heir.* Once one hundred pounds had exchanged hands, he'd turned the sickly looking heir over to Delaney's ministrations—while he watched. Sutherhorne himself never participated in these illegal physical acts, but he did quite enjoy observing.

Regardless, how to exact the rest of his vengeance on the red-haired brute would require further thought.

But it would be soon. Very soon.

* * * *

The next afternoon, Julian and Garrett strode toward the Eaton residence and the upcoming talk with Jonas. Their breaths huffed out in icy clouds as their boots sunk into the snow. A few inches had fallen overnight.

"I am not looking forward to speaking with Jonas about male desires, human anatomy, and reproduction," Julian stated.

"You must have had the talk with the twins," Garrett replied.

"Yes, when they were of a certain age. Thinking about it, I suppose intellectually Jonas is the same age the twins were when I spoke to them."

"I will have to keep Jonas's condition in mind and hold my temper in check," Garrett said.

"Overreacting is never prudent, though I suppose I should heed my own advice in most situations," Julian replied.

Garrett smiled and winked. "I'm sure you're looking forward to seeing Alberta."

Julian had stayed away from Alberta too long. Perhaps embarrassed that he'd fallen apart in her arms. But hearing the news about Aidan had broken him in two. Garrett had known it would, and had the foresight to ask Alberta to come to the hall in order to comfort him. His brother knew him well, and true to his character, looked out for him. When was the last time a woman held him, soothed him, and wiped away his errant tears?

Fiona. The doctor had informed the family that there would be no recovery from the carditis and her heart would fail. Julian had lost control at the news and Fiona had bravely comforted him. Though he'd spent a lifetime keeping his emotions hidden, he was like the rest of the family: emotions could appear with no warning whatsoever. The Wollstonecraft men felt things deeply, loved fiercely, and were passionate about justice and the rightness of the world.

"Yes. Thank you for having Alberta come to the hall when you told me about Aidan."

Garrett exhaled. "I understood the information would be devastating. It is plain to see that you care for her."

Why deny it? "I do. Not sure what to do about it. I'm not a young man any longer. To become involved with a woman at this late date? And of course—the curse. It gives one pause, as you well know."

Garrett laughed cynically. "But here are Abbie and Megan in fine health. It is making me question everything. Like you, I am not sure what to do about it. Could they be in fine fettle because I was not with them? Who is to know?"

Julian didn't know how to respond. Who was to know? Drama wherever he turned. Did he really wish to insert himself in *this* particular drama?

Yes, he did. He was fond of Jonas, and perhaps more than fond of Alberta. He was honored that she had asked him to speak to the lad.

Pulling his hat lower to avoid the bracing winter breeze, Julian picked up his pace, and Garrett met his stride. Truly, he had enough on his plate with what had befallen Aidan, and now the dramatic discovery of Garrett having a daughter and a former love. Facing Riordan the day after tomorrow and informing him of his brother's fate would not be easy. "Father will be coming with me to Carrbury to see Riordan."

"I would have, Julian."

"You have enough to contend with. I *am* tempted to head to Hertfordshire, but I will heed the doctor's suggestion for now."

"I believe it best."

Once they arrived, Julian was disappointed to find that Mrs. Claxton answered the door. She stated that Alberta and Jonas were awaiting them in the parlor. He'd hoped to get Alberta alone for a moment. After their coats, hats, and gloves were taken, Julian and Garrett were shown into the parlor. Jonas looked apprehensive.

Alberta stood. "I will leave you alone. Will you stay for a drink after, Julian? Garrett? A brandy perhaps?"

Hell, yes. Julian would need the drink. "Of course."

"I thank you for the invitation, but I should return to the hall," Garrett replied.

She smiled and exited the room, closing the door behind her.

"Bert told me why you're both here," Jonas mumbled, looking contrite. "I shouldn't have kissed Meg."

Julian and Garrett sat across from him. "Did your body react?" Julian asked. Might as well steam ahead directly into the delicate subject at hand. Jonas nodded. "It is nothing to be ashamed of, lad. It is a perfectly natural response when you kiss a young lady."

Garrett leaned forward. "The key word here is *young*. Megan is far too young to be involved with a man. And you *are* a man, Jonas. Fully grown. Ten years older."

Jonas met Garrett's gaze. "I liked kissing her, though."

"Yes, but it cannot happen again. Not until Megan grows up a little more," Garrett replied.

Jonas's eyebrows knotted with worry. "But she won't want me when she grows up."

Julian's heart tightened at the dismay in Jonas's voice. "That's not necessarily true. You must be patient. I know it will be difficult. But in this situation, *you* must be the grown-up. Remain firm in the belief that you must wait. In the meantime, you can visit, write, stay in touch. Can I rely on you to be the grown-up here, Jonas, regardless of your feelings?"

"I love her, Tens. I want to marry her."

"How do you love her?" Garrett asked in a soft voice. "Do you understand what marriage will mean?"

Jonas paused, and Julian could see him working out the proper response. "Bert and Reese were married. It means sharing things: food, thoughts, kisses, laughter, and more. Sleeping in the same bed. Sitting together in the evening, happy to be with each other." Jonas smiled. "And love? I want Meg with me always. I want to keep her safe. I'm happy when she looks at me. Smiles at me. I feel strange inside when she's near."

"What you described about love and marriage is very astute," Julian said. Jonas arched an eyebrow in question. "Astute means smart."

Another broad smile spread across his perfect features. "I'm smart? Truly, Tens?"

"More than you may believe. If Megan loves you as much as you love her, she will wait. As I said, you must be the grown-up and remain strong. Will you be able to do that, Jonas? Allow proper time to pass before you take your relationship farther? No kisses, no improper touching. It will be difficult, but Megan must be allowed to grow and mature. And if she loves you, she will want you, do not worry." Julian gave Jonas an encouraging smile.

"I will be the grown-up, I promise. I want to marry her someday, Tens. But doesn't the man have to have a job? Make money to live? Reese did; he was a barrister. What can I do?"

Julian sat back in his chair. Well. Didn't expect that. He glanced at Garrett and they exchanged looks of surprise. As he surmised, Jonas was not simpleminded, but had many limitations. Those precincts would be difficult to handle not only for him, but for any woman who married him. It would take an extraordinary young lady indeed. Was his niece up for the challenge? It remained to be seen.

"Let us ponder on it for a while, Jonas. Do you have any other questions?" Garrett asked.

"Is Meg your daughter? For real?"

"Yes, for real. It has been a happy surprise for us all. It is a long story, but it shows what happens when young people give in to passion and love and don't consider the consequences," Garrett answered. "Society is harsh toward unmarried young women who find themselves carrying a child. It is entirely unfair that young ladies receive the brunt of the censure. Society is unforgiving; they call it a scandal, and it's another reason that you and Megan must remain strong and wait. You do not want Megan to find herself in such a situation."

Jonas shook his head vigorously.

In as many brief words as they could muster, Julian and Garrett explained the act of human reproduction. Jonas absorbed the information, his expression contemplative. "I won't do that with Meg, not until we're married, I promise."

"Good lad." Damn, he could only hope that the young couple curbed their desires. From experience, Julian knew it was difficult. He glanced at his brother. Garrett was the living proof.

Jonas stood. "I'm going to feed Poppy. Do you both want to come with me?"

Julian laughed. "And have your llama spit at me again? I think not. Besides, I am going to share a brandy with Alberta." He rose to his feet. "Any time you have questions, Jonas, you come to me. Or Garrett. We are all friends."

Garrett stood as well. "Julian is correct."

Jonas smiled, his blue eyes sparkling. "Tens. Garrett. We're very *good* friends." He scampered from the room and Julian blew out a cleansing breath. *Thank Christ that was over.*

Moments later, Alberta entered, smiling warmly. "Forgive me. I listened outside the door. I couldn't sit still in my room."

Garrett smiled and gave her a slight bow. "And on that note, I will take my leave. You and Jonas will come for dinner the evening after next? Cook will be pulling out all the stops. I know it is short notice, but we would be delighted if you accepted."

"We would love to attend."

Garrett nodded toward Julian and exited the room. Alberta sat next to Julian on the settee. "I thought you would have returned to London by now."

"Prime Minster Peel ended the autumn session prematurely and is reluctant to call us back. He knows he is in danger of losing the house. The Factory Act does not go far enough, and I and others are pushing for further reforms. Also, many of us are pushing for a repeal of the Corn Laws. It all makes for contentious sessions, to say the least."

Alberta smiled. "Obviously you are not of a conservative bent."

"Far from it. Nor am I in the House of Lords. Viscount Tensbridge is a courtesy title. I am a Member of Parliament for this district."

She nodded. "My uncle often wrote of the earl's causes. Some he agreed with, others he did not. Neither am I conservative. I take interest in what goes on at Westminster, though I know it is not fashionable or acceptable for a woman to do so."

"I applaud you." He returned her smile. "And I look forward to future conversations."

"Concerning Jonas, from what I heard, you were wonderful. And how very frank you were in your descriptions." Alberta winked good-naturedly. She teased him and he loved it. With a crooked grin he stood and gathered her up in his arms. "All the talk about kissing and desire has had its effect on me. I have not kissed you yet. I mean to correct that." He rested his forehead against hers. "A proper kiss."

"Kiss me then," Alberta whispered.

Gently grasping the sides of her head, he stared into her glorious golden-brown eyes. Slowly, he leaned in, making the anticipation flare between them. He nibbled on her lush lips, then took it deeper, taking complete ownership of her mouth. Alberta kissed him in return, tangling her tongue with his.

How gratifying to react this swiftly to a devastating kiss at his age. At forty-five, he had a number of good years left; why not embrace everything life had to offer? Encircling Alberta's waist, he brought her in tight against him. Against his stiff and aching prick.

She replied with a moan, which heightened his desire to a level of wild fierceness he'd not experienced in years. "Julian," she whispered against his mouth as he trailed hot, fevered kisses down her neck.

Reluctantly, he ended it by cupping her flushed cheeks and gazing into her eyes. "I'd better have that brandy," he rasped.

"Brandy?" She smiled. "Of course." Alberta left his arms and walked toward the sideboard. He felt her absence keenly.

This had moved beyond a flirtation with an attractive neighbor. How far he wished it to advance was another question entirely. Julian understood Garrett's reluctance. Hell, he'd lived it, and he never wanted to live through burying a woman he loved ever again. At least, not before reaching old age. Logic dictated that he walk away from what was developing between him and Alberta. But when did logic ever enter into emotions?

Caution was needed. To keep his emotions tightly reined.

Easier said than done.

Chapter 9

Later that night, Garrett paced about his room. He hadn't had a decent night's sleep in more than two weeks. There were a number of reasons: one was finding out he had a daughter. To discover her kissing a man with decided enthusiasm was a swift kick to his guts. Megan stood on the cusp of womanhood, and Garrett had missed so much of her life. It put him in a somber mood, mourning the time he had lost.

His talk with Jonas had made him realize that the young man was passionate and intuitive about the world around him. He had come to know Jonas better the past several weeks, while he'd been supervising the improvements about the small Eaton manor house. Perhaps he should include Jonas more in the planning of repairs. Though he may be slow, Jonas did possess an innate intelligence that could be channeled into something worthwhile. The young lad had mentioned an occupation. He would give it serious thought.

His reflections turned to Abbie. Bad enough she had haunted his dreams all these years, drifting around the corners of his subconscious, tormenting him with heated memories of their youthful affair. But to have her down the hall was more than he could bear. How tempting it would be to march to her room, kick the door in, and make love to her until she writhed and cried out his name. Lick and taste every inch of her silky, sweet skin. No other woman had ever affected him in such a stark way. If he allowed this attraction between them to go further… Could he push her from his life once again? How could he with Megan in the picture?

Garrett stalked to the sideboard and poured himself a scotch, the family Mackinnon's own special single malt. His rooms were laid out much like a large flat, with the front section serving as a combination library-study.

Through to the rear were his large bedroom, dressing room, and bathing room. He had a custom-made copper tub built to accommodate his large frame. Water pipes had been installed two years past, eliminating the need for servants to fill the tub, so he indulged in a daily soak, especially after working in the stables all day. The rooms garnered him the privacy he desired. All of the men of Wollstonecraft Hall had similar floor plans in their respective wings.

After slumping into his leather wingchair, he stared moodily into the fire as he sipped his whiskey. His muddled emotions brought their first meeting to the forefront. Leaning back, he closed his eyes and was drawn away somewhere in time. He was riding the horse he had owned before Patriot, a black stallion called Midnight Thunder. He had come upon Abbie on one of the numerous horse paths meandering through and around the estate.

Garrett brought Thunder's reins up short and called out, "Whoa." Everything around him came to a complete standstill. Before him stood the most beautiful creature that he had ever laid eyes on. Could it be a fairy princess from another realm?

It was a young lady wearing a lavender walking dress. She wore no hat or gloves, but he couldn't blame her, as the air was hot and humid. She carried a small matching parasol, but did not use it to keep the sun off her face. Instead, she seemed to be enjoying soaking up the rays.

The lilac shade of her gown enhanced her porcelain skin and glossy black hair, which was piled high on her head; a couple of loose strands framed her glowing, lovely face. The surrounding countryside faded away, leaving only...her. She was all that existed for him. Garrett's heart pounded with a fierce beat, the blood rushing to his ears.

"Hello," she said. "You have a beautiful horse." She shaded her eyes from the sun as she looked up at him. "And I must say that you are beautiful as well."

He threw back his head and laughed. Bold minx. He gave her a wicked smile as he slid off Thunder. "I am Garrett Wollstonecraft."

"I hope you don't mind me perambulating about your property. I am staying with Sir Walter Keenan, your neighbor. His niece is a dear friend of mine." The young lady returned his smile. "We arrived yesterday and are here for most of the summer." She held out her right hand. "I am Abigail Wharton. Pleased to meet you, Mr. Wollstonecraft."

Her voice was light and musical, as if someone were clinking crystal champagne glasses together. The enticing sound caused shivers to run along his spine and his breath to catch. Taking her hand, he bent over it, somewhat awkwardly. He wasn't used to the falderal of parlor manners.

He'd only attended one ball, in London, and he had spent most of the evening in the card room. "And you, Miss Wharton." His voice sounded husky to his own ears. It was as if he'd been hit by a bolt of lightning. He dropped her hand a little too quickly and took a step in reverse.

"Will you walk about with me, show me your property?" she asked politely.

What an audacious female. Not only speaking her mind, but daringly meeting his gaze. Weren't young ladies supposed to giggle and avoid eye contact with men, instead batting their eyelashes coquettishly? Not this one, and he liked it. More than liked it, for he couldn't seem to catch his breath. "If you like."

"Oh, dear. I am about to do something entirely scandalous." She stepped before him, rose on the tips of her toes…and kissed him. The suddenness of it shocked him to the heels of his dusty boots. Then came the sensations that followed: the softness of her lips, her evocative scent of wildflowers, fresh air, and sunshine. If sunshine even had a scent. Dropping the parasol, she rested her hands against his chest. Since he was riding about his own property and because of the warm weather, he only wore breeches, tall boots, and a billowy white shirt open partway down his chest.

When her hands made contact with his bare skin it seared his flesh, and he dropped the reins and riding crop and pulled her into his embrace. Already aroused, his cock stiffened to the point of pain. Garrett deepened the kiss and she gasped, opening her mouth enough that he could slip his tongue into it. The taste of her made him moan. Every part of him sizzled from her heat. More…he needed more…

Soft rapping at his door brought him out of his dreamlike state. Bloody hell, he was aroused. Scrubbing his face with his hand, he glanced at the mantel clock. Past midnight, who in hell… No. *She. Wouldn't. Dare.*

Garrett was shirtless, his trousers undone and riding low on his hips. He shot to his bare feet and slammed his glass on the nearby table. Whoever knocked at his door past midnight deserved to be traumatized by his appearance. He marched to the door and pulled it open.

Abbie.

God, she was gorgeous, still the fairy princess from another realm. She wore a sheer pink nightgown and matching wrapper, with pink fur trim about the neckline and the cuffs. He glanced down. Her small feet peeked out from under her ensemble. Slowly he trailed his gaze across her tempting curves. Giving birth to Megan had only enhanced her lush figure. "Abbie, what…"

She pushed past him and entered his room. Exhaling, he closed the door.

Abbie spun about to face him. "You asked me a question when we were out riding. I never replied."

"You don't have to tonight, perhaps—"

She nodded briskly. "Yes, I do. Who can sleep?" Abbie's heated gaze slid across his torso. "Lord, you are a finely put-together man. The years have made you more enticing and attractive, blast you. I have never been this forthright and outspoken with anyone but you."

"I was thinking of our first encounter when you knocked."

A shy smile curved about Abbie's lips. "Yes. I acted boldly from the beginning. I said that you were beautiful. We exchanged a couple of sentences and suddenly I was kissing you. And finding myself overwhelmed by your embrace."

Garrett stepped closer. "We were drawn toward each other."

Abbie nodded. "Always. The answer to the question that you asked this afternoon is… Yes, I want you. I never stopped." He opened his mouth to speak, but she held up her hand. "I deluded myself into thinking I had safely hid away what we'd shared. As soon as I saw you in Standon it all flooded to the surface. I couldn't pretend any longer. I realized that it was well past time to inform you about Megan."

Clasping her hands in front of her, she met his gaze. "We have both apologized. As you said, there are scars on both sides. We will carry them for the rest of our lives. But I wish more than anything for the healing to begin in earnest."

"Abbie, you…"

"This is far more intense than I thought it would be," she whispered, interrupting him again. "My first instinct is to flee to my small house and hide. Forget it all. But I cannot." Abbie stepped closer and laid her hands flat against his bare chest as she'd done during their first meeting. His skin burned from her touch, and because of it, he couldn't stop the husky moan from leaving his throat.

"Though I want you, I yearn more for a fresh start. But we can only accomplish that if we place the past and all its scars behind us." Her words were direct and honest, just as he remembered. Abbie tunneled her fingers through his thatch of ginger chest hair and he moaned again. "Which means that you must leave the curse behind you. It has ruled your life for far too long." He stiffened at her statement. "Do not get your bristles up or allow your temper to say something you may regret."

"As I have in the past, you mean?" His brows furrowed. "I pushed you away because I was genuinely concerned for your safety. Hell, I still am. I would do anything to protect you."

"To the detriment of our young hearts." Abbie glared at him, her mouth twisted in disapproval. "I waited three long weeks for you to show up at my door; I told you more than once that I lived in Brighton. I sat on our porch for days, waiting like a fool. You never came." Her lower lip trembled. "You didn't love me enough to ride in and claim me. I cursed you, for how could you do such a thing to us? Deliver such a mortal blow to our love?"

Her voice trembled, and Garrett's heart squeezed at hearing the raw emotion in her words. "Then to discover that I was with child...I felt all at sea. Completely lost and alone. You had truly abandoned me. I had no choice but to inform my parents of my condition. At that exact moment, mired in despair, it struck me. *I* left. *I* did not stay and fight for our love. The blame did not all lay at your feet. Then I thought perhaps it was never meant to be. Perhaps I did not love you as deeply as I believed."

She exhaled shakily. "To lessen the aching pain, I convinced myself that what lay between us was nothing more than base lust. With the decision made, I went to my parents, then, shortly thereafter, agreed to the marriage and promptly put you out of my mind." Abbie laid her head on his chest and he slipped his arms around her, bringing her in tight against him. "But not out of my heart. No matter how much I denied it to myself and to my husband, Elwyn knew the truth. Despite it all, I loved you still."

Garrett smoothed her hair. "Loved? Past tense?"

"Do not ask me to try and sort through my emotions in that regard. Not tonight."

"Fair enough. But hear this truth from me: I deeply regret that I did not come and claim you. It is a regret I will carry all the days of my life. Could you truly find it in your generous and brave heart to forgive me? Perhaps we can salvage something consequential from this youthful wreckage."

She sighed. "Not if you insist on placing the curse between us as a shield. If you cannot commit to me or love me with your entire heart and soul, then I do not want you at all. I won't settle for any less. Elwyn taught me that much."

He remained silent, taking in all that she had revealed. Abbie, as always, spoke from her heart. She deserved the same from him.

"Truly, Garrett. I don't deny your family, past and present, has suffered wrenching personal tragedies. But we cannot allow it to keep us apart any longer," she continued. "Nothing has happened to Megan or me. Perhaps the curse is broken at long last. Perhaps...our love was true. Isn't it the requirement for breaking the curse?" she murmured.

"Supposedly, true love breaks it, but there is no unequivocal proof one way or another." Could she be correct? It would go against everything that he believed in. "I watched my stepmother die horribly. She literally rotted away from a childbed infection before our eyes. Three weeks later, my infant sister gasped her last. At ten years of age, I swore never to let anyone close. But you burrowed into my heart and soul regardless. You hold them both captive. Even after all these years."

He continued to smooth her hair as he spoke. "My sister-in-law, Fiona, languished of a heart infection for months, turning into a ghostly figure I did not recognize. My mother, whose memory I tried desperately to cling to but it faded from my recall anyway. Cancer ate at her until I was no longer allowed into her room. My earliest memory I have is of them lowering a casket into a dark grave. I was four.

"Death and mourning were the sum of my childhood. Watching how broken Julian was, how hurt. Thankfully, the twins kept the worst of the sorrow at bay. They livened up the house and brought us all out of misery. But I vowed, then and there, that no one would own my heart or break it, because I would refuse to love any woman." He laughed cynically. "It was all for naught."

He clasped the sides of her head, forcing her to look at him. She met his gaze with unshed tears gathering on her long lashes. "From the moment I saw you on the trail all those years ago, I knew you would shatter my plans to stay detached and removed from emotion. From love. I foolishly thought that we could enjoy a brief assignation and go our separate ways. God, I *am* an idiot." He kissed her forehead. "I denied what was happening. Refused to accept what my heart told me. I believed that the only solution was to be malicious enough that you would never wish to see me again. It worked better than I had hoped. And it shattered me."

"I am truly sorry for your childhood losses. I understand better why you believe in the curse as deeply as you do, but to let it come between us." She gazed up at him. "We did not speak like this in the past."

Garrett smoothed her hair once again. It was as soft as spun midnight silk. "There was not much opportunity for speaking. We used our bodies to communicate more than anything."

"May we talk? Here?" Her look was eager and hopeful and he didn't have the heart to refuse her. "I wish us to become acquainted. The people we are now."

He nodded, then stepped away from her and motioned to his sideboard. "Would you care for a drink? I have Mackinnon single malt, my mother's family's own scotch."

"Yes." Abbie curled up in one of the wingchairs before the hearth. Once he poured the drinks in crystal tumblers, he handed her one and sat opposite. "Tell me about your wild streak in your twenties."

His eyebrows shot up in surprise. "How in hell did you hear about that?"

"Sir Walter was a hermit, but he did enjoy sharing gossip in his correspondence with Alberta. She told me the other day. I am curious."

"And what of your past?"

"Let us speak of you for the remainder of the night."

Garrett curled his lip and took a long draw on his scotch, clenching his teeth as the burn trailed down his throat. A brief dissolute episode in his life and she honed in on it. "I could blame Aidan, for even at sixteen he was rather naughty. He confided in me that he lost his virginity the year before at The Crimson Club. It is a place in London that the men in my family like to frequent on occasion. It is a tasteful and respected brothel."

"Did you lose your virginity there as well? Is it a rite of passage for the men of your family?" she asked, her tone curious.

"Since you wish to discuss my secrets, here is one I have shared with no one: I lost my virginity...to you. There was no other young lady before you." Garrett gave her a heated gaze. "Emotionally speaking, there has been no woman after you. The encounters meant nothing."

"Oh, my," she murmured. "I am rather shocked about your virginity. I assumed most sons of peers indulged as young as Aidan. Forgive me for feeling rather satisfied at the fact I was your first, and pleased that the only encounter that meant anything...was ours." She sipped her scotch. "However, I was not your last. Hence the adventures with your nephew. Do tell."

Did he hear a tinge of hurt at her statement that she was not his last? Perhaps he imagined it. "I was twenty-one and hadn't been with another female since I stupidly pushed you away. Aidan proposed a short jaunt to London. It lasted close to two years."

Abbie's eyes widened. "Good heavens. What did you do in all that time?"

"When we were not staying at the London townhouse, we were at The Crimson Club. Or other houses of ill repute. Gambling, attending scandalous parties. As the months clicked by, the places grew increasingly seedier. Aidan strived for more stimuli, more thrills, and did not care where he obtained them." Garrett threw back another swallow of scotch. "I should have seen the signs then and there. Regardless, I eventually grew bored with the meaningless, indiscriminant sex. Aidan did not." He caught her gaze. "We agree to tell the absolute truth?"

She nodded.

"You haunted my nightly dreams from the day we parted. It became torturous. I thought that I could effectively erase you from my subconscious with other women. It was a complete and utter failure." He exhaled. "I was determined to not think of you during the day, but you entered my dreams without fail, night after night. Taunting me."

"I cannot find it in me to be smug at this information. It merely proves how mistaken we were to so cavalierly toss what we had aside. For you haunted my dreams as well." She took another drink. "This is rather good."

"Care for another?"

"If it keeps us talking civilly and truthfully, then yes." She held the near-empty tumbler out and he strode to the sideboard and refilled the glasses. Blast it all, he had been in a state of arousal since before he opened the door to find her there. Talk? He could think of a more strenuous and sensual activity than conversing. But he innately understood that Abbie needed this. And truth be told, he did as well. For how could they move forward—if that is what they truly wanted—unless they discussed what had happened, and what was to come?

Garrett stood before her and held out the glass, and her gaze lingered on his low-riding breeches. His erection was plain to see. Pink color washed her cheeks as she clutched the glass and looked away to stare at the dancing flames in the fireplace.

"Did you have any serious relationship with any woman?" she whispered, still staring at the fire.

"There was one." Abbie turned to look at him. "In Scotland. I visited my grandparents the summer after ending my debauched journey. I was twenty-three, the age a young man should begin to shop about for a prospective wife. The Wollstonecraft line did not depend on me procreating; what was the rush? I met her at a social in Edinburgh. Lovely young lady. My grandparents were thrilled. Perhaps, they thought, I would settle in Scotland."

God, it had been ages since he thought of Elspeth. How much to reveal? *All of it, you fool.* "I thought myself half in love. Elspeth was beautiful, her hair a rich caramel shade, her eyes shining with a matching incandescent color. We kissed, touched, and even came close to having actual sex. There is nothing quite like rolling about in the heather kissing a pretty young lass..." His voice trailed off and a smile curled about his lips at the memory.

"I do not think I care much for this bit of your past," Abbie stated, her mouth pulling into a taut line.

"Nothing came of it, for I did not want to be responsible for breaking another woman's heart or placing her in danger because of the curse. But more importantly, *my* heart was not completely engaged. I ended it before it became too serious. It did not come close to what we shared, and I discovered that I would never settle for less. If that meant I would be alone the rest of my days, so be it. I had already vowed to live a solitary life anyway."

Their gazes caught. The heat between them could easily ignite a raging forest fire.

"What happens now?" she whispered.

"Come to my bed."

"Bounder," she replied softly, her eyelids lowered. "Beyond that."

"You tell me. You have my complete attention."

"I do want you, Garrett. But could we possibly...take things a bit slower? As I told you, I do not know exactly where this will lead, if anywhere."

He couldn't believe what she had just said. Garrett stared at her incredulously. "You come to my room, claim you want me, bare your heart, and ask me to bare mine; now you state that you want to take things slow? Are you out to purposely torment me?"

She placed her glass on the nearby table. "Good God, no. All I ask is we not have actual sex *tonight*. Touch each other, by all means... I am not sure how to explain this... By our own admission we are not the same people. I want us to—I want you to—"

"Court you?"

She smiled, and the warmth of it made his heart skip a beat. "Precisely. I wish to be courted. Just a little. I never have."

No, he supposed she hadn't. After their first meeting, they'd agreed to meet the next afternoon. Once in each other's arms, they'd found a private area in the woods, rolled about in the grass, feverishly touching and kissing until passion overcame them and, at her eager invitation, they lost their virginity. Abbie was his first. By God, if he had any say over fate and curses, she would be his last.

Her arranged marriage also negated any courting. In this, he would not deny her. "I would be honored to court you." He stood and held out his hand. She slipped hers in his and rose to her feet. "Define touching," he teased. "Like this, perhaps?" Cupping her rear, Garrett brought Abbie in tight against his hard-as-oak cock.

Bold as ever, she slid her hand between them and grasped his cock, squeezing hard until the groan escaping him sounded similar to a beastly growl. "And like this." Abbie stood on the tips of her toes and nuzzled his neck. "This...and more. Until we reach our peaks. Licking, tasting. Kissing." Her breath came in short pants. "But we must keep it our secret, until—"

"We are certain we wish to make this permanent? If my courting you will even sway you to consider permanence?"

She nipped his earlobe playfully. "Already you are finishing my sentences."
"Come to my bed, and we will do all you described. I want you to put your mouth on me, make me..."

She kissed him with a hot wildness, causing him to groan in response. Then she broke from him. "I think it best I head to my room. We must show some restraint. A little, at least. Besides, there is always tomorrow night."

God, he was on fire. "Stay one more day here at the hall." He wanted her for one more night. "We have more to...discuss."

"I will ask Megan. The decision will be up to her." Abbie kissed his chest, then stepped away. "Good night, Garrett. The sweetest and heated of dreams to you." She winked, then in a swish of sheer pink material, departed his room leaving him hard and aching. *Minx. Vixen. Tease.* He loved it. He could not wait until tomorrow night, for they would be doing far more than teasing if he had any say in the matter.

Chapter 10

As difficult as it was to leave Garrett's arms, Abbie thought it best to return to her room. It would have been simple to acquiesce to his blatant invitation to go to his bed; however, a small amount of prudence was warranted. She was glad she'd decided to go to his room, for she debated with herself for over an hour before appearing at his door. More than anything, they needed to discuss the past and, more importantly, the future.

Sleep came quickly, and it was restful, if not exactly long. She awoke shortly after dawn, read for a while, then, after asking a footman for directions, she and Megan joined the family for breakfast. Thankfully, Megan agreed to stay one more night at Wollstonecraft Hall when they spoke privately before the meal.

What an abundance of food. The earl certainly did not exaggerate when he stated it was their favorite meal. After the men loaded their plates they all ate heartily, exchanging conversation on all manner of topics, ranging from horses to current affairs and social reforms.

A whirlwind of activity filled the rest of the day, from another tour of the hall, lingering in the libraries selecting books, afternoon tea, and then a light supper of roast beef. Through it all, Abbie was a bundle of nerves, anticipating her meeting with Garrett later in the night.

Once Abbie was sure Megan was fast asleep, she crept to Garrett's door once again and lightly tapped on it. He swung it open, wearing the tight breeches he'd worn last night and a billowing white shirt, open and displaying his broad, muscled chest. His long hair hung forward, shadowing part of his face, giving him a deliciously dangerous air.

She wore the same pink confection she'd worn the previous night, as he'd seemed to like it. Grasping her wrist, he gently pulled her across the threshold, then closed the door with his bare foot. He swept her up in a wild, hungry kiss that made the room spin. Garrett tunneled his fingers through her hair, scattering the few pins holding her style in place. Her wavy locks tumbled past her shoulders and he nuzzled them. "Wildflowers," he murmured. "I never forgot your scent. It stayed with me, all these years."

Oh. Her insides tumbled at his soft but husky voice whispering in her ear. *Stay strong.* Reluctantly she stepped away from him, immediately missing his rock-hard body and sizzling heat. "We have more to discuss, as you mentioned last night."

He closed his eyes as if trying to gain control. Watching him struggle with his emotions caused her stomach to tremble. "Right. Talk. I need a drink. You?" He opened his eyes and the intense heat emanating from them tempted her to say to hell with conversation.

Once he poured them a scotch, they took the same seats they'd occupied the previous night. Abbie stared into the amber contents of her glass. "You will think me bold—"

"Be bold. I loved it then, I yearn for it now," he rasped.

"I said I don't know where this will lead. But I do have an inkling of where I would like it to lead."

He crossed his long legs and sipped his scotch, watching her intently over the rim of the glass. "Tell me. Everything. Honestly and succulently."

"I had accepted that I would remain a widow for the rest of my days. The bungalow was paid for. Elwyn arranged a small stipend for me, along with money for Megan's education. I was comfortable. At peace. I even had an open marriage proposal if I ever changed my mind."

"What?" Garrett thundered.

"It was from Gethin—Dr. Bevan. We are friends. He suggested an alliance of sorts. I think he was lonely and assumed I was as well."

"The bloody cheek," Garrett growled.

"I was actually enjoying my independence and privacy. Then you rumbled into Standon. All my carefully laid plans were torn asunder. I came here without thinking things through, for that is the affect you have on me. I do want you to court me a little, but I want more. Perhaps we can work toward the permanence you spoke of." She took a long draw on the scotch, its fiery contents giving her the courage she needed. "But not if you insist on placing the curse between us as a shield. If you cannot commit to me or love me with your entire heart and soul, then I do not want you at all. I won't settle for any less. Elwyn taught me that much." She met his gaze. "We could tumble headlong into another scandalous affair. I could return to my life in Standon with yet another heated memory to keep me company as I slide into my dotage. But I've decided that I will only move forward if you agree to put the curse aside." There. She'd said it. There had to be rules of engagement.

Garrett remained silent, and her nerves sparked. Abbie had no idea what option he would choose.

"And if I do not place the curse aside?"

"Megan and I will return to Standon as soon as I can arrange it. Now that she has met your family, I would never deny her visits. She and your father have already formed a bond."

He laughed cynically. "Yes. But not with me."

"It will come... in time," Abbie replied softly.

"Do you know what you are asking? The curse has been a part of me since I was a child."

"I understand. I even empathize. But if we are to have a future..."

"You want us to have a future?"

She bit her lower lip. "I'd like to attempt it."

"As would I. You wish a fresh start? I will try."

She cried out with relief as tears trickled down her cheeks.

Garrett continued, "For I cannot deny my feelings any longer, nor can I push you away. Not again. It would kill me, completely hollow me out until nothing remained but an empty shell of a man. The curse is still with me, Abbie. It is seared on my soul the same as you are. God help us if the curse rears its ugly head. But I vow I will do all I can to not allow it to rule my life." He slammed his glass on the table, rose to his feet, and walked toward her. Garrett helped her stand, then brushed the tears away with the pads of his thumbs. "Let us start over."

She gave him a shaky smile. "Get to know one another, learn to love again?"

"Again? *A ghraidh, mo chridhe.* I never stopped loving you. Ever." He captured her mouth in a desperate, wild kiss. Abbie returned it, caressing his tongue with hers. Everywhere their bodies made contact increased the heat crackling between them.

"I haven't heard those words for years. I remember clearly when you first said them to me. 'My love, my heart.' You mean it, truly?"

"Besides a couple of other short phrases, it's the only Gaelic I know. I often heard my grandfather call my grandmother such during my visits. Grandfather Mackinnon said, 'Heed me, laddie. 'Twill melt a woman's heart if ye whisper these words in her ear.'" She laughed at his Scottish burr. "I have not spoken them to anyone...not since you." He brushed a lock of hair from her cheek. "Yes, I mean it. Truly."

Garrett had never stopped loving her. Abbie's heart soared with joy. But caution bade her not to return the sentiment. Not yet. She had to be completely sure of his feelings and see if his claim of tossing the curse aside held truth. Beyond that, no more teasing. She kissed him, running her hands through his silky, ginger locks.

Scooping her up in his arms, Garrett ran to the bedroom, lowered her, then kissed her deeply. Abbie fumbled with the buttons of his breeches, and when she finished she broke the kiss, grabbed fistfuls of the wool material, and yanked it, along with his drawers, down his hips until they fell to the carpet. "Oh. As I remember."

"Allow me to see you," he rasped.

"One of us must stay dressed. Tonight will be all about touching and kissing. Nothing more. Another night, I promise." She crooked her finger as she backed up. "Remove your shirt, lie on the bed, and allow me to explore every muscled valley and plane. Every hard part of you."

Bloody hell, he was near to bursting. All she would have to do is touch him and he would explode. First, better ensure their privacy. He strode to the door, closed it, and turned the key. No one would be interrupting them if he had anything to say about it. Next, he did as she commanded and lay on the large bed, eagerly awaiting her. The fireplace was large, the flames casting the room in a golden glow and enhancing the sensual mood.

"Stunning," she murmured as she crawled toward him from the foot of the bed. He spread his legs to make room for her, and she immediately ran her tongue along his hipbone up to his waist. Abbie grasped his shaft and he quaked with desire, using all his inner strength not to climax. Giving him a couple of strokes, she continued to lick and kiss him until her mouth was inches away from the head of his prick. How often had he dreamed of this only to deny it the next morning?

Her mouth enveloped him and he cried out. Abbie's cheeks hollowed, her tongue busily trailing across his distended veins. His hips rose on their own accord, eager for her to take him deeper. Take him all. "Yes, taste me," he moaned, keeping his voice low. "Please," he pleaded. He never said please to any woman. Only Abbie.

It didn't take long, as he'd been on the edge of the precipice since she'd appeared in his life once again. Watching her head bob between his legs was a memory that he would savor forever. He wrapped her coal-black hair about his wrist as he gently lifted his hips. "Abbie... God... Hell." Colors burst behind his eyelids, his neck cords straining with the force of his release. His entire body bucked and shuddered.

Abbie released him, then smiled as she cuddled in next to him. "You taste as enticing as I remember."

He couldn't catch his breath. Finally, he found his voice and pulled her close. "And you are still the sensuous siren of our youth." They lay together for several moments. Sated, but energized, he turned Abbie on her back and pushed her nightgown past her waist. "Allow me to return the favor."

Hot. Wet. Glorious. He ran his tongue across her folds, then spread them with his fingers and dived in deeper as his thumb worked her sensitive nub. Abbie moaned. It would not take long for her either. Garrett feasted, and hardened once again. With his free hand, he stroked himself in concert with the licking motion of his tongue. The wet sound of their oral ministrations, the musky scent of arousal. There was no one else in the world but the two of them, exactly how it had been in the past.

Abbie arched her back and cried out, her head hitting the pillow over and over with each tremble of her body. Garrett pulled her close to his heart, savoring her release while he continued to stroke his shaft. A moment later he joined her, burying his face in her neck, his eyes burning from intense emotions. Bloody hell, he loved her.

Garrett lay on the bed and motioned for her to follow him. "Stay. Sleep in my arms."

Abbie sighed wistfully. "I would love nothing more, but we don't want to cause a scandal."

His eyebrows rose. "What do you think we've been doing from the moment we met?"

"Well, true enough. But we agreed to keep this quiet for the time being. Plus, think of Megan. I want us to be completely sure before revealing this. Besides, there is the getting-to-know-you business to see to."

Garrett laughed. "I believe that we have moved beyond the boundaries of courting."

"Not for us, my darling." She playfully swatted him. "I will stay for a short while, then I must return to my room."

As Garrett lay with Abbie curled around him, a warning bell tolled in his head. He would never forgive himself if he placed Abbie and Megan in danger. He spoke the truth when he stated the curse was still with him. Vigilance was warranted. But when she lay in his arms like this, nothing else mattered. Not curses, past hurts, youthful mistakes, or regrets. He was in love with a glorious woman—the same woman—for the first and last time in his life.

Chapter 11

Once they had indulged in a late brunch, Megan and Abbie were escorted to the Wollstonecraft carriage with a promise that it would return later in the evening for dinner. Abbie did not own a fancy gown, but the earl had assured her that it would not be a formal affair.

As the footmen unloaded their cases and carried them into the residence, Abbie placed her hands on her cheeks. Still flushed and tingling from her passionate encounter with Garrett the night before. How would she be able to keep this secret? Much had been resolved, truths spoken, feelings admitted, but nothing pleased her more than him agreeing to a new beginning and to place the curse aside. It was as if a black cloud had been lifted from her heart, at least partway. She would remain optimistically cautious.

Alberta greeted her warmly, calling for the tea tray as they all settled into the parlor. Megan and Jonas exchanged shy glances but did not speak.

"How was the visit, Megan?" Alberta asked.

Her face lit up. "Oh, Mrs. Eaton, the place is a palace, or at least as large as one. The earl gifted me with a signed copy of *Frankenstein*. The author is his fourth cousin. Can you imagine! He and the viscount were ever so kind, and the food! I thought I would burst."

The housekeeper entered with the tea tray and a plate of lemon biscuits and placed them on the table in front of Alberta. "Thank you, Mrs. Claxton." As she poured, she asked, "And what did you think of Garrett Wollstonecraft?"

Abbie's insides tumbled with apprehension as she awaited her daughter's reply.

Megan's mouth turned down. "At first glance he's frightening, with his size and all. But he kept us busy going for rides around the estate,

playing parlor games, and giving tours of the libraries. They have three."
She paused as Alberta handed her a teacup and saucer. "Perhaps someday
I will like him well enough. I am still angry, in here." Her daughter placed
a closed fist to her chest. "I do not need or want a father, and I feel as if I
am being forced to accept him."

Not a ringing endorsement at all, and Abbie was disappointed. What
did she expect, her daughter to claim him as her father after only a few
days? How unrealistic. "No one is forcing you."

Megan sniffed. "I was not given a choice to meet his family.
You made me go."

Well, she had her there. Abbie did not wish to tell her daughter it was
mostly to have her focus on something else besides Jonas. She couldn't
relay that fact, what with the man in the room drinking tea with them.
Megan's approval of Garrett was of paramount importance *if* Abbie was
to have a future with him. It was an immense *if.*

Abbie accepted the tea from Alberta. If she did decide to reconcile with
him, it would mean a major upheaval to their lives. Leaving Standon and
the only home that Megan had ever known. Abbie was wise to suggest
that they keep their budding relationship slow and secret.

"I like Garrett," Jonas stated as he reached for a biscuit. "He helps
people. He's helping us by paying for supplies."

"True. We are on a fixed income," Alberta stated. "I know talking about
finances is frowned upon, but there is no possible way I could afford to
renovate this place entirely out of pocket. I argued, but to no avail. Garrett
has contributed lumber and labor. When I protested further, he stated that
I was giving a number of his tenants much needed work. How could I say
no?" Alberta sipped her tea. "The entire family is generous to a fault."

Alberta's statement made Abbie admire Garrett all the more. If only
Megan would take the words to heart.

The large landau arrived promptly at thirty minutes past seven. Once
they were all seated, the carriage departed, and Abbie was filled with
anticipation at seeing Garrett. She wore a sapphire blue gown with an
off-the-shoulder style, the neckline trimmed with three layers of lace.
There would be no crinolines for her, not only for the cost, but because
Abbie did not care for the current style. Instead, she used several layers
of petticoats to emphasize the wideness of the full skirt.

Though the gown was more than adequate for a Standon event, it hardly
suited for dinner at an earl and viscount's estate. Alberta's silver gown was
of a similar style. On the seat opposite was Jonas, looking rather stunning
in a black suit and a snow-white cravat. Megan kept giving him clandestine

glances. Garrett had informed her of the conversation he and his brother, Julian, had with Jonas. She could only hope that the young man would keep the promises he'd made to Garrett and Julian.

Megan wore a new purchase: her first gown that hung to her ankles. Another sign her daughter was growing up. Pale green in color, it accentuated the emerald in her hazel eyes and showed her crowning glory of red hair to perfection. She still wore her hair down to show she wasn't completely mature. But she and Alberta had styled it attractively, using a pearl hair comb to hold the locks of her thick hair in place.

When they arrived a phalanx of footmen assisted them from the carriage while Martin, the butler, welcomed them. Once their cloaks and capes were taken, they were all shown into a room Abbie did not recognize.

The formal parlor had three crystal chandeliers, and Abbie smiled at the bright illumination. Gas lighting was not to be found in Standon yet. The walls were gold, the velvet curtains red, and in the far corner, tables and chairs were set up for cards and the like. Enhancing the elegance of the room was the expert workmanship of the cornices and moldings.

After the earl and viscount stepped forward to greet everyone, Abbie found she was alone with Viscount Tensbridge. "Where is Garrett?" she asked.

"My valet is assisting him. By their own choice, he and my sons do not have their own, so we share for dinners and such."

Here lay the perfect opportunity to converse about his son. "Speaking of sons, my lord, Garrett has asked me to speak to you regarding Aidan."

Tensbridge clasped her elbow and pulled her farther away from the others. "You have news?"

She stared up into his worried eyes; the pain was plain to see. "He is doing as well as can be expected, my lord. Allow me to explain about the sanatorium. My late husband started the clinic years ago, and when he passed his friend and colleague, Dr. Gethin Bevan, decided to continue his work. They had been friends since their boyhoods in Wales, attended Cambridge together, and decided on Standon, of all places, because of the privacy and peace such a community could afford." She smiled. "Also for the fact the Knights Hospitallers lived and worked in the area in the fourteenth century. My husband wished to carry on the tradition of helping others in need."

"Very worthy; I admire him for it. And Dr. Bevan."

"The point I am making is both were made members of good standing in the College of Physicians. Well qualified and professional. Dr. Bevan believes as fervently as my late husband in the facets of addiction and how to treat it humanely. For they believe it is a disease, not a result of weakness or a bad habit." She laid her gloved hand on Tensbridge's arm. "I was there during the first few days of Aidan's treatment, my lord. Since Elwyn passed I often volunteer, and have learned much about the condition." "Tell me everything. Hold nothing back."

Abbie did as he asked, relating the symptoms of withdrawal: the nightmares, the tremors, and the sickness. As she described his physical condition, the pain in the viscount's eyes increased. "The good news, my lord, is that he's through the worst of it. Now comes the difficult part, recovery and staying sober. He will need fresh air, exercise, and a proper diet. Those aspects alone will take months. He will also have to come to terms with everything that has happened. Learn to respect himself once again. Dr. Bevan and his daughter, Cristyn, will ensure he receives thorough and compassionate care."

The viscount laid his hand on top of hers and squeezed. "Thank you," he whispered, "for telling me this. It has helped. Please call me Tensbridge, I cannot abide all this 'my lord' business."

"Of course I will." She smiled warmly.

"Also, thank you for introducing us to Megan. I look forward to getting to know you both better. You are a welcome addition to the family."

"How very kind, I..." The words died in her throat, for Garrett had walked into the room. He wore a red kilt, sash, and an accompanying black dinner jacket and vest, along with matching hose and black shoes. His long hair was tied back, revealing his handsome face to perfection. A smile crept across her lips as he headed toward her. It was as if he stepped out of a Scottish castle. He took her breath away.

Garrett took her gloved hand and kissed it. "Good evening, lassie."

She laughed at his sensual Scottish burr as warmth moved through her. He looked every inch a Highlander. How utterly appealing—and arousing.

"Quite the entrance, Brother." Julian slapped him on the back. "Excuse me as I see to our other guests."

Neither she nor Garrett acknowledged his departure, for he still held her hand as they stared in each other's eyes. "The tartan is Mackinnon, my mother's clan," he said as he kissed her hand once more before releasing it.

"How handsome you look in it." She leaned in and whispered, "I would love it if some evening you wore the kilt and nothing else."

Garrett moaned softly. "Naughty woman. You're tempting me to show you how much your words have...excited me."

She dare not look down. Instead she glanced about the room to find that they had become figures of interest to everyone else. So much for keeping their mutual attraction concealed.

Garrett murmured, "For you? I will wear the kilt and nothing else." Louder he said, "Shall we join the others?"

He held out his arm and she took it as they walked toward the group. Megan was frowning, and Abbie fought not to roll her eyes in response. What now? As drinks were served—Megan was given sparkling cider—polite conversation broke out and Abbie took the opportunity to pull Megan aside. "What is wrong?" she whispered to her daughter.

"Nothing, Mama," she replied in a flat, emotionless voice.

She knew her daughter too well. "You did not like the way we were looking at each other, did you?" Megan's lips pursed in response. "I have every right to live my life the way I wish, as you have pointed out to me more than once. Your papa is gone, my dear. I mourn him still. But I will not deny having feelings for another man. Have I asked you to deny yours for Jonas? As inappropriate as they are at this time of your life."

Megan blinked. "No, Mama."

"Perhaps you believe my attraction to Garrett is inappropriate."

Megan shrugged, then gave a slight nod.

"I will not be rushing into anything. I will remain circumspect in my dealings with Garrett, as we have much to discuss. But I also will not deny that I still harbor deep feelings for him. Nor will I deny that I am somewhat frightened by those intense emotions." Abbie paused. Should she be bearing her soul to her daughter like this?

Yes. She had to make Megan understand that relationships between men and women were fraught with myriad complications such as overwhelming passion and crippling doubt. "This is all part and parcel of falling for a man who brings his own fears and desires into the mix. It can be entirely messy and exhilarating. Bear with me as I come to terms with this uncertain situation. Be patient if I act impulsively or out of character. Allow me the courtesy to live my life as I see fit." She took her daughter's hand and spoke in a soft tone. "Garrett is a good man. Permit yourself to like him. Even a little bit. He is not replacing your papa; he never could. I know it as well as he. But life does march on, despite the fact that we miss those no longer with us."

Megan bit her lower lip. "I understand. I will try, really I will."

"Good girl. Now let us join the others."

By the time they were shown to the dining room Megan's mood had improved. Abbie now understood that she and Garrett were walking a fine line, their renewed relationship fragile. Any manner of outside forces could break it to bits, and it worried her. But staring at him across the table caused her heart to beat faster. Was this moving too quickly? When she was in his arms, it felt as if they were not moving fast enough.

After everyone was seated, the footmen brought a tureen of soup and other delicacies. The table was impeccable, with white linen cloth, napkins, three gold candelabras, elegant white china with gold trim, and more utensils and glasses than Abbie knew what to do with.

"We decided not to be too formal," the earl stated. "We are going with five courses instead of ten." He winked teasingly. "Since there is no lady of the house, I approve all the menus. We will start with an onion and potato soup, then a salmon mousse, a chateaubriand of beef, asparagus casserole, roasted carrots, and assorted cheeses and pickles. Dessert will be a raspberry trifle and assorted biscuits. How does that suit, Megan?"

She smiled at the earl. "Sounds delicious, my lord."

"Excellent. I hope you brought your appetites; be sure to tuck in."

Everyone laughed.

"The flowers in the centerpiece are beautiful, my lord. What are they?" Abbie asked the earl. The orange, red, and yellow color scheme was attractive, as were their daisy-like petals.

"Cape heaths, from the south of Africa. A particular favorite of mine. Do you like them, Megan?" the earl asked.

She nodded. "I do, my lord. I adore flowers and plants."

The earl snapped his napkin open and laid it across his lap. "Excellent. Pick a day next week and I will take you through our greenhouse and orangery. I should return from my journey by then."

"Father and I are heading to Carrbury tomorrow morning for a short visit," Tensbridge offered. "We thought it best to see Riordan in person and inform him of developments. Carrbury is south of here, in East Sussex. Riordan is schoolmaster there."

"A schoolmaster? How lovely," Megan stated. "Will I meet him soon, and your oldest son, my lord?"

It amazed Abbie how at ease her daughter seemed around the earl and viscount. If only she would extend it to Garrett.

A pained smile touched Tensbridge's lips at the mention of Aidan. "Of course. Both are busy at the moment, but when they hear of you, they will be eager to make your acquaintance."

Pleasant conversation continued as the courses were brought out, and Abbie was relieved when Megan finally asked Garrett a question about horses. Jonas joined the conversation as well, asking questions on breeding. Two hours passed swiftly.

When they had finished their meals, the earl stood. "I believe the gentlemen will forgo the brandy and cigars, and instead we shall all move to the parlor. Tea and coffee will be served, along with aperitifs and spirits."

As everyone headed toward the parlor, Garrett clasped Abbie's elbow and pulled her along the hallway into a vacant room. He closed the door, then swung her about until she found herself leaning against it, Garrett's left hand lay flat on the wall near her head. Abbie could barely make out his features in the darkened room; only one gas lamp was lit in the corner. But he stood close enough that she could see his smoldering gaze, the green in his eyes glittering with emotions she could not name.

"All through dinner, I wanted nothing more than to push the dishes aside and lay you on the table. Lift the hem of your gown, touch you." He kissed her with a ferocity that caused her stomach to drop clear to the floor.

The kisses trailed across her cheek to her neck, and she moaned. "When will I see you again? Tonight? How? Where?" he murmured as he nibbled on her earlobe.

Abbie could not think straight, her mind whirling. "I...I don't know."

He pressed his hard body against her, rotating his muscular hips against her so there was no mistaking his arousal. "I need you, Abbie. To be *inside* you."

Where could they meet? Abbie could hardly smuggle him into her room; Megan was next door, and Alberta and Jonas not far away. They certainly hadn't been quiet during lovemaking in the past; no doubt nothing had changed, if last night in his room was any indication. The stables were not a viable option; they would freeze, regardless of any woodstoves. The orangery? The greenhouse? *Oh, he feels good.* Clasping his broad shoulders, she inhaled. *And smells good.* It was a different cologne from before, but enticing. Sandalwood, or perhaps—

"Abbie. When?" His tone was pleading, desperation clear in his husky voice.

How tempting to say, "Here, against the door," except Garrett would follow through on her suggestion without hesitation.

"Tomorrow night. Find a place we can meet far from the residences. A place not too chilly." Abbie could no more deny him than she could deny herself. She wanted him, too. Most desperately. Who could think of caution when he was near? When he nibbled enticingly on her earlobe, causing shivers of desire to ripple through her?

Garrett captured her mouth once again, exploring, making her ache in places she thought would never ache again.

"Garrett, we must—"

He broke away, his chest heaving. "Rejoin the others? Before they suspect? *Mo chridhe,* they already suspect."

She touched her flushed cheeks. "Well, perhaps it is wise we not give further evidence to the contrary." This time she glanced down. Thankfully, his furry purse hid most of the evidence of his arousal.

"Staring at my sporran? Vixen." He winked teasingly.

"Is that what the purse contraption is called, or are you referring to another appendage?" Abbie winked in return.

Garrett threw back his head and laughed. Tears clustered on her eyelashes, for she had not heard his masculine, full-throated laughter since they first met all those years ago. This is the Garrett she fell in love with upon first meeting. This is the Garrett she wanted to spend the rest of her life with. Abbie would do all she could to see this lighthearted, happy man enjoy life, embrace love, and not become lost in the gloom of the curse ever again.

Her earlier conversation with Megan replayed in her mind. What was between her and Garrett was chaotic, passionate, invigorating, and because of it she must remain vigilant. Be open to the emotions swirling between them, but not allow herself to plunge headlong into this desire as she had all those years past. For she was scared witless that he would break her heart again. If he did, Abbie knew, this time she would never recover.

Chapter 12

Once Garrett saw to the business of the stables, giving instructions to the head groom and the stable lads, he headed to the Eaton residence. His father and brother had already departed for Carrbury, taking the landau carriage, William, the coach driver; the earl's valet; and Thomas, the footman.

Riordan and Sabrina were renting a townhouse instead of staying in the small cottage supplied by the education board. Since his true name was known now, Riordan wanted to give his bride a comfortable residence, and one large enough to accommodate her friend, Mary Tuttle, and any family that may visit. Riordan had also borrowed a maid and one of the cook's assistants from Wollstonecraft Hall until the end of June.

Instead of walking, he tasked one of the stable lads to drive him in the brougham. It gave him time to gather his thoughts. While a weight had been lifted from him in agreeing to place the curse aside, a part of him acknowledged that it still lurked in the background, ready to push its way to the forefront at the first sign of any hint of a tragic event. It had ruled his life for decades, firmly entrenched in the very fiber of his being. It was not easily dismissed.

But he was willing to take another path. Abbie was worth it. If only he had been adult enough fourteen years ago to see it. Now with Megan in the picture…a *daughter*. His heart ached when he looked at the young girl. In his initial observances both of them were evident in her, physically and personality-wise. His heart ached for the fact that his daughter acted awkward around him, yet he could hardly blame her. Finding out her beloved late papa was not actually her father would be a shock. It would tear anyone's life to shreds.

Garrett was envious of a dead man. For the years that he'd lived with and loved Abbie and Megan. Thankfully, by all accounts the doctor had been a kind and devoted man. Her arranged marriage could have turned out as horrific as Sabrina's. But enough ruminating on the past. The future lay before him, and he remained determined to embrace it all. A fresh start, as Abbie claimed.

The carriage pulled up by the front entrance and Garrett immediately exited. "Samuel, head to the kitchen and I'm sure Mrs. Claxton will fix you with a warm drink."

The young man touched his forelock. "Thank you, sir."

Garrett knocked and Alberta answered. "Mr. Garrett Wollstonecraft calling on Mrs. Abigail Hughes."

Alberta smiled. "Come in, sir. Everyone is in the parlor. You arrived in time for afternoon tea." After removing his cloak and gloves and handing them to the housekeeper, he entered the room, carrying the box he'd brought with him. Once he exchanged pleasantries, he opened it and handed Abbie a bouquet. "For you, Mrs. Hughes. You stated you wished to be courted."

Her face lit up, and it caused his heart to skip a beat. "Cape heaths? From your greenhouse?"

"Yes. Hope you like the color combination." They were blue and purple.

"I love them, thank you." Her voice trembled with emotion, and his insides warmed at pleasing her.

"I made an early morning expedition to Sevenoaks and stopped by the sweet shop. First for Megan; I do hope she enjoys chocolates." He passed her the small wrapped box. "Mostly buttercreams and orange fillings."

"Thank you, Mr. Wollstonecraft." She gave him a brief, genuine smile that arrowed straight to his heart. He'd bring his daughter chocolate every day in order to bask in the kindness of her smile.

"And I did not forget you, Jonas." He passed the young man a decorative bag tied with a ribbon.

Jonas opened it and peered inside. "Humbugs! Thank you, Garrett." He tossed one of the hard candies in his mouth.

"Alberta, I hope you are partial to chocolate peppermints." Alberta took the box he held out to her.

"I am, thank you. My goodness, it appears you are courting all of us."

He laughed as he held a larger box to Abbie. "This is for you, Abbie. An assortment of sugar-coated nuts, lemon drops, and hand-dipped chocolates with various fruit fillings." The large, silk-covered box had cost a pretty penny, but Abbie was worth it—and more.

"We should leave you two alone," Alberta offered.

"No need. I thought Abbie and I would take a ride in the carriage. Would you be up to a short jaunt?"

"I would. Heavens! Candies, flowers, and now a ride in your carriage. You *are* courting me. I could not be more pleased," Abbie replied, her cheeks flushing attractively.

"Excellent. Then perhaps tomorrow you, Megan, and I could journey to Sevenoaks for the afternoon? There are a couple of shops to explore and a lovely tearoom."

Abbie looked to her daughter. "Megan?"

"Yes, Mama."

Not overly enthusiastic, but not quite as cool as past encounters. He would take the small victories when and where he could acquire them. "Then we shall. Now, Abbie, if you will fetch your cloak. There are warming bricks in the carriage, along with woolen throws to ensure you stay comfortable."

Alberta stood. "I will arrange the flowers in a vase while you are gone."

"Alberta, if you could ask Samuel to return to the carriage? He is in your kitchen. If he's not done with his warm drink, tell him to bring it along."

"I will. Come with me, Jonas, Megan."

He found himself alone in the parlor, pleased that his gifts had been appreciated. Now to see if Abbie would be agreeable to his next surprise.

Once bundled in the small carriage, Garrett knocked on the roof, then gathered the throw and placed it across their laps. "January does not translate well to courting. If it were summer, there would be other options, like taking in a Sunday afternoon concert at the bandstand in town. Cricket matches, teas, picnics, and other socials. We will have to make do. The warming bricks are at your feet. At least the sun is out and offering a modicum of warmth."

"This is quite exciting. Where are we heading?"

He laid a gentle kiss on her lips. "Around the perimeter of the Wollstonecraft property, then beyond. However long you wish to be cuddled up with me in this small carriage."

Abbie laughed. "There isn't much room, but I adore cuddling."

"See? I am learning new things about you already. The getting-to-know-you part, as you suggested." He sobered. "I would also like to know more about the man who raised my daughter. The man who held your affection. Tell me about your past."

"He did hold my affection. Elwyn was also my dear friend." Her eyes sparkled as she spoke of him, and Garrett experienced a stab of envy. "He was of average height and build. A pleasant-looking man with a ready smile and twinkling brown eyes. His patient and kind personality served

him well as a physician. He was much loved and admired. He knew my
father through the army; Elwyn was a young medic. They became friends,
and after the war in Spain my father moved to Brighton and Elwyn took
a position at St. Bartholomew's Hospital in London."

Abbie smiled, seemingly happy to talk of her late husband. "It was there
he first came across those with addictions, and it moved him greatly. So
much he decided to start his own clinic. He wanted to place it in a serene
setting, and Hertfordshire proved to be ideal. Also, it was far enough from
London to ensure privacy. He used a large portion of his own money to start
it, and many high-profile clients funded further expansions and renovations.
It left little time for socialization or finding a wife, so when my father
contacted him... Well, he thought the marriage would benefit us both.

"It did," Abbie continued in a soft voice. "He took a broken-hearted
girl expecting a child and welcomed me into his life and home. He never
spoke down to me. Instead, he included me in all aspects of his professional
life. Elwyn treated me as his partner. He was also gentle and patient and
did not rush me into consummating our marriage. And when Megan was
born, he couldn't have been more proud or loving. You may rest assured
that he loved her with every part of his generous heart."

A damned saint. Garrett grudgingly had to admit the man merited
praise. "I am glad and gratified that Dr. Hughes proved to be exactly what
you and Megan needed and deserved. It is to my everlasting shame that
I cannot say with certainty I would have been at age eighteen. As you
stated, I was self-centered. Perhaps I still am, for I am far from perfect."

"I don't require you to be perfect, Garrett. I never have. I adore you
the way you are. Believe me, Elwyn was not perfect; there were times he
annoyed me and I him, I imagine. He was untidy, leaving piles of clothes
and papers throughout the house. He was also a picky eater. But those
quirks of his personality merely made him human. Real."

"Why didn't you have children?"

Abbie sighed wistfully. "We tried, and seeing as I had Megan, Elwyn
came to the conclusion that the fact that I had not conceived lay with him.
In typical fashion, he did not allow it to make him bitter or sad. Instead,
he cherished Megan all the more."

Garrett took her hand and kissed it. "Thank you for telling me about
him. I'm pleased that Elwyn was there for you both, but I am entirely
envious. Which makes me human. Real."

She leaned against his shoulder. "Oh, yes. You are very real."

"Perhaps you will tell me more about yourself while we ride."

"What do you wish to know?" Abbie asked.

He slowly removed her glove with his teeth and let it drop to the floor of the carriage. Then he took her hand. "Your favorite music, books; do you like to dance? What is your favorite color, dessert?" He stroked the pulse point of her wrist with his thumb. "What is your favorite position for sex? I recall you particularly enjoyed being on top and riding me like Boudicca heading into battle."

There was the attractive blush to her cheeks again. "Oh, you wicked, sinful Scot," she murmured sensually.

"Scot? I suppose I am in many ways." He kissed her hand. "I certainly look the part."

"Especially last night. Oh, Garrett, you were glorious, absolutely splendid in your mother's tartan. As I said, you must wear it more often. Even if for me alone."

"Aye, lassie. The kilt and nothing else. Och, but ye are a demanding wench." He mimicked his grandfather Mackinnon.

Her eyelashes fluttered. "And you must speak to me with that exact accent when you wear the kilt. Special occasion. Not every time we...we..."

"Make love?"

"Yes. Oh, what is this place?" Abbie pointed out the window as the carriage slowed and came to a stop.

"This was a hunter's hut from my great-grandfather's time. It's in remarkable condition, as my own grandfather and father kept it in minimal repair even though none of us hunt. I hired a few of the tenants in need of work to ensure the place is in tip-top shape: the fireplace working, the walls, roof, and floor sturdy. I told them that I wished to have a private area to write, so new furniture will be moved in this afternoon. This will be our place, Abbie."

He took her hand and kissed it. "I will meet you at the rear entrance of the Eatons' residence at the stroke of midnight, and we will ride here on Patriot for a stolen hour or two. If you are amenable." *Hell, say yes. End my torment.*

"This is entirely outrageous. You *are* proposing an affair?"

"Yes, a surreptitious one, as we court and come to know one another. As we move forward, we will need to discuss what the future holds. For I want a life with you Abbie, and my daughter. If you do not foresee one with me, tell me now, and we will progress no further." Christ, his insides were in knots.

"I did not come here looking for this, not really. Or perhaps I did," she demurred. "Yes, Garrett, I yearn to explore and see what the future holds."

Abbie paused, then gave him a shy smile. "I will not deny us showing how much we yearn for each other."

He gathered her in his embrace and kissed her hard. As always, it turned fierce, then gentled, until they were playfully nibbling on each other's lower lips. "Do tell. Your favorite music, books, do you like to dance? What is your favorite color, dessert?"

"I adore Mozart," Abbie whispered. "Books by Dickens and nonfiction books of English history. I haven't had much opportunity to dance; I long to learn the waltz. I adore all shades of purple, hence the reason I loved the flowers you brought me, and I am mad for multitiered cakes slathered in sweet butter frosting, along with scones with whipped cream and strawberry jam."

Garrett laughed. "At the tearoom tomorrow, I will ensure we order cake and scones." He nuzzled her neck. "I will teach you the waltz. Though I haven't attended many balls through the years, that is one dance I do know." Reluctantly he released her, but Abbie slipped her arm through his and cuddled in close, laying her head on his shoulder again. He banged the roof of the carriage and it moved forward.

Having her close like this, he would make damned sure they stayed out for the entire afternoon. Never had he felt as happy and content as he did at this moment.

* * * *

At five minutes before midnight, Abbie stealthily made her way to the rear entrance of Alberta's home. It was utterly exciting to be meeting Garrett secretly like this. She gathered her wool cloak about her neck as she stood in the doorway. For a brief moment, doubt overcame her feelings of exhilaration. What happened to her conviction of remaining discreet, even judicious with her emotions? No matter what happened tonight, she must cling to her vow of remaining cautious. It was her only defense against being hurt once again.

Earlier today she had said to Garrett, "I did not come here looking for this, not really." But to be honest, deep down she ached for it. In the years that she'd been married to Elwyn, she'd never stopped loving Garrett. Because of it, she had not been free to give her heart to her kind and thoughtful husband.

The decision she'd made years past, of not revealing who the father was, had affected far more lives than her own. Garrett's and Megan's.

Garrett's family. Her own parents, instead of supporting her, all but cut her from their lives. Their initial rejection had hurt. But Abbie took solace in knowing her life with Elwyn had given her the peace and contentment she needed. A chill curled about her heart. How selfish she'd been, but what other options did she have pregnant at eighteen?

Abbie had decided it would be prudent to settle on an approximate date of departure. This visit could not continue forever, even though Alberta encouraged her and Megan to stay until the middle of February. Winter travel was tedious, but more than anything, Abbie felt she must set boundaries that aligned with her oath of vigilance as far as Garrett was concerned.

The unmistakable sound of thundering horses' hooves brought her out of her diverse thoughts. *No more regrets.* The past lay behind her, and all that Abbie wanted was to live for today and guardedly look to the future. Garrett's silhouette took shape as he came into view. The moon's illumination cast him in shadow, and with his greatcoat billowing behind him he had the appearance of a mysterious highwayman. Pulling up on the reins, Patriot halted before the entrance, snorting and whickering. Abbie closed the door behind her as gently as she could.

Garrett outstretched his arm and she reached up and clasped it. With a smooth motion, as if she weighed nothing at all, he pulled her up behind him and she slipped her arms about his slim waist. "Hold on," he said. Clicking his tongue twice, he sunk his heels into Patriot's flanks and the stallion set off at a gallop.

The wind whipped about them, and Abbie's heart hammered with excitement, not only for being nestled against Garrett's tall, imposing frame, but because of the speed of the horse. This would be her life with Garrett: exhilaration, passion, and endless love. With her eyes burning with unshed tears, she laid her head against his back and held him tighter, never wanting to let go.

They arrived at the hunter's hut in mere minutes. Garrett slid off Patriot, then held out his arms. Clasping her about the waist, he held her aloft and slowly allowed her to descend along his body. Sparks ignited everywhere they touched. With a wicked smile he released her, then tied the reins to a tree, giving Patriot an affectionate pat on the neck. "Shall we go inside?" he asked.

Abbie nodded as Garrett opened the door. The tiny stone hut, complete with rough-hewn wood beams, was cozy and warm, as a fire blazed in the hearth. She stepped across the threshold. Garrett followed her in and closed the door behind him. In a swift motion he removed his coat and gloves, tossing them to the nearby armchair. Then he assisted her in removing her cloak.

A large chaise longue, decorated with a quilt and pillows, stood against the far wall. It certainly appeared able to accommodate the both of them. Along the opposite wall were a writing desk, a chair, and a cabinet. Above the desk, there was a shelf with various books. A pile of chopped logs sat by the hearth. "I admit it is rustic."

She turned to meet his gaze. "I adore it. You went to a good deal of trouble."

After lighting a candle, Garrett moved to the cabinet and opened it. Inside were various decanters, glasses, and covered dishes. "I wasn't sure if you even drink spirits beyond wine and scotch, so I brought a few selections. Also water, biscuits, cheese, and fruit. Would you care for a drink? I have the Mackinnon single malt scotch, sherry, brandy."

"I find sherry cloyingly sweet. But I will have the Mackinnon single malt."

"A girl after my own heart," he laughed. Then he grew serious. "Damn it all, Abbie, you've always had it."

This honest side of Garrett was a welcome development. Years ago, it had been obvious that he kept the majority of his emotions under tight rein. The sporadic moments she thought of him through the years, she'd chalked up his reticence to youth and immaturity. For it could not be that he didn't love her. There was one truth that she had taken from their indiscretion: no matter how cruelly he'd denied it, the love between them was genuine.

Abbie stepped closer. "You always had mine, Garrett. Full possession. I tried to offer it to another."

He clasped her upper arms, and she gazed into those beautiful hazel-green eyes. "And I'm bloody glad you were unable to do it. Selfish of me, but then I've always been selfish where you are concerned."

"Yet you pushed me away," she murmured.

"And you never told me you were pregnant with my child," he admonished gently.

"It will always be between us. Scars, as you said."

"We've apologized, cleared the air, but yes, Abbie love, the scars are permanent. Instead of picking at them, it is to our mutual benefit to embrace the fresh start you spoke of."

Abbie caressed his cheek, trailing her fingers across his rugged jawline. Heavy whiskers outlined the contours of his chin. He laughed. "I should have shaved before coming here."

"I don't mind."

"Shall we have that drink?" he asked, giving her a wink.

He wore a white shirt open halfway down his impressive chest, and a pair of tan breeches, and high boots. "No," she said, her voice low. Abbie unbuttoned his shirt and pushed it apart. She sighed longingly at his muscular torso. "I have waited years for this. I'd rather we made love. Immediately."

He gathered her in his arms and kissed her. It turned desperate, eager, and wild. "Abbie, I confess I will not be able to take things slow. Not tonight. I need to be inside you now."

She pushed his shirt off his shoulders, then licked one of his nipples, causing an agonizing moan to escape his lips. "Slow can come later. Take me, Garrett. This very minute."

Clothes, hairpins, boots sailed through the air, not that she wore much, as she'd left off all her undergarments in anticipation of tonight. Once naked, they tumbled headlong onto the chaise, kissing, nipping, touching. As Garrett turned her slightly to lay kisses on her bare back, he froze. "Oh, Abbie." The tips of his fingers followed the trail of criss-crossed scars spanning across her shoulder blades. In a low, dangerous voice, he said, "Who did this to you? Who would mar such perfection? Give me a name and I will see them suffer."

"My father," she replied softly. "When I told him of my condition."

"Still living in Brighton is he? I'll leave at once. He deserves to be horsewhipped," Garrett barked.

Abbie laid a hand on his arm, strangely pleased he would leap to her defense. "It is yet another reason my parents and I are estranged. He took his riding crop to me, sliced my dress—and my back—to ribbons. My mother stood by and watched. I decided then and there that I would reveal nothing about who the father was, and I would have nothing further to do with my pious and heartless parents. I accepted Elwyn's marriage proposal more to escape them than anything else."

"God, Abbie. You've suffered this because of me and my selfish, reckless behavior. I will never forgive myself." The anguish in his voice touched her heart. "No wonder you hated me. I deserve your censure. Your contempt."

She cradled his cheek. "Please, do not allow this to ruin our time together. We spoke the truth when we agreed about having scars. These ones have healed. If it is any consolation, Elwyn also threatened to horsewhip my father when he discovered the scarring. It ended their friendship." Abbie smiled sadly. "It is why I readily accepted Elwyn's suggestion that we delay consummation of our marriage. I was ashamed."

Garrett turned his head slightly to kiss her palm. "I respect and admire Elwyn the more you tell me of him. Damn your miserable father. And mother, for acting as willing accomplice."

"We should leave this in the past, where it belongs. Please, continue what you were doing," she encouraged, giving him a sensual smile.

Garrett gently and tenderly kissed her scars, causing moisture to collect on her lashes. He slid his lips to hers and kissed her deeply. Abbie returned it, the passion between them soaring. He halted and opened a small box on the table next to them. "When I journeyed to Sevenoaks the other day, I also paid a visit to the apothecary and purchased condoms. New from America. Made of rubber, if you can imagine."

"How forward-thinking you are. I was going to suggest withdrawal, but this is a better solution." She gave him a teasing wink. "Shall I assist you?"

Garrett rolled over flat on his back and handed her the envelope. "Sheath me, Abbie love."

A curious contraption, but Abbie managed to roll it on. Garrett then clasped her hips and brought her on top of him. "Ride me, my wild vixen," he teased. Then he sobered, his expression smoldering. "Do not make me wait, I beg you," he rasped.

Abbie clasped him, rose above him, and positioned his shaft. She plunged down on top of him, which caused them both to cry out. Oh, how he filled and stretched her. She stayed perfectly still, savoring their joining, becoming used to a man being inside her again. Never believed it would ever be Garrett, except in her dreams.

"Sweet Christ. If I could only live all my days like this," Garrett moaned. "Inside you forever."

"Yes," she whispered. Abbie understood exactly what he meant. It had been too long. Why had they denied themselves this bliss? No longer. Placing her hands flat on his chest, she started to move. Garrett clasped her hips, moving her back and forth as he captured her gaze. He looked splendid, his long, fire-in-the-hearth colored hair spread out on the pillow, his eyes burning with an intensity that took her breath away.

The sensations were building at a rapid pace; it would not take her long. She leaned forward to give her swollen nub more direct stimulation. Garrett clasped her breast with his left hand, his thumb rubbing the erect nipple. She moaned with the pure joy of his touch.

"Yes, love, come for me. Don't close your eyes. I want you to look at me." He raised his hips to meet her rocking motion and she gasped. As he commanded, Abbie met his gaze once again. Faster he pumped into her and she met his rapid pace. A sheen of perspiration already covered them both from their exertions.

Then it happened. A roll of stinging pleasure rocked her senses. A joyous explosion. Crying his name as if it were a prayer, her release caused her to freeze in place, her back arching with ecstasy.

"I'm close, keep moving," Garrett growled.

The room still spun about her, but she threw herself into his rhythm, this time she bounced up and down on his stiff prick and his thrusts went deeper, became wilder. "Ah!" He sat upright from the force of his climax, his body shuddering all around her. He gathered her in his arms, nuzzling her neck, groaning with each tremble and shake. "I love you, *mo chridhe*. Love. You."

"And I love you, my Scottish warrior." Abbie could not stop the words from slipping out. Caution be damned, at least in this moment. He chuckled as she held him tighter. A teasing remark, yet it held truth. She wanted nothing more than for him to fight for their love. Protect it with his last breath. Claim her as if there were no other woman on earth for him.

Abbie exhaled. *Oh, be my warrior, Garrett. Never hurt me again. Love me.* But in the dark corner of her heart, doubt lingered. She couldn't help it. Though the love was always there, hidden, sometimes forgotten, the trust would have to be earned anew on both their parts. Especially for her, for a nagging part of her still did not trust him fully, specifically where the curse was concerned. And that chilled Abbie to the bone.

Chapter 13

As he had revealed to Abbie the previous night, there were affairs through the years, brief sexual episodes with women of all shapes and ages. Nothing remotely serious; his emotions had not been engaged at all. The meaningless sex grew boring, and Garrett found he'd rather stay close to home than venture into London to The Crimson Club for a discreet erotic encounter.

Regardless, it had been close to a year and a half since he'd had actual sex. This could explain the passionate climax he'd experienced moments ago. In truth, Abbie had caused his explosive reaction. As he'd revealed when she first returned to his life, no woman could compare. He and Abbie had shared a rare, sensual bond from the first moment they touched.

Holding her close like this, skin against skin, all was right with the world. If only they could stay in the small, isolated sphere he'd built for them. They lay on the chaise, a sheet across their hips, a plate of cheese, fruit, and biscuits on their laps. Garrett lazily fed Abbie grapes, popping a couple in his mouth for good measure.

They couldn't remain here; real life beckoned. Besides, Garrett couldn't leave Patriot out in the elements all night. The stallion was a thoroughbred, used to warm comfortable barns and paddocks, not standing outside with bitter January winds whipping about his flanks. "As much as I would love to linger, we must head to our respective residences. Especially before your absence is noticed." He caressed her cheek with the tip of his finger. "There is no reason we cannot return here tomorrow night."

Abbie reached for a chocolate biscuit. "And every night thereafter? I must return to Standon at some point."

"Why?"

She leaned up on her elbow and stared down at him as she nibbled on the biscuit. "I have a home, responsibilities. Megan has school and has missed too much time already."

Her words chilled his heart. Hell, he didn't want her and his daughter to leave. "And what of a future, the one that you said you wished? With me? We do have a schoolmaster in the family. In fact, Riordan informed us, before returning to his position, he will be starting a progressive school here in Kent. He will put in place an education board of local members, similar to the one in Carrbury."

"I am pleased for your nephew, but it would be a year or more before it comes into existence. What will Megan do in the interim?" Abbie gathered the sheet about her lush body. "No, I must set a date for our departure. By the end of this month, or perhaps sooner. I will discuss it with Megan."

"That leaves barely more than two weeks." Garrett frowned. He did not like this development at all.

Abbie stood and gathered up her garments, then began dressing. "Don't pout. I assume you wish us to stay in touch. You can always return with us for a short visit." She gave him a warm smile. "Perhaps Aidan will be amenable to visitors by then."

Garrett pushed the tray of food off his lap and sat upright. "Of course I wish us to stay in touch. Regarding Aidan, according to Dr. Bevan, the family should stay well clear. Perhaps it will be difficult to comply. But the family agreed to wait until Aidan allows visitors." He swung his legs around and reached for his trousers. "On the subject of us, there is still much to work out it seems."

Abbie cupped his cheek. "Fourteen years past, there was no one else to consider but our youthful, selfish selves. But don't start to think that I do not wish us to be together. On one hand I yearn for it, but I also wish for us to remain cautious. It is the prudent thing to do."

Garrett stared at her incredulously. "You don't trust me, not fully."

"The curse has ruled your actions for decades. I wish to be certain that you've truly placed it behind you before we move forward. That is all." She caressed his cheek with the pad of her thumb. "Considering our past, and the way you hurt me..." He stiffened at her words. "You did hurt me, Garrett. Deeply. You *abandoned* me. As a result, I need time. Perhaps it is selfish of me, but I am asking you to understand."

He stood. Arguing with her would serve no purpose, for she was not completely wrong with regard to caution—or the curse. Or about him hurting her. Yet it stung. "I will try my best to understand. In light of this, I'd best return you to the Eatons."

They did not speak as he hurriedly dressed. Then he put out the fire and locked the cabinet. Garrett struggled with his emotions, with whether to allow them to rush free or keep them under tight control. This aspect of his personality simultaneously annoyed and amused Abbie. She'd told him so in the past.

He cast a quick glance and her eyes smoldered. It was not as if she were tossing him aside—quite the opposite. No, he couldn't blame her for wishing to take what was quickly developing between them at a slower pace. Abbie gave him a playful wink. How tempting it was to toss off his clothes, carry her to the chaise, and make love to her again. And again.

Abbie turned and reached for her cloak and the spell was broken.

Once they arrived at the rear entrance of the Eaton residence, he slipped off Patriot and helped her down.

"Well, good night." She gave him a brief smile.

Abbie was about to head toward the door when he grasped the sides of her head, forcing her to look at him. "You're mine, and if that sounds domineering and possessive, good, because where you are concerned, I am. I'll be damned to a fiery hell before I let you leave me again for whatever reason."

Annoyance sparked in her dark brown eyes. "Let me? I am going home, I am not *leaving* you. Besides, you threw me away.... Never mind. We will not travel down *that* path once again. What time do you wish us to be ready for our excursion to Sevenoaks tomorrow?"

He kissed her hard. At first she stubbornly resisted, but she soon softened, returning his kiss with equal passion. Garrett broke the kiss and marched away from her, then mounted Patriot. "I will call for you and Megan at one o'clock. And tomorrow night, I will be here at the stroke of midnight. Agreed?"

Abbie gave him a sultry smile as she touched her well-kissed lips. "Agreed."

Taking the reins, he gave Patriot a touch of his flanks and he was off, galloping toward Wollstonecraft Hall. Tonight was not near enough, it barely took the edge off his arousal. Perhaps a brisk dash would cool his ardor.

The extreme emotions tearing through him concerned him. He never wanted to love a woman like this. It was dangerous to love to distraction, to be obsessed. Yearning for every touch, smile, and kiss. Surely he could gain control of his emotions. Well, the maelstrom was exhilarating, at least. But did he wish to live the rest of his life in such turmoil?

With Abbie by his side, in his arms, lying under him as he thrust in and out? God, yes. *Forever.*

* * * *

Sitting in the Rose Crown Tearoom, Garrett noticed they were attracting attention from the townsfolk. On the rare occasions he'd ventured to Sevenoaks, he hadn't lingered in tearooms or engaged in conversation with the locals. He'd left that to his father and brother, the peers in the family.

The owner of the tearoom waited on them personally, bringing a three-tiered cake stand stuffed with cream cakes, tarts, and scones. Megan's eyes lit up at the bounty. His daughter had a sweet tooth, make no mistake.

"May I say I'm heartily glad to see you in my humble tearoom," the owner, Mr. Crook, gushed. "I would be obliged if you recommend us to the earl and viscount."

Good God. "What jams do you offer?" Garrett asked as he laid the linen napkin across his lap.

"I have blackberry, strawberry, peach, apricot, a Seville orange marmalade..."

"Excellent," Garrett replied. "The marmalade and apricot jam. Ladies? Any preferences?"

"Your selections are perfect," Abbie smiled.

Mr. Crook bowed. "Right away, sir." He scurried off, leaving them mercifully alone.

Abbie picked up the china teapot and filled their cups. "What an advantage being born into an aristocratic family. He couldn't do enough for us."

"Believe me, the bowing and scraping becomes tedious very quickly. All it does is draw attention." Garrett stared at the women at the next table. He scowled and they looked away, blushing and whispering behind their hands. He could well imagine what they were saying. No doubt wondering who Megan and Abbie were to him—although one glance at his daughter and conclusions could be drawn.

Abbie chuckled. "Ignore them. Instead, let us enjoy the company and the food. Goodness, I hardly know where to begin. Megan?"

"Mama, you have to ask? Cake, of course!"

Garrett laughed as Abbie used the silver tongs to load her plate. "I believe I will begin with scones, if Mr. Crook would make haste with the jams."

The older man hurried to their table and served the condiments. "Anything else, sir?"

"No, thank you. We have everything we need, and it is lovely."

Mr. Crook beamed in response, then moved to another table. Garrett placed three scones on his plate, slathering them with apricot jam and dollops of fresh cream.

"The Wollstonecrafts are involved in progressive causes. Will you tell us which ones?" Megan asked as she placed a piece of strawberry cake on her plate.

"Of course. Your grandfather is in the House of Lords, and your uncle, Julian, is a member of parliament, since his viscount title is courtesy only. Both are working toward factory reform and revising the current inadequate Factory Act by limiting the number of hours of work during the day, especially for women and children. They are also crafting revisions concerning improvement of the horrendous working conditions." Garrett sipped his tea. "Riordan, your cousin, is involved in education reform. It is why he took the position of schoolmaster, to test his ideas. He found the profession enriching and wishes to build his own school here in Kent."

"How wonderful," Megan said. "And you, sir?"

He and Abbie locked gazes. "I recently found a worthy cause in the medical field. Treatment of addiction."

Megan's eyes lit up. "Oh, my, like Papa used to do. Dr. Bevan is continuing his work."

"Yes. I'm toying with the idea of setting up a grant for young doctors to train in this field, eventually leading to funding sanatoriums similar to the one…your father ran." Garrett nearly choked on the word "father," but Dr. Hughes had brought her up. "My nephew, Aidan, will join me in this venture, I'm sure."

"I believe he will," Abbie replied softly.

"I have a cause," Megan announced. "I believe people like Jonas, who are challenged either physically or intellectually, should have a safe haven if they have no family to care for them. The asylums are not the place for those with special needs."

Garrett felt a surge of pride at Megan's statement. "Then we shall see it done. I will raise the subject at our next family meeting."

Satisfied, Megan began to eat her cake. A smudge of frosting dotted the tip of her nose, and Garrett gently brushed it away with the tip of his finger. At least she didn't shrink from his touch. She giggled when he showed her the evidence.

They conversed pleasantly, and Garrett could not remember when he had spent such an enjoyable afternoon. Finally, his daughter appeared to be warming toward him, at least a little.

"Megan and I have decided on a date to return to Standon," Abbie stated. "We discussed it this morning."

Frustration, tinged with sadness, speared him, though he fought showing it. So much for the lovely afternoon. "Oh?"

"Next Monday, the twenty-sixth."

Less than six days. Blast it all, he hurt inside. Garrett took a bite of his scone and did not reply.

His disappointment must have been obvious, for Abbie said, "Alberta and Jonas have their own lives. As do we, as I've explained earlier. Megan must return to school. Do you think your father and brother will return home by Monday next? We certainly do not wish to leave without saying goodbye."

"They will return in a day or two. By Sunday at the very latest," he replied gruffly.

"Wonderful. Megan has something to ask you."

He looked to his daughter, and she met his inquiring gaze shyly. "I hope, well, both of us hope, you will come for a visit. Perhaps you can even return with us to Standon. I know it is a lot to ask on short notice."

Garrett had the distinct feeling that Abbie had put their daughter up to this, but found he didn't mind. In fact, he was touched by her suggestion. She may have even meant it, which helped alleviate the gloom overtaking his mood. "Thank you. I will be visiting, you may count on it. If I'm not able to return with you, it will be shortly thereafter. I will stay at the George Inn."

"I thought you would stay with us," Megan said.

Abbie laid a hand on her arm. "My dear, for propriety's sake, it is best Garrett stay at the inn."

"Yes, I suppose—"

"Mr. Wollstonecraft?"

The three of them turned toward a young messenger carrying a satchel across his shoulder. "Your butler said I could find you here in town, sir." He passed Garrett an envelope. "From Scotland, sir. Important. The butler said for me to bring it to you with all haste."

Garrett reached in his pocket and gave the lad a shilling. *Hell.* A feeling of foreboding took root. He broke the seal and pulled out the officious-looking paper. From his grandfather's solicitor.

I regret to inform you that Alec Roderick Mackinnon died January the tenth. Allow me to offer my sincerest condolences. As per his request, your grandfather will not be buried until the snows melt, as travel would be impossible for you at this time. Please inform me at your earliest possible convenience of when you will travel to Edinburgh, and we will make arrangements for his interment and the settling of his estate.

Garrett didn't bother with the rest. *Damn it all.* He swallowed hard as tears formed on his lashes; he refused to show any emotion in a public place. His grief was private. With shaking hands, he placed the letter in the envelope and sat it on the table.

"My dear, what is it?" Abbie asked, worry in her tone. Try as he might to hide his emotions, she read him easily. She always could.

He cleared his throat. "My grandfather passed away. January tenth. Alec Roderick Mackinnon, age eighty-two."

Megan touched his hand. "I am sorry, Garrett."

A wayward tear slipped from the corner of his eye and trailed down his cheek at his daughter using his first name. He laid his large hand on top of hers. "Thank you, my sweet. I do regret that you will never meet him. He is...was...as red haired as we."

Megan smiled, though it had a touch of sadness in it.

"Perhaps we should take our leave," Abbie suggested.

Garrett removed his hand, but not before giving Megan's an affectionate pat. Then he wiped the tear from his cheek. "Not at all. It was not completely unexpected, as he was eighty-two. The last letter that I received mentioned that he was not well. And when he hadn't answered mine the past five months... Well, as I said, not unexpected."

"But hurts nonetheless," Abbie replied kindly.

"Yes. It bloody hurts. Sorry for the language, ladies."

"When did you last journey to Scotland?" Megan asked.

"Five years past, when my grandmother died. Once I grew up the trips grew less frequent, but we kept up a vigorous correspondence." Garrett sighed wistfully. "He was a large man, braw, as they say in Scotland, with a quick temper and a generous heart. A genuine twinkle in his eye. My mother was his only child. His older brother, who never married, died about ten years past. I am the only living relative in the direct line." He nodded toward his daughter. "And Megan."

"Goodness, you will be the sole heir," Abbie marveled.

"Well, I won't be inheriting a Scottish castle or pots of gold. My grandfather lived modestly; he owned a small share in Mackinnon Spirits and Liquors, based in Edinburgh. The company belongs to another branch of his family—his cousin's, I believe." Garrett drank some tea, savoring the warmth. A cuppa always helped in times of stress, so his grandfather claimed. "He never traveled beyond Hadrian's Wall, not even when my mother passed, even though my father invited him more than once. He despised travel." He raised his teacup. "I will miss him. To Alec Mackinnon."

Megan and Abbie raised their teacups and they all took a drink. Regardless of hearing of his grandfather's death, he would not sink into despair. It was a sunny day. He sat with the woman he loved more than his life and his lovely daughter. His grandfather used to say: "Be happy while you're living, for you're a long time dead." The Scottish saying held a good deal of common sense and truth.

Time to get on with the living—and loving.

Chapter 14

When they arrived at the hunter's hut shortly past midnight, Garrett wasted no time and gave her a passionate kiss. "I need you. I want to forget..."

"Your grief? I understand." Abbie caressed his cheeks, trailing the tip of her finger across his prominent cheekbones. "When someone we care about dies, we need affirmation of life, in whatever form." As she had when Elwyn passed. Instead of seeking physical contact with another man, Abbie had decided to volunteer at the sanatorium. She was eager to contribute, to play a role in her husband's legacy. But obviously Garrett needed a more direct confirmation of life. His erection pressed insistently against her.

He spun her about until she faced the stone wall. "Forgive me, I will withdraw, I swear it."

"Yes, all right." Garrett pushed up the skirt of her gown, moaning when he discovered she was not wearing undergarments once again. His hand slid between her legs. Already she was wet, thrilled at this wild, carnal side of him. Most of their past encounters were like this, rushed, frantic, feral. He kicked her legs apart and entered her with a swift, deep thrust, causing her to cry out at the sheer delight of him filling her.

Slipping an arm about her waist, he pounded into her, careful that her exposed skin did not scrape against the rough stone wall. Her feet lifted from the floor and she gasped in surprise. Garrett held her aloft, yet firmly pinned against his hard, unyielding body. As he slid in and out of her, he nuzzled her neck, whispering fiercely in her ear. "You are all I want, all I need. I love you, Abbie. Never stopped. Never will." He uttered a rough oath as she cried out with her swift release.

Garrett's thrusts grew wilder, and she placed a hand against the wall to steady herself. Then he left her, groaning as he lowering her to the floor.

Gasping for air, Abbie turned to face him. He held one hand over his shaft. As promised, he did not come inside her. Reaching in the pocket of her skirt, she handed him a handkerchief.

"Would you?" he asked, still breathing unevenly.

Abbie moved his hand and gently wiped away the proof of his desire. It was intimate, standing this close, assisting him as their breathing returned to normal. Garrett then undressed, and did the same to her.

He swept her up in his arms and carried her to the chaise. Laying her on it, he covered her with his large body, then began to build the passion between them once again, but at an agonizing, slow pace. Garrett only stopped long enough to place the rubber condom on his stiff shaft. Once sheathed, he kissed and licked her skin, suckled her breast until she writhed and moaned under him. He threaded his fingers through hers and lifted their arms above their heads.

When he entered her, tears gathered on her lashes. It had never been this intense between them before, but when had they had the opportunity to love each other so unhurriedly? His languorous, deep thrusts urged her onward as she lifted her hips to meet him. The sounds and odors of sex filled the small hut and mingled with their moans. Abbie lost all concept of time, and lost track of how many occasions she reached her peak. His free hand rested at her hip, and Garrett started to alternate between quick plunges and deliberate slow withdrawal.

Oh, Abbie was ready to come apart. Fly to pieces. Then she did, as if she soared with the clouds. She had read such passages in books and thought them exaggerated. Then she remembered her past encounters with Garrett. No exaggeration. This one topped them all.

His release directly followed hers. He lifted his head, gritted his teeth, and all the cords in his neck pulled taut as he shuddered. "Sweet, suffering Jesus," he groaned. Burying his face in the curve of her shoulder, he trembled and Abbie held him close to her heart. They lay like this for interminable moments, until he finally lifted from her and lay flat.

Exhaling shakily, he gathered her into his embrace. "My God."

She sighed contentedly. "Yes, indeed. I am the most fortunate of women."

"And I the most fortunate of men. Abbie, will you wait a few days before your departure? A week even?"

"Why?"

"I need you, I want more of…this. Besides, how can I court you if you are in Standon? You claim that you wish us to know each other better, then announce you're leaving. What is going on? Second thoughts?" He frowned. "Or is it the caution you mentioned?"

How to explain? Her emotions had not been caught in a maelstrom like this since they were last together all those years past. It was all on her, for she was the one who'd come here to stir them up. Now she was retreating like a besieged coward. God, *was* she having second thoughts? Abbie snuggled in closer. No second thoughts about loving him. Abbie needed him as she needed to breathe. "Yes, a little caution. Also, there is scandal..."

"What? Scandal? What are you on about? You keep mentioning the bloody word."

"In the eyes of society, what we did fourteen years ago is as scandalous as what we are doing here and now."

Garrett bolted upright, staring at her as if she were off her head. Perhaps she was. "To hell with society. All that matters is us. Together. Never to part. Say you agree, Abbie. Return to Standon by all means, but know this: it is temporary." There was an edge of anger and exasperation in his voice. "You belong with me. At my side. In my bed. Damn it all, I want us to wed and be a family with our daughter, and more children besides. I want us to share the future. You said that you wanted one with me. Have you changed your mind?"

"If I hadn't come here, you never would have sought me out," she accused. Bitterness unfurled inside her once again. "Let that sink in. You broke my heart. I kept waiting for a knock at the door. A letter or note. Any word. *Something.* But it never came. *You*...never came to me. I had been discarded like an old pair of boots."

Garrett threw his arms in the air as he stood. "God above, Abbie, we've agreed to put the past behind us—to allow the acrimony to heal. But it never will. Not for you. Not completely."

She rose, holding the sheet to her chin. "Perhaps it never will. Can you blame me? Which makes me traveling here on an impulse all the more troubling." Her voice quivered with emotion. "Yes, scandal is on my mind, for I paid for it as you never have. I was alone and pregnant, rejected by my parents, beaten by my father, married to a stranger—thankfully a kind one, but a stranger regardless. I carried the brunt of it all these years. It has affected me. It still does."

"You should have come to me," he snapped. "The moment you discovered you were pregnant."

"And be humiliated again? *You* should have come to *me*," she retorted.

"Damn it all, I've said that I'm sorry for my youthful, immature actions. And I *am* truly sorry. I didn't seek you out because I was ashamed of my cruel words and behavior. I believed that you were better off without a selfish, self-absorbed young man with a stubborn streak as long and wide as the Thames. You were better off without a superstitious man who allowed an ancient curse to rule his life. I would have made a terrible husband and father."

She blinked rapidly, trying to stave off tears from forming. "And now you've changed?" she asked skeptically.

He gave a short bark of cynical laughter, then frowned. "I'm still stubborn. I like to believe that growing older and wiser has made me less selfish. And the curse? I'll not lie, it's still there. I believe there is merit to its existence. But I've decided that it will no longer rule my life. I've *told* you this, Abbie. I love you too much to set you aside again. It would destroy me more than any damnable ancient curse." He smoothed her cheeks with the pads of his thumbs. "How to make you believe it? You will have to trust me. Trust, Abbie. It is holding you back. You love me, but the trust is not there. Not one hundred percent. And until it is, there can be nothing permanent between us."

A lone tear trailed down her cheek. "I do so *want* to trust you. There is such a hollow feeling inside me and it's been there for years."

He kissed her forehead. "Since I hurt you."

Abbie nodded, sniffling. "When I saw you in Standon, I was breathless. Stunned. Thrilled. I had to see you again. Talk to you. Touch you. All the feelings I had hidden away roared to life, and without properly thinking it through, I journeyed here. For I had to know: Was what we shared all those years ago real or merely a youthful, reckless folly? And beyond my own desires, you needed to be told of Megan. Bitterness was not a sufficient reason to keep her existence from you."

"Allow me to declare once again: You are bold and courageous for coming here. Because you are correct. My stubborn self refused to seek you out, even though you've haunted me, especially in my dreams. But here we are, my love, flaws and all. Acknowledging our mistakes, our frailties, and our faults. Where do we go from here? You spoke of a fresh start. I would advise both of us to embrace it."

Abbie leaned against his chest. "And someday live at Wollstonecraft Hall?"

"It is large enough to accommodate us. The men of Wollstonecraft Hall are a strange sort, all living together as we do, but we are a solid, supportive family, and they would welcome you and Megan warmly."

"They have already," she whispered.

"There. All that remains is for us to decide what to do next. Marriage is the logical step, but I will not rush you. I promise."

Garrett made it sound so easy. Being here, after what they had shared, it would be tempting to agree to anything he proposed. Which made it all the more imperative that she remain cautious. Abbie also had to think of Megan. Her daughter already had her life upended, and though she appeared to be adjusting a little, she needed more time. Truthfully, Abbie did as well. "Since I've already decided on the Monday departure date, I should follow through. If it were only myself to consider, but Megan—"

"I have a suggestion. I would like you both to accompany me in the early spring to Scotland. A few weeks at most. Discuss it with Megan. I understand that you have concerns about her schooling, but we will make it up somehow. Think about it. Will you?"

Abbie gave him a stern look. "You must cease interrupting me, Garrett. I don't like it."

"I stand admonished. And you're right. I will endeavor to not do it again."

His words were sincerely meant, and she smiled in response. "Thank you. I will discuss the journey with Megan. We've never been to Scotland, and we would like to be there to support you in dealing with your grandfather's burial and estate. I can't see her saying no, but there is a chance she may prefer not to go."

Garrett took her hand. "I believe she is warming toward me."

"How could she not? But in the interim, we will return to Standon, as there is much to consider."

He kissed her hand, a sly smile curling about his sensual lips. "I've been thinking; if we do decide to marry—and I am not pressuring you, mind—your house in Standon could be donated to the sanatorium, as a place for family to stay when visiting patients. Or, when I set up the foundation, young physicians fresh from university can reside there as they study under Dr. Bevan. If he is amenable to the scheme. Ultimately, it is your property, your decision. I would never presume to interfere. Ever. I am a progressive Wollstonecraft, after all."

No pressure? Good heavens. "My, you have been making plans."

"Merely seeing my way clear to that fresh start. A new path to follow."

"I will not be led about like one of your prize horses. I make my own decisions concerning my life, as I always have." Abbie told him this in a matter-of-fact tone, not angry, but firm.

"Absolutely. As I said, your decision. Always."

She cupped his cheek. "I will discuss all this with Megan once we return to Standon. We will plan from there. I have much to mull over. As you say, there is no rush." She kissed him gently on the lips. "For now, we will make the most of the time remaining, especially the nights."

Garrett pulled her close and began kissing and caressing her, Abbie understood that the trust between them was fragile. As far as marriage, she could not think about it now, for deep down in her soul she was frightened witless that he would hurt her again. More proof she hadn't been thinking clearly when she impulsively made this journey. The love? It was growing stronger than ever. But would it be enough to carry them forward?

* * * *

Aidan Wollstonecraft opened one eye and looked about, taking in his surroundings. It was as if he were staring down a dark tunnel. Considering the dimness and the fact that all was blurry, he could not see much of anything at all. He'd been in and out of a haze for who knows how long, with strange people hovering around him. Often he wondered if he'd conjured them in his dreams, especially the attractive young lady with the kind voice and gentle touch. Thankfully, she felt real enough. But most of his dreams had been disturbing, revealing flashes of appallingly depraved scenarios that couldn't possibly be real. Or were they?

One event haunted him more than others. A vague memory replayed in his mind: Aidan offering himself for money in order to purchase opium. Surely, he had not sank to such depths. He had often resorted to thievery when funds ran low since he'd stopped collecting his quarterly payment. It hadn't seemed right to use his father's money for his vices, though last month he'd been desperate enough to consider it. Aidan had even stood outside the bank, debating whether or not to collect it.

Another recurring reminiscence tied in with selling himself for coin: In his dream there had been a brute of a man with a lustful gleam in his eye. Aidan banished the image. It was only a nightmare. It had not happened. But hell, it seemed real enough. Dismissing the disturbing thoughts, he rubbed his forehead as a sharp pain throbbed behind his eyes. If only he could focus and see things clearly, literally and figuratively.

With a great deal of effort he tried to sit up, but he discovered that his right wrist was bound to the bed rail. *What in the hell?* Aidan gazed about the room, which still lay in shadow. More hazy images, though he could focus on a glass of water sitting on the table by his bed. Grunting with the effort and hampered by his restraint, he tentatively reached for the glass. It slipped from his hand and fell to the floor with a resounding crash.

The door opened, and someone entered. "Oh, you're awake." A female voice.

"Sorry...glass..." His voice was rough and gravelly, his mouth dry.

"It's all right. Silas, could you please clean this up, then fetch Mr. Black a fresh glass of water."

"Right away, Miss Bevan."

Mr. Black? Aidan's fuzzy and fevered brain began to doubt his own existence until he recalled that his brother, Riordan, used Black, their Irish mother's maiden name, when he'd accepted the schoolmaster position. Fine, he would go along with the facade. An image of Garrett carrying him from a carriage filled his mind. "My...uncle..." Blast it, why couldn't he string more than two words together?

Miss Bevan moved to his right side and unfastened the leather strap binding his wrist. "Allow me to bring you up-to-date: Your Uncle Garrett and another man, Edwin Seward, brought you here from London approximately three weeks past. You were deathly ill from the effects of an opium addiction. My father, Dr. Gethin Bevan, is the physician who runs this sanatorium. My name is Cristyn Bevan. I'm his assistant and am training to be a nurse. You are in Standon, Herefordshire. Today is Thursday, January twenty-second. I will fill in more details when you are better able to process the information."

Aidan rubbed his wrist as he watched Miss Bevan move efficiently about the room. Perhaps it was wise that she not enlighten him too much; he was having a hard enough time following what she'd just said. Garrett brought him from London. How mortifying. Flashes of sin and vice filled his mind and he shook them away. Bad enough that they haunted his dreams; he did not need them invading his lucid state. Not that he felt altogether coherent.

Taking hold of the heavy drapes, she pushed them aside and blinding sun filled the room, causing Aidan to wince in pain. "I believe we shall endeavor to sit you upright in a chair today, and see that you partake in a meal."

The thought of food caused his stomach to lurch. Who could think about food when every bone in his body throbbed and his head pounded? His angel of mercy returned to his bedside and smiled. With the draperies open and the room illuminated he could see her more or less clearly for the first time, and she was not some blurry figure hovering about his subconscious. God, she was beautiful. Her hair was as black as his, her skin as luminescent as the finest string of pearls. But it was her eyes that caught his attention. An indescribable shade of blue-violet that he'd never seen before. How easily he could get lost in them. Apparently, he was still an unrepentant rake if attracted to a woman in this sorrowful physical state. *Cristyn.* What a lovely name. "You're shockingly malnourished. We must see that you eat, but we'll start slow and build your appetite. Ah, here is Silas. Assist me in placing Mr. Black in the chair."

Aidan groaned as this Silas person and Miss Bevan hauled him out of bed. Damn it all, he was as weak as a kitten—could not even place one foot in front of the other, let alone stand on them. Once they situated him in the chair, Silas turned him toward the window, causing Aidan to recoil once again at the bright light. However, the little warmth from the late January sun consoled him. When had he last felt the sun on his skin? He'd lived as a shadow creature from a gothic horror novel for so long, he could not recall.

Miss Bevan handed him a full glass of water and he could barely hold the damned thing. With a concentrated effort, he lifted the glass to his mouth and sipped. *Ambrosia.* Aidan nearly groaned with the pleasure of it. Using his free hand, he trailed it along his torso. He could feel his ribs even through the wool nightshirt. Glancing at the bandages on his hands, he tried to recall what wounds he'd obtained. Worried, he continued to sip the cool water.

Moments later, Miss Bevan placed a table and a tray of food in front of him. She took the glass from his quaking hands and set it on the tray. "Beef stew, fresh bread, and stewed apples. You must eat, Aidan."

Hell and damnation, he didn't want food—he wanted a hit of opium. The shaking in his hands increased. Cold perspiration broke out on his temples.

Miss Bevan—Cristyn—pulled up a chair in front of him and sat. His reaction must have been plain to read for she said, "Take what you need, not what you desire or crave." She placed her hand on top of his and he jolted from her touch. "And you need food. It is critical that you begin eating solid food this very day."

Desire? His gaze glided along her torso and slowly upward again, halting at her breasts. They were ample, the swell of them clearly visible through her plain wool gown and long apron. As sick and skeletal as he was, he desired *her*. Sex often staved off his more serious and damaging vices, though it hadn't during the past few months in London.

Cristyn held up a spoonful of stew encouragingly, as if he were a helpless babe. He supposed he was. Anger and annoyance replaced arousal. How tempting to knock her arm aside and send the tray careening to the floor. But he'd done that enough already. Reluctantly, he closed his mouth over the spoon and forced himself to fight the gag reflex. He swallowed and tasted nothing. It could have been a spoonful of ash for all he knew. Aidan took another, then another, until the bowl stood empty.

"Well done! I'm extremely proud of you," she enthused.

His angel spoke to him as a master might speak to an obedient dog. The food sat like a lump in his stomach. It roiled and churned and tried to claw its way up his throat, but he forced it down again. Nausea made his head spin.

It would be easy to slip away, stop eating, fight his recovery. The torment would end, at least. It also had been easy to slide into the dark pit of utter irresponsibility and depravity. But looking at this beautiful woman who'd invested time and energy into his recovery, Aidan did not have the heart to disappoint her. Quite the revelation. He rubbed his chest. Yes, the damned organ still pounded out a steady beat. For more months than he cared to count, he'd thought that he no longer possessed a heart.

Aidan stood on the edge of a precipice. Live or die. The choice was that bloody simple. Cristyn gave him the courage to at least *try*.

Chapter 15

Since the sun was out, Garrett suggested to Abbie that they all ride about the property and the woods beyond. They rode three abreast, with Megan between them. Garrett made certain they crammed all sorts of activities into their daily plans. Some of the activities consisted of Megan skillfully playing the pianoforte with him and Abbie acting as an enthusiastic audience. Other entertainments included various parlor and card games. The assorted recreations also kept the grief he was experiencing over his grandfather's death from the forefront of his mind. It hit him hard, and Garrett was grateful that Abbie and Megan were there to soften the blow.

If they were to leave on the twenty-sixth, he was going to make the most of the time remaining. Keeping occupied also ensured that he was distracted from their upcoming departure. Should he convince them to stay? Yes, blast it all. Tonight, when he and Abbie met at the hunter's hut, he would do exactly that. Even if he had to drop to his knees and beg.

The afternoons were not excessively cold, which made the horse outings pleasant, as long as pots of hot chocolate and plates of sweets were waiting on their return. Last evening he'd been invited to dinner at the Eatons. What concerned him during the visit were the shy, heated gazes Megan exchanged with Jonas. Despite their promises, the young couple would bear watching.

Today was another bright day, a slight chilly breeze, and the snow accumulation from last week had all but melted, except for places where the sun could not reach. On their horses, they chatted amiably as they traveled the well-worn trails twisting about the perimeter of the large property. Garrett glanced at Abbie, who smiled in return.

Their discussions had helped to ease the underlining tension between them, had perhaps even alleviated a part of the hidden resentment. They had a future, and would be a family. It was a matter of degrees on how to get there. Patience would be needed, as he understood all too well the tumultuous emotions at play.

Another emotion filled his thoughts of late: guilt. How he'd treated Abbie in the past. Not visiting his grandfather more often before he died. But more importantly, Aidan. Not only for ignoring the signs of his steep decline into dissoluteness, but for not staying and assisting in his care. Though he supposed he would only be in the way. How arrogant to think that he could make a difference in Aidan's recovery.

If he'd stayed in Standon, his stables could function without him for a few weeks. Though he would miss it, for Garrett reveled in the sights and smells. The sweet odor of hay, how it crackled under his boots, and the musky scent of the horses. Hell, he didn't even mind the smell of shit.

The head groom, MacAdam, and the well-trained stable lads and grooms could easily see to the daily routine. Yet he liked to keep a hand in. The breeding of his horses, the training, the daily care, just being around the noble creatures enhanced his life and ultimately kept complete loneliness from overtaking him.

He recalled something that his grandfather had said to him when he sank into a brooding mood, as Wollstonecraft men were prone to do: "I've no use for self-indulgent behavior. Get over it, lad. Stop yer wallowing and live yer life!" About bloody time he followed that sage advice.

"Mama, when I woke last night, I stopped by your room. You were not there. I waited thirty minutes, but you didn't return."

Megan's question tore Garrett from his indulgent thoughts. He and Abbie exchanged glances.

"I was with Garrett," Abbie replied. "We need privacy to become reacquainted, and meeting later in the evening affords us the time we require."

Megan's expression turned serious, as if contemplating what Abbie had revealed.

"I love your mother, Megan. I never stopped," Garrett said.

Megan's eyebrow arched as she turned to stare at him. "If you loved her then, before you even knew about me, why didn't you marry her?"

A direct and pointed question, and Garrett was not about to lie to his daughter. "There is blame to go around, although most of it lands on me. We were too young, with harsh words exchanged on both sides that caused lasting scars. There are other, more private reasons I do not wish to discuss today, but our meeting again has revealed a new path for us to travel."

"Are you going to marry, then?" Her tone was questioning, but not angry. Thank God for small mercies.

"I have asked her," Garrett replied. "Your mother believes—and I concur—that it must be discussed between the two of you. Hence the reason you will be returning to Standon for a short while. How do you feel about it, Megan?"

They rode in silence for several moments, and he and Abbie exchanged apprehensive glances once again. They couldn't marry if Megan was adamantly opposed. Well, they *could*, but it would start off their nuptials on a tense footing.

"Would we live at Wollstonecraft Hall?" Megan asked.

"Yes. It is certainly large enough for us to have part of an entire wing to ourselves. We would have to work out about your schooling, of course..."

"I would be living with my grandfather, uncle, and cousins." Megan's eyes sparkled. "Jonas will be nearby." Her smile slipped. "Which would make you my..." Her voice trailed away. He understood what she meant.

"As I said before, I would never try to replace your beloved papa. Not in any way. You may continue to call me Garrett, and refer to me any way you wish. Father, stepfather, or friend." He smiled warmly at his daughter as he pulled up on the reins to halt Patriot. "I would like, above all things, for us to be friends. But I will not force it."

Abbie and Megan stopped alongside Garrett. "Megan, we will discuss it further when we return to Standon next week, but are you willing to consider a future marriage between myself and Garrett?"

"Mama, I wish for you to be happy, and I believe—"

The sound of a rifle shot cracked and a bullet whizzed over Megan and Abbie's heads. Instinctively, Garrett moved in front of them to protect them. Another shot rang out, causing him to reel in his saddle. White-hot pain tore through his shoulder and blood seeped through his greatcoat. "Uun," he grunted from the impact. *Hell, I've been shot.* He'd been about to call out for Megan and Abbie to follow him to the hall with all haste, as remaining stationary was not wise under the circumstances. But he never even had a chance to speak.

The reins slipped from his hands and he fell to the ground. All around him the landscape blurred and started to spin. Abbie and Megan screamed, rushing to his side. *Go. Leave me.* But Garrett could not speak the words. If anything happened to them he'd never forgive himself. Life would not be worth living. All grew dim. Damn it all, he was losing consciousness.

* * * *

"My lord, you should've allowed me to fire the shots," Delaney stated in a bored tone.

"Well, I hardly see how it is my fault that he moved into my crosshairs. The cumbersome beast is so damned tall it is a wonder I did not take the top of his head off." The Marquess of Sutherhorne shrugged indifferently. "I did not intend to injure or kill, but it appears that fate had other plans. So be it. Is he dead? I cannot see from this angle."

"The women are panicked, as he's on the ground." Delaney continued to look through the opera glasses. "Ah, there is a slight movement of his hand. I see blood at his shoulder."

"Not a fatal wound, then." What an unexpected windfall. All Sutherhorne had wanted to do was give Garrett Wollstonecraft a fright. Delaney had discovered that the woman and the girl were visiting neighbors, and the Scottish swine had been spending time with them. Their names were Abigail and Megan Hughes, from Standon, Hertfordshire. What were they to Wollstonecraft? He *must* discover the connection.

Regardless, vengeance was required, and what better way than to let the horse breeder experience true fear? The way Sutherhorne had when Wollstonecraft had manhandled and threatened him three months past in Carrbury.

The plan took shape rather quickly, especially when Delaney reported that the red-haired girl bore a slight resemblance to the beast. Related? Wollstonecraft obviously cared for them, and firing a rifle over the ladies' heads would strike terror in the man—and give Sutherhorne a balm for the slight he'd endured.

"My lord, I suggest we take our leave."

Delaney's gravely monotone voice pulled him from his thoughts. "Of course. The plan for our departure is in place?"

"Yes, my lord. Your carriage awaits, a mile through these woods."

Sutherhorne handed the rifle to Delaney, who then slipped it in the saddle holster. "I will require you to take a quick sojourn to Standon and gather any information you can on the woman and the chit."

"Of course, my lord. And what of the young heir?"

Sutherhorne narrowed his eyes. "The dissolute grandson, Aidan? Why, do you covet the man?"

Delaney's expression turned stony and he did not reply. Recalling the events at the naughty party, Delaney had thrown himself into the carnal activity with a good deal of enthusiasm. He regarded his employee shrewdly. What did he know about this man? Next to nothing, though Sutherhorne did not care to delve into the man's past. As long as he fulfilled a purpose and provided a service, Delaney could continue with his illegal boxing and other personal pursuits, illicit or not.

"I am about to spread the tale of Aidan Wollstonecraft's decline throughout London. The salacious tidbit of gossip regarding selling himself for opium should destroy his family's bloated and exaggerated good reputation quite thoroughly. I may even toss in his exotic sexual proclivities as an added bonus."

"The talk in Sevenoaks is that the young heir has taken a sojourn to Italy for the winter months, to recover from a chest infection," Delaney stated.

Sutherhorne laughed. Did the family truly believe they would get away with this fiction? There were at least two other peers in attendance at the wicked party who could corroborate. Then he sobered and cast a sidelong glance at Delaney. His employee was dangerous and unpredictable—he knew that much about him. Could he have developed an obsession with Aidan Wollstonecraft? Why else was he asking questions in Sevenoaks?

"I do hope you were discreet in your inquires regarding the heir." Delaney gave him a brisk nod. "The lie will not hold up once word starts to spread. Come. Let us depart before we are discovered."

The two men rode silently through the thick cluster of oak and fir trees.

"Delaney, I want you to stay in the area. Not at the local inn, but elsewhere. Find out if the Scottish barbarian dies of his wound. Once you have an update, return to London with all haste. Then you will be free to carry out my other request."

"Yes, my lord. Consider it done."

Sutherhorne smiled and glanced at the blue, cloudless sky. A beautiful day. He breathed in the cool, crisp air, then exhaled.

By God, revenge was sweet indeed.

* * * *

Abbie looked about frantically. Since they were surrounded by woods, the shot could have come from anywhere, though it appeared the sound had come from north of where they stood. They were exposed here, on open ground.

Megan stood by, wringing her hands. "Mama, what should we do?" she cried.

Abbie laid her head against Garrett's chest. His heart still thumped with a strong beat. *Thank God.* She tore off his wool muffler, bunched it up, and held it to his wound. Pressure would stem the bleeding. She'd learned this much from her physician husband. "Listen to me, Megan. Calm yourself. You must ride immediately to Wollstonecraft Hall. Inform Martin, the butler, about what has happened. We need a wagon and footmen, and the physician should be called."

Megan's eyes widened. "But—"

"Go, Megan," she urged, "and tell them to bring weapons in case they are needed."

Her daughter glanced worriedly at Garrett, then mounted her horse and set off at a brisk gallop. *Please God, let her be safe.* She was taking a chance asking Megan to do this, but if the person who fired upon them was still out there, Abbie would rather the perpetrators fire on her and Garrett. At least a moving target was harder to hit.

And they *had* been fired upon. Abbie had heard and felt the bullet dash past their heads, far too close to be accidental. When Garrett moved in front of them, he took the impact of the second bullet. *Oh, my love.* He'd done it to protect them.

There was too much blood. From a shoulder wound? The slug must have hit a major vein or artery. Abbie pressed harder as her frightened mind struggled to remember things that Elwyn had told her or something she'd read in one of his medical books. On the rare nights she could not sleep, she'd often read them.

Think, Abbie. The subclavian artery was in the shoulder, which fed to the main artery in the arm—she couldn't recall the name. That could explain all the blood. Was bone shattered? The artery or veins destroyed? Nerves and tendons damaged beyond all repair?

Garrett groaned, his eyelids fluttered. "Abbie..." he croaked.

"Yes, I'm here. Stay with me. Help is on the way," she soothed as she pressed harder on the wound.

"Safe..."

"We are safe. Do not worry."

He clasped her hand. "Love...you." His eyelids closed and his grip slackened.

"Garrett!" Again, she listened to his chest. Still beating. He was a strong man; he would fight this. Interminable moments passed. Silence surrounded them, except for the haunting, hoarse screech of a hawk circling overhead. Finally, the unmistakable sound of thundering horses' hooves filled her hearing. Four men on horses galloped toward them, followed by a wagon with three others riding on it.

An older man pulled up on the reins, halting the horse before her. "MacAdam, ma'am. The head groom. What direction did the shots come from?"

As he spoke, the men from the wagon jumped down and rushed toward them. Abbie pointed toward the cluster of trees. "There, I believe. My daughter?"

"Miss Hughes is well, and bravely explained in detail what occurred. Martin has sent for the physician in Sevenoaks, and sent word to the earl's personal physician in London. He also sent a runner to Carrbury. The earl and viscount will want to be informed. As would Master Riordan."

"Yes, of course," she murmured.

It took five men to lift Garrett and carry him toward the wagon. Abbie followed behind and one of the men helped her up. She knelt beside Garrett and continued to hold pressure to the wound.

"Do you believe it was deliberate, Mrs. Hughes?" MacAdam asked. "Miss Hughes was not sure."

"Yes. The first shot sailed over our heads, far too close for comfort. The second hit Garrett when he moved in front of us, to protect us."

"Thank you. Lads, take the wagon to the hall. Quickly now. Inform Martin that Jacob, Samuel, and I will search the woods." MacAdam pulled his rifle from the saddle. "Off with you!"

They had tied Patriot and the gelding to the rear of the wagon, and with a snap of the reins, they lurched forward, the pace growing quicker as the horses built up speed. Garrett mumbled as he slipped in and out of consciousness. Hot tears clustered on her lashes, but she blinked them away. She must stay in control—Garrett's survival depended on it. The ride was rough, and Abbie almost lost her balance more than once as the wagon hit ruts in the semi-frozen ground.

Once they arrived at the front entrance of the hall, she was swept up into a beehive of activity, with Martin efficiently and confidently giving orders to all and sundry.

As she was being assisted from the wagon, Martin rushed to her side. "We shall place Master Garrett in the morning room, Mrs. Hughes, as it is on the main floor and there is a chaise large enough to accommodate him."

"Yes." She followed Martin and the footmen as they carried Garrett inside. He moaned twice, still wandering in and out of awareness. Abbie slipped out of her coat as the footmen did the same for Garrett. "Remove his shirt as well; tear it off, if you must."

"Gordon, if you please," Martin said.

The young footman unbuttoned the waistcoat and removed it, then did the same with the white shirt. Part of it stuck to the wound and Garrett moaned as it was pulled away. They sat Garrett upright partway, and Abbie took the opportunity to inspect his back. An exit wound, which meant that the bullet had passed through. Thankfully, the blood escaping there was a mere trickle. But what damage had it wreaked in its journey? She moved in beside Garrett and placed further pressure on the wound, which had bled profusely while he was being situated.

"What can we do until the doctor arrives?" Martin asked, worry clear in his tone.

Heavens, what to do? "Fetch hot water, clean rolls of cloths to use as bandages, scissors, and—blast it! I have no idea what else."

"Gordon, go to the kitchen directly. Mrs. Barnes is there and will collect what we need. Hurry now," Martin instructed.

The young man sprinted from the room, and he'd no sooner departed when another footman announced, "Dr. Phillips from Sevenoaks."

"Ah, Doctor. If you please. Master Garrett has been shot. If you would attend him posthaste?" Martin asked.

Abbie glanced up. An older man with a white beard came to her side and rudely bumped her out of the way. "This is no place for a lady. See she is removed."

Fury colored her vision and her blood boiled. Regardless of what this man said, she would persist and hold her ground. "See here, Doctor. You may address me directly; in any case, I will *not* be leaving this room."

He finally met her indignant stare with a sniff of disdain. "Suit yourself, but do stay well clear." The doctor roughly lifted Garrett, causing him to groan in protest. "Ah, the bullet passed through. He is losing too much blood. All that remains is removal of the arm to stem any infection. At the shoulder should do it."

Even the ever-dispassionate Martin could not keep the look of horror from his face at the doctor's wild diagnosis.

"This is hardly the seventeenth century, Dr. Phillips. I suppose you'll be bringing out the leeches next," Abbie snapped.

"I will not be spoken to in such a tone from a woman," he sniffed. "And leeches still have their place in today's medicine. Besides, who are you to be giving such decided opinions?"

"I am the widow of a doctor; I know a little of the profession."

Dr. Phillips laughed mockingly.

Abbie chose to ignore it and soldiered on. "There have been great strides in treating wounds such as these. Removing appendages is no longer the first option. You must do all you can to save the arm." She bustled past him and applied further pressure to Garrett's shoulder, which had started to bleed profusely once again.

"Ma'am—"

"The lady's name is Mrs. Hughes, Doctor. I apologize for not introducing you," Martin interjected.

"Mrs. Hughes, then. You see how the wound is seeping. He will bleed out if we do not remove the limb and cauterize the wound. Removing it will also lessen the chance of infection."

My God, this man had stepped out of the medieval age. Abbie protectively stepped in front of Garrett. "Listen to me, all of you. We will not proceed with this butchery until the earl's doctor arrives from London. I demand a second opinion." Abbie pressed harder on the wound. "I will stand here and apply pressure until he *does* make an appearance. I am most determined, and nothing will shift me from Garrett's side unless you drag me kicking and screaming from this room." It took all her self-control to stem her anger. Abbie kept her tone respectful, but firm.

"There is no call to be dramatic," Dr. Phillips replied in a clipped tone. "It could be another two hours before this London doctor arrives."

"I will stand here all blasted night if that is what it takes!" she cried.

"Doctor," Garrett coughed. "I...I would listen to her."

"Is this what you want, Mr. Wollstonecraft?" the doctor asked.

"It...is."

The doctor pursed his lips. "As you wish. We wait for this London doctor."

Garrett gazed at her, pride and admiration reflected in his beautiful eyes. And love. Oh, always the love. "My angel."

The overwhelming urge to cry nearly swamped her, but she would save the tears for later. When she was alone. Garrett needed her, and Abbie would not leave his side.

Fight, my Scottish warrior, fight.

Chapter 16

There were not many places in Riordan's small townhouse where Oliver could steal a few private moments with Mary Tuttle, but he had managed it right after afternoon tea. The visit to Riordan and Sabrina's home in Carrbury had been bittersweet. After informing Riordan of Aidan being found, and the circumstances surrounding it, there were plenty of recriminations to go around. Why hadn't we seen the signs? Why hadn't we done more? Considering they prided themselves on being a supportive family, they had failed miserably with regards to Aidan.

But the men soon moved past such self-indulgence and concluded that they would give Aidan time and space to heal. When he was ready, they would be there for him—in whatever capacity.

Oliver and Julian had decided they would return to Wollstonecraft Hall on Sunday. In the meantime, Oliver was enjoying the visit regardless of the situation. Yesterday afternoon he had sat in on Riordan's class, completely caught up in the lesson, bursting with pride and admiration for his grandson's skills.

Then there was Mary. Oliver had not believed that he would see her quite so soon after their emotional parting, but he welcomed her company and the diversion from worrying about Aidan. Alone in the small library-study, Oliver closed the door, then turned and faced Mary. His heart banged furiously in his chest. By God, to have such a rush of passion at his age proved that he still had plenty of living to do. And loving.

Their gazes caught, and Oliver strode toward her with a decided purpose. To hold her. To kiss her deeply. As if reading his mind, Mary started toward him and they met in the middle of the room and shared a kiss so devastating Oliver thought his heart would burst. She tasted sweet.

Enticing. As he trailed his mouth across her cheek and down her soft neck, he murmured, "Is it terrible that I wish to forgo all propriety and make love to you here and now?"

Mary moaned. "Oliver, what are we to do? For I feel the same. It has been so long."

Mary had informed him last night, when they managed to take a short walk, of her sailor fiancé and his tragic death on the same ship as her father. How she had not been with a man since. Hell, he was tempted to suggest they go away together, find some isolated cottage by the sea. Revel in each other's company, make love whenever the mood struck them. It would be impetuous and scandalous, but certainly in line with being a man of Wollstonecraft Hall.

He cradled her face. "All my talk of a correspondence and deciding what we want...what damned nonsense. I know my mind. I know what is in my heart."

Mary smiled. "And I know what is in mine as well. You are a sinfully handsome man who has aged well—like a fine wine. I want you, Earl of Carnstone. I want you to make love to me until we are completely spent and I—"

Oliver kissed her fiercely. How he adored this lovely woman and her plainspoken ways. Aching, he took the kiss deeper, then moaned when Mary trailed her fingers across his stiff prick. Bold as well. As he nibbled on her lush lower lip, he said, "I don't want some brief dalliance, Mary Tuttle."

"I am to be your mistress, then?" she teased as she squeezed him.

"No. Much more than that. My companion. My friend. My lover. Perhaps more, as—"

There was a sharp rap at the door and they sprang apart. Oliver buttoned his coat as he called out, "Come in."

It was Julian, and he looked pale. "Gordon has arrived from Wollstonecraft Hall with disturbing news: Garrett has been shot."

The news hit Oliver as a forceful blow to the solar plexus and he staggered from the shock. Mary immediately came to his side and held his arm. All at once, he felt like an old man.

"It happened when he was out riding with Megan and Mrs. Hughes. He was shot in the shoulder—not deemed fatal, but serious nonetheless. The doctor from Sevenoaks has been summoned, along with Dr. Faraday from London. I suggest we depart with all haste."

"Yes, of course," Oliver murmured, still trying to process the news. Hell and damnation, what else was going to happen to this family?

"Riordan was there when Gordon relayed the news. He and Sabrina will be coming as well, as soon as he makes arrangements for his students." Julian slid his worried gaze to Mary. "I believe, Miss Tuttle, that he will be asking you to stay and assist in his classroom."

"Yes, I will do anything to help," she replied.

"Are you all right, Da?" Julian asked.

Julian had not called him that since he was eighteen. Once Garrett was old enough to talk, he'd always called Oliver "Da," and for a few years, Julian had followed suit. It touched him, hearing it again from his oldest son. At times, Julian could be too self-contained. But not here. "Yes, just give me a minute."

"I will prepare for our departure." Julian exited the room, closing the door behind him. Oliver groaned, and Mary assisted him to the settee, then sat beside him, holding him close.

"I cannot lose him, Mary. Garrett is precious to me. It will destroy me if..." His voice shook, his eyes grew moist.

She held him in her arms; her comforting warmth calmed him. "I understand. He is the living link to your lost love. I saw her portrait in your study. Moira was beautiful. You love her still."

"I do, but not to exclusion of allowing love into my life once more. And I have allowed it, with you, Mary."

They held each other tight. God, he needed and ached for this. As soon as Garrett was recovered, Oliver would not waste another damned minute. He was in love, as he predicted—for the last time in his life.

* * * *

Time passed far too slowly as Abbie, Dr. Phillips, and Martin took turns keeping pressure on the wound. She'd managed to coax Garrett into drinking cool water during the short periods he was lucid, but he'd remained unconscious for most of the two hours.

Blast, had she made the right decision? Garrett had agreed, but was he in his right mind to make any type of conclusion in his present state? This was not a wound they could bind and hope for the best.

Martin ordered a tray with tea and sandwiches, and Dr. Phillips immediately helped himself. Abbie could not think of food. Her insides tumbled and shook with worry and fright. The thought of losing Garrett tore her asunder.

At last, Martin announced, "Dr. Faraday from London."

"Good God, a blackamoor!" Phillips gasped, clearly shocked.

The young man appeared to be no more than thirty. He had an air of self-confidence that Abbie immediately admired, and he did not flinch at what she considered a derogatory term.

"I assure you, sir, I am neither Muslim nor from Africa. I was born in Chelsea," the young doctor stated, his tone even.

"There must be some mistake," Dr. Phillips prattled. "This cannot be the earl's personal physician." He turned to face Dr. Faraday. "What are your credentials?"

"My father is white, does that suffice? Do I have enough Anglo-Saxon in me to warrant the consideration I am due?" Dr. Faraday kept the emotion in his voice under control, but Abbie could hear the annoyance nonetheless.

Dr. Phillips merely sputtered, mumbling unintelligibly.

"I graduated from Cambridge, and am a member of the College of Physicians, which I believe are adequate credentials by anyone's standards," Faraday continued. "Now, is this the patient?"

"Yes, Doctor. I am Mrs. Hughes. I have no credentials except that my late husband was also a physician. I demanded that we wait for your arrival; Dr. Phillips diagnosed removal of the arm."

Dr. Faraday sat his large satchel on the table they had placed near the chaise Garrett laid upon. "Well, we will determine if amputation is necessary; however, an examination is in order first. Will you assist, Dr. Phillips?"

The older man seemed stunned at the request, then cleared his throat. "Yes, of course."

"Mrs. Hughes," Faraday said in a kind voice. "You may remain, as we may need your assistance. Martin as well. Allow me to see the wound."

Nodding, she reluctantly stepped away from Garrett, and as soon as she released pressure, another spurt of blood thrust out, tricking down his chest.

"See how it pumps? Definitely an artery. A vein has more of a steady flow. I am assuming the artery is still intact or he would have bled out by now. How long since Mr. Wollstonecraft has been shot?" Faraday asked.

Abbie glanced at the mantel clock. "Two hours and fifteen minutes."

"There is no time to waste. I will require boiling hot water to sterilize my surgical apparatus, and we will need plenty of brandy for the patient."

"I will see to the water immediately." Martin rushed from the room.

"Dr. Liston, at St. Bartholomew's, is testing using ether, a compound from America. It renders the patient unconscious during operations and various procedures. Alas, we will have to dull Master Garrett's senses with spirits," Faraday stated.

"Ether? How fascinating," Phillips murmured, temporarily forgetting his previous prejudice.

"Will you be able to assist, Mrs. Hughes? A warning: there will be a good deal of blood," Faraday said as he unpacked his satchel.

Abbie nodded shakily.

"Then let us make preparations. Dr. Phillips, place pressure on the wound while Mrs. Hughes assists the patient in drinking a copious amount of brandy. I will prepare."

Everyone went about their duties silently. With the knives boiled, and sleeves rolled up, Dr. Faraday insisted that they wash with carbolic soap before handling any of the sterile instruments.

The doctor placed a padded stick in Garrett's mouth, and as soon as he made the first incision, Garrett moaned and passed out. Using clamps, he spread open the wound. "There. By God, he *is* lucky. There is a small tear in the subclavian artery. The surrounding veins are intact, and it appears that the brachial plexus is whole." Faraday turned slightly toward Abbie. "That is the bundle of nerves controlling arm function. Whether he will have complete control of his arm remains to be seen."

"The bullet must have passed straight through, nicking the artery on its passage," Phillips stated.

"Yes. Will you clamp the artery closed, Doctor?"

Phillips gave Faraday an astonished look. "I have never done anything remotely like this before…"

"There is always the first time. Mrs. Hughes, pass me the curved needle."

The next several minutes passed in silence, as more oil lamps were brought in to cast further illumination while the sun set. Abbie watched, fascinated, as the two unlikely doctors worked in tandem to close the tear.

"My word. The neatest, tightest stitching I've had the honor to witness," Phillips remarked, awe in his voice.

"Thank you, Dr. Phillips. Will you finish closing the wound?" Faraday stepped aside, and Abbie's admiration for the young man increased. Regardless of Phillips's rude tone and prejudicial comment, Faraday had kept his composure and included the older country doctor in the procedure.

"Despite our care, infection will be the next hurdle to overcome." Faraday turned to face her. "May I say that I admire your instincts, Mrs. Hughes? By keeping constant pressure on the wound, I can honestly state that you saved Garrett Wollstonecraft's life. Well done."

Faraday joined Phillips, and together they addressed the exit wound, then bound Garrett's shoulder with the torn, clean cloths.

She had saved Garrett's life. Abbie exhaled shakily as she sat in the nearby wingchair.

Phillips passed her a cup of tea. "Well done, indeed, Mrs. Hughes."

She gave Phillips a polite nod and sipped. Closing her eyes, she sighed as the warmth from the tea spread through her, giving comfort and calm as only a cuppa could.

While reveling in the quiet peace, a clamor rose outside. Loud voices grew closer, then the earl and viscount burst into the room with Martin and one of the footmen hard upon on their heels. Abbie stood, as did Phillips.

"My son. Bastian, tell us everything," the earl said to Faraday, his voice shaking with worry.

The young doctor gave a compelling narrative, including Abbie and Phillips in the telling. "I gave your son a strong dose of laudanum, and along with the brandy, he will sleep for hours. We can only hope that infection and fever do not take hold. He should stay here for the night and may be moved to his room tomorrow." He laid a hand on the earl's shoulder. "Though your son lost a goodly amount of blood, my lord, I do not feel a transfusion is warranted. We have Mrs. Hughes to thank for ensuring the situation did not become dire, even fatal."

Abbie blushed under the praise, and the earl and viscount came to stand before her. "How can I thank you, Abbie? May I call you Abbie?" the earl said, a shaky smile curving about his mouth.

"Of course, my lord."

He clasped her upper arms gently. "No more of that. You are *family*. I am Oliver."

Julian nodded as he clutched her arm, pulling her from his father and into a crushing embrace. Goodness. She was not used to such emotion from Garrett's older brother, but this proved she did not know these men at all. Abbie found that she wanted to. Family. How utterly astonishing. "And I am Julian. Thank you, Abbie."

Momentarily dumbfounded, she returned the embrace and basked in its welcoming warmth. They broke apart and laughed, more from the relief that Garrett would no doubt survive.

"Martin, see there is a light supper laid out for our guests in about an hour. Bastian, you will be staying the night?" Oliver asked.

"Of course," Dr. Faraday replied. "I assumed as much and brought my valise. I left word at the hospital that I would be staying until Garrett is on the mend."

"Brilliant." Oliver turned toward Martin and said, "Riordan and his wife, Sabrina, are following directly behind us. He had to make arrangements for his students. See that rooms are prepared for everyone."

Martin bowed. "At once, my lord."

"Dr. Phillips, will you stay for a meal?" the earl asked.

"Well, I..." The older man was obviously flustered at being asked to dine at the earl's table. "I would be honored, my lord."

"Martin, please show the doctors to the library and offer them a drink. We will join you directly."

With the doctors' departure, Oliver turned his attention to her. "Can you tell us what happened?"

"I will, but first I *must* go to Megan. She must be wondering what is going on. It was she who rode for help."

Oliver smiled, his eyes twinkling. "Ah, my stout-hearted lass."

"Sit with Garrett and I will return shortly." Abbie turned to leave, then halted. "I will take a light meal in here. I will not be leaving his side."

"As I surmised," Oliver said. "I will make the arrangements."

Abbie lifted her skirts and hurried upstairs. Glancing at the front of her riding habit, she shuddered at the sight of the blood. The outfit was no doubt ruined, but she didn't care. Garrett was alive. It was all that mattered.

Megan stood as soon as Abbie entered the room. "Is he..."

"Alive, yes. The earl's physician arrived from London and stitched the artery closed. Garrett is resting."

Megan exhaled and sat on the edge of the bed. Abbie joined her and slipped her arm about her daughter's shoulders. It was then the floodgates opened. Abbie cried, sobbing piteously, allowing all her pent-up emotions free.

Megan hugged her. "Oh, Mama. You do love him."

Abbie laid her head on her daughter's shoulder. "This has hit me hard. I do have deep feelings for Garrett. Yes, I love him. Perhaps I never stopped. Are you upset to hear this?"

"No," Megan hedged.

"You don't mind?" Abbie sniffled as she wiped the tears from her cheeks.

"I admit that finding out Garrett Wollstonecraft is my father was, and is, shocking. Upsetting, even. However, I believe we will become friends. I've also gained a grandfather, uncle, and cousins. Megan laughed lightly. "And if you do decide to marry him someday? We can live here at the hall, with horses and servants. And with Jonas nearby? How exciting!" Megan sobered. "How selfish I sound. Truly, your happiness comes first, Mama.

I do wish you to be happy above all else. The decision is yours to make. I will not stand in your way."

"My, you are growing up. How very wise of you, my dear," Abbie replied softly.

"I'd like to do something for Garrett. He sounded sad when he spoke of his grandfather and the Scotch collie. Is it possible for us to buy him another? Having a new puppy will help him recover, I'm sure of it. And it will keep him company when we return home."

"How considerate," Abbie smiled. "I will broach the subject with the earl."

Abbie hugged her daughter. Thank God she was softening toward Garrett at last, enough to make a thoughtful suggestion. It was a good start. First, Garrett had to recover before anything else was decided—and Abbie would not get a moment's rest until he did.

* * * *

Garrett could not make sense of where he was. His mind was fuzzy; his surroundings lay in shadow and chaotic confusion. Last he remembered he was out riding with Abbie and Megan. *I was shot.* Yes, he understood he'd been wounded. Drifting in and out of consciousness, he'd managed to pick up snippets of conversation. Arguments. Talk of amputation. Possible infection. Fever. And of death.

A narrow band of light lay ahead of him. Walking toward it, he realized the light was actually a wall of flame. He was carrying something, a log for the fire? He glanced down and screamed.

He carried his own severed arm.

His eyes popped open and Abbie wiped his brow, speaking soothing words. His arm! He found it was still attached, though he couldn't move the damned thing. Bloody hell, why wouldn't his eyes focus? There were people in the room, but they all disappeared in a swirl of mist. *Stay awake.* But he could not. Fatigue washed over him and all grew dark.

* * * *

"Is there anything we can do, Doctor?" Abbie asked, her voice filled with anguish over Garrett's delirious state.

"Unfortunately, we must allow the fever to run its course. There is much we can do to assist it along. I am not a believer in sweating out a fever. Garrett must be kept cool. Keep the windows open. Put out the fire. We will need tarps to lie across him and the bed. And we will need ice. Plenty of ice to lay on the tarps. We must bring his temperature down," Faraday stated, his voice grave.

"Martin, see it done. Bring enough ice from the ice house to cover Master Garrett and the bed itself," the earl ordered.

"I will prepare a nostrum that I often use for fevers," Faraday said. Oliver nodded and the doctor exited the room, closing the door softly behind him.

Riordan also stood nearby, an apprehensive look on his face. He'd arrived later the first night, and Abbie had been immediately struck at the weariness etched in his countenance. First, to hear of his twin, Aidan, and now his uncle. Gazing at Riordan, it was clear that he loved his uncle fiercely.

"I will do the ice collecting," Riordan murmured. "I need something to do."

"Very well," the earl said. He watched worriedly as his grandson departed. Turning to Abbie, he said, "He took the news about Aidan hard, but this. Sabrina has been a rock. As are you, Abbie."

Already she and Sabrina had become fast friends, though the socializing came to an abrupt halt when Garrett succumbed to this lingering fever. Abbie continued to wipe Garrett's feverish brow. "There has certainly been a good deal of drama in the Wollstonecraft men's lives of late. And it appeared when women entered your sphere."

Oliver raised an eyebrow. "Are you saying that this is the curse? It affects the women, not the men."

Abbie met his steady gaze. "And you think that we are not affected by all this?"

"No, that is not what I meant," he snapped. Oliver shook his head. "Forgive me. My nerves are balanced on the edge of a knife, the same as everyone else's. The curse is a sensitive subject. We do not speak of it if we can at all help it, but it hovers over us nonetheless. A curse of the broken-hearted." Oliver frowned. "What disturbs me is that this was a deliberate act. I would call for the constable, but there is nothing to report."

"I understand. It is frustrating. At first, I thought that it could be a hunter or poacher. But why the second shot so quickly after the initial one, and in the same general vicinity? Too much of a coincidence."

"My thoughts exactly."

Abbie dipped the cloth in the basin of cool water and continued to wipe the perspiration from Garrett's flushed face. "To change the subject, Megan mentioned she would like us to purchase a Scotch collie puppy for Garrett. Do you know of where we could procure one without traveling to Scotland? Do you believe Garrett would welcome such a gift?"

Abbie saw doubt flicker across his face—doubt that Garrett would recover. But as quickly as it appeared, a resolute look replaced it. "When you told me that Alec Mackinnon had passed, I experienced a genuine sadness. Garrett adored him. Though I extended numerous invitations through the years, both before and after Moira died, he remained a creature of habit and loathed traveling. So I allowed Garrett to spend several summers in Scotland with his grandparents." He smiled. "Alec gifted Garrett with a collie years ago. A collie puppy would be welcome, not only to assist with recovery, but a remembrance for his grandfather. Permit me to make inquiries."

Abbie gave him a warm smile. "Thank you, Oliver."

"Alberta Eaton has made overtures. I thought to invite her and Jonas this evening. Company for you and Megan. She also wishes to assist, and I do not have the heart to refuse her." Oliver laid a hand on her shoulder. "Join us for an hour or two. You need a short respite. Bastian can sit with Garrett while we share a meal."

The thought of leaving his side filled her with fright, but what better person to watch over Garrett than a competent doctor? "I thought Dr. Phillips would suffer apoplexy when he strode into the room. How do you know him?"

Oliver clasped his hands behind his back. "He is impressive. Bastian is the son of a ship builder and a lovely lady from the West Indies, more specifically, Jamaica. She is the daughter of a successful sugar producer. Even though the Faradays are rich in their own right, I wished to sponsor someone at Cambridge. Someone outside Society's accepted norm. It was a particular achievement, seeing Bastian's maternal grandfather was a freed slave."

"I abhorred the existence of a slavery trade. I am relieved it was finally abolished in the commonwealth."

"It should have passed long before 1838. A stain upon the empire, and I fear it shall be for generations to come. Despite his achievements and the successes of his mother's family, Bastian, for all his tall, good looks and intelligence, will never fully be accepted into Society. I aim to do all I can to further his cause. Hence the reason I made him my personal physician. Well, that and the fact that he is highly capable."

"He certainly took charge and saved the day." Abbie stared at Garrett. "Though this fever worries me."

"I believe it will pass. Garrett is strong and has much to live for."

Oliver left her alone. The room was quiet except for Garrett's ragged breathing. As she trailed the cool cloth across his broad, muscled chest, a distant memory filled her thoughts.

By this point in her summer visit she had fallen desperately in love with him. One afternoon she took a walk. She and Garrett had made plans to meet later in the evening, but she longed to see him—even if it was only a distant glimpse. Her journey had been rewarded. Garrett stood outside the stables, shirt removed, giving his black stallion a wash. Hidden behind a cluster of shrubs, she watched as the play of muscles in his back rippled with each swirling rub of the horse's glossy coat. Garrett wore a large glove, rubbing in the soap, talking in a quiet tone. Midnight Thunder whickered the occasional response, showing how relaxed he was in Garrett's presence. Garrett was as finely muscled and sculpted as his stallion. Arousal gripped her as she continued to observe man and beast in perfect harmony.

Yes. Strong. Virile. Formidable.

"Fight, Garrett. Come back to me."

Chapter 17

Summer 1830
They had been meeting everyday for three weeks. Garrett, randy at the
best of times, found he could not draw breath without thinking of holding
and kissing Abbie. Perhaps he suffered from an obsession, a fever of the
heart. For he would not accept that it was something deeper. Like love.
Must be lust, for they could not keep their hands off each other. Inexpert
in the ways of sex, they both caught on quickly enough, experimenting with
different positions. The previous night had been particularly wild, with
him behind her, pounding fiercely, reaching for...he wasn't sure what. How
could they keep up this pace? Abbie was here for another two weeks yet.
Candidly, Garrett understood it wasn't only the scorching physical
aspect. They got on well, had many similar interests. They had become
friends. He admired her boldness, especially during sex. Shaking his head,
he glanced about the tool shed. It was becoming more difficult to find places
for their secret assignation. It was a wonder they had not been found out,
for they were not exactly quiet during their multiple heated joinings.
And what about the future? He had plans, already had discussed the
possibility of a horse breeding operation with his father. It would be quite an
undertaking. The stables would have to be doubled in size, a breeding shed
and different paddocks for the mares, stallions, and yearlings constructed.
Larger feed storage facilities and an indoor training area. It would be
years before he saw a profit, but Garrett could not wait to begin. He'd
always loved horses.
Abbie loved them, too. Could he make her part of his future plans?
Where had that thought come from? The door opened and Abbie stepped
inside, causing his breath to hitch and his heart to pound.

She ran to his arms and he caught her up in a fierce embrace. He kissed her, hot, sweet, and deep, but Abbie pulled away, gazing up at him. "May we have a conversation before we lose ourselves?"

Talk? When every part of him throbbed with yearning? "We may not have much time..."

"Then we will not talk long." Abbie grabbed his hand and dragged him toward the crates. She sat, pulling him down beside her. "Tell me more about yourself. What are your plans for the future?"

How fortuitous. Why did she wish to know any of this? His future would not include her. But staring at her beautiful, eager face, he hadn't the heart to refuse. He spoke of his plans for horse breeding and she listened intently. "I will be attending Cambridge for the autumn session, though I'm still undecided where to focus my studies," he said.

"You are the second son, there is always the church." He made a face and she laughed. "Well, there's the law. Or medical studies. Many second sons buy a commission in the army after university. But you would prefer to breed horses."

"I've no interest in fighting wars. They are usually fought to further the ambitions of the rich, with the poor used as cannon fodder at the front lines." He thought for a moment. "Learning estate law interests me; perhaps I will consider it. I would like to learn the ins and outs of running Wollstonecraft Hall. Our steward is elderly, his retirement is imminent. I believe I would enjoy taking over the position and would excel at it."

"You would make a fine steward," she beamed.

What was her point in asking these questions? Garrett was about to inquire when she vaulted herself at him, kissing him soundly. He was lost, drowning in her fresh wildflower scent, her feminine softness, the ferocious beating of her heart. As he kissed her, he cupped her full breast, his thumb brushing past her erect nipple until she whimpered with need.

There would be no rolling about the floor in this dusty shed. Instead, Garrett stood, bringing Abbie with him. He backed her up against the wall, pinning her there. While he kissed her, his hands roved over her curves and the bold minx clutched his stiff shaft and squeezed. A ragged moan tore from him.

Frantically fumbling with their clothes, he freed himself and entered her in a swift fashion, burying himself deep in her heated core. He stilled, nuzzled her neck, savoring the exquisite joy of being inside her. Then something happened—shifted, as if his soul opened to take her in. His heart swelled as he moved inside her. Lifting her high enough to meet his eager thrusts, Garrett gave everything he was and could ever hope to be.

Abbie threw her arms about his neck, clutching him tight. Accepting and open, allowing him to take control. Be dominant. Take complete possession. If he could live the rest of his life like this—inside her, loving her—then his life would be complete.

This coupling was not quick; he thrust into her for interminable moments, each seared in his memory. His heart and soul. Lost on some higher plane of passion, he was aware that Abbie had reached her peak twice and was building on a third. Still he pumped into her, completely absorbed. When at last they reached their climax together, it became the most perfect and awe-inspiring moment of his young life. Nothing going forward could equal this bliss.

Love. He acknowledged it. It poured through him like molten gold, and he allowed it to saturate him. But only for those few moments they were still joined, clasping each other, breathing hard. When that passed, he would reflect on it no more, nor would he accept the turbulent emotions for what they actually were. He would remain stalwart in his conviction of loving no woman. The curse must be at the forefront of his decisions. And if it meant turning away from this glorious young lady, then he would do it.

Until then...love. How powerful. How breathtakingly perfect.

The memory was soon replaced by Garrett standing in the middle of a frozen wasteland. A chill climbed up his spine, and his breath expelled in an icy fog. Damn it all, he was cold. When he had turned Abbie away at the end of her long-ago summer visit, this is where he'd resided ever since. In a barren, cold state.

At least he no longer carried his severed arm about. However, he could not will his injured arm to work. He was wearing the garments he'd worn on their ride. *Ah. This is a dream. A metaphor for my life.*

A lone wolf howled in the distance, the sound mournful and lonely. It grew ever closer, until the beast stood before him. The creature was huge, its ice blue eyes staring at him hungrily. Garrett dare not move. Wolves were rare in England. He'd never seen one except in paintings or picture books. The beast growled, its teeth long and sharp. With blinding clarity, he understood what this animal represented—a wolf was on the Wollstonecraft seal. The name itself meant "wolf stone."

The curse. The wolf symbolized the curse.

It had returned with a vengeance and had come to consume him. Tear him to shreds. The wolf ran toward him, teeth bared. Blast it, he must fight, stand his ground. How could he with only one functioning arm and no weapon? The beast vaulted toward him, knocking him to the ground, ready to tear out his throat.

"No!"

* * * *

Abbie tried to keep Garrett's good arm from thrashing about, but he was too strong, even in his weakened state. "When will the fever break, Dr. Faraday?"

The young man stared at Garrett, his brows furrowed. It had been close to twenty-four hours since they'd encased Garrett in a cocoon of tarps and chunks of ice. The room was frosty, as the windows were wide open, allowing the late January air to pour in. Abbie wore her wool cloak and still felt chilled. "I believe the crisis will be later tonight. The wound does not appear to be infected; however, there could be inflammation within. I will order more willow bark tea."

"Abbie, come to the main parlor. Alberta and Jonas are here. We have tea and sandwiches. You must eat," Julian said in a kind tone.

"I will stay with him," Faraday stated. "Go. You must keep up your strength."

Truly, she was hungry, as well as exhausted. Reluctantly, she stood, and gazed at a feverish, perspiring, and shivering Garrett.

Julian took her arm and escorted her from the room. "He will recover. He is too stubborn not to."

Abbie gave Julian a shaky smile as they stepped into the main parlor. She'd never been in this room. It was huge, at least the size of a small ballroom. There did not appear to be gas lighting, as candelabras surrounded the perimeter, causing the gold wallpaper to shimmer. The polished parquet floor and high ceilings also gave the appearance of a ballroom.

"In the early days of my grandfather, this room saw many a country dance, and a couple of formal balls. Lately it has been used as a gathering place. At Christmas, we entertain the tenants and neighbors, hire an orchestra, and even indulge in a waltz or two. Father is not one for elaborate entertainments."

"It is stunning." Abbie stared up at the tiled ceiling. As with other rooms in Wollstonecraft Hall, a certain welcoming warmth and coziness beckoned despite its formal appearance.

Kind and sympathetic faces turned to her. Riordan and his wife, Sabrina. Abbie had been surprised to learn that Sabrina's former lady's maid, Miss Mary Tuttle, lived with the couple as a family member. And, Sabrina revealed, Mary had caught Oliver's eye. Mary had stayed behind in Carrbury to look after Sabrina's kitten and attend to Riordan's schoolroom, with assistance from his oldest student, who was training to be a schoolmistress.

Alberta and Jonas smiled warmly. Megan left Jonas's side and rushed toward her, hugging Abbie tight. "There is a late supper laid out on the sideboard. I informed the cook of your favorites," Megan said.

"Thank you, my dear." Her daughter escorted her to the vast array of food on display. Roast chicken, sliced hard-cooked eggs, lettuce, cheese, butter rolls—much like a picnic in January. Abbie did not stand on ceremony; she loaded her plate and took a seat at the long table in the center of the room. Everyone fell in line, selected food, and joined her.

Biting into the butterflake roll, Abbie nearly moaned aloud. *Melt-in-your-mouth delicious.* How could she enjoy a meal with Garrett upstairs fighting an infection? Perhaps even fighting for his life? She halted, and Alberta laid a comforting hand on her arm.

"It is perfectly fine to enjoy a meal," her friend soothed.

"Yes," Abbie murmured in response. She continued to eat, but not with the same enthusiasm.

"Where was Garrett shot? I mean, where outside?" Jonas asked as he buttered his roll.

"Not far from Wolf Stone Woods. Why, lad?" the earl asked.

Jonas's nervous gaze darted around the table. "I...heard something." Everyone ceased eating. "What did you hear?" Alberta asked.

"Well, on the day Garrett was shot, I was in the woods. I wanted to feed the rabbits. I know I'm not supposed to leave the property, Bert, without telling you. I'm sorry." Jonas looked down, contrite. "It's why I didn't say anything."

Abbie glanced at Oliver, and it was plain he struggled to hold his temper. Megan laid her hand on Jonas's. "It's all right. No one is angry with you. Please tell us everything." Megan's touch and soft words mollified Jonas. Looking at him, one could forget he was still a child in many ways, and because of it, there was no use in becoming annoyed with him.

Jonas looked up. "I couldn't see much, but I heard two men talking. I hid behind one of the large oaks. One man called the other 'my lord.' The lord said something like, 'Stay here, see if the Scottish barbarian dies, then return to London.'" Jonas paused, as if replaying the conversation in his mind. "I remember! He called the other man Delaney."

Riordan vaulted to his feet. "Delaney is Sutherhorne's bullyboy, the one who attended debtor's court with him."

Abbie blinked rapidly in confusion. "Sutherhorne? The marquess that kidnapped Sabrina?"

Oliver slammed his fist on the table. "The very one. This is all on me. I encouraged the family not to take any steps in bringing him to justice. I thought it futile. Damnation, I should have at least attempted it."

"No, Oliver. We all agreed," Sabrina stated. "We're well aware that peers are rarely penalized for any crime. As you said, Sutherhorne has Prince Albert's ear. And his friendship."

"Regardless, I should have made a case to garner some sort of punishment." Oliver banged his fist once again. Abbie had never seen the earl this angry.

"You all did it to protect me, to spare me censure from society. I hereby remove the impediment." Sabrina's mouth pulled into a taut line. "Bring him down, whatever it takes."

Riordan sat, leaned in, and kissed his wife on the cheek. "My darling. Consider it done."

"Did you see them at all, Jonas?" Julian asked.

"I did peek. One man is nearly as big as me, but I didn't see his face. The other man had a white beard. And he was skinny."

"Sutherhorne. Damn him. There is no mistake. Grandfather, we should head to Sevenoaks immediately. See if this Delaney character is still about," Riordan said.

"The sun has set. If he's at the inn, he will be there in the morning," Oliver replied.

"Oh," Jonas cried. "I remember, the old lord told the man not to stay at the inn."

"Where else could one stay?" Julian asked.

"There are a small number of homes that take in guests. Perhaps we should head to Sevenoaks after all. Riordan, come with us. You have seen this Delaney and will be able to identify him," Oliver replied.

Jonas stood. "I want to come, too. This man tried to hurt my Meg. And Abbie. He hurt Garrett. I can help."

The men exchanged dubious looks, then Julian said, "Of course, lad. Garrett is usually the muscle of this clan. You will stand in his stead."

Abbie was awed as the Wollstonecraft men sprung into action. In less than ten minutes they were ready to depart, with Julian carrying a large revolver. Abbie, Megan, Alberta, and Sabrina were left alone in the parlor.

"We might as well finish our meals. Megan, would you please refresh our tea?" Alberta asked.

Megan nodded and stood to fetch the teapot from the sideboard.

"Goodness," Abbie murmured. "They are not to be crossed, are they?"

"No. They are fearsome men when provoked. You should have seen them when they broke in the door to rescue me from Sutherhorne." Sabrina sighed. "I was anxious to put the episode behind me. When Oliver suggested not pursuing justice on the matter, I was silently relieved. But not because I was ashamed or feared Society's wrath." She dashed a lone tear from her eye. "Regardless of how my father treated me with such cold indifference, and the fact that he tried to sell me in marriage more than once, he *is* my father. I did not want him sent to Newgate Prison. A small part of me still loved him. How utterly pathetic."

Abbie smiled warmly. "It speaks well of your kind heart that you feel empathy for him. And it's perfectly understandable. When I had discovered I was pregnant at eighteen, my parents turned on me. Branded me a sinner, and worse. They threatened to throw me to the cobbles if I did not marry. Our relationship is strained to this day. Yet a small part of me will always love them, despite their abhorrent treatment of me."

Megan stood with teapot in hand. "Truly, Mama? They treated you horribly! I am glad I've never met them."

"I fear you never shall."

"Well, you have a family now," Sabrina smiled. "We stick together, and are loyal to a fault. And I include you in this, Alberta, if the heated looks that Julian gave you tonight are any indication."

Alberta blushed and smiled in return. "We shall see where it leads."

Megan refreshed everyone's tea and took her seat. "I do hope they will be safe and find this terrible man. How can a marquess be capable of such a heinous act?"

Abbie frowned. "Unfortunately, there are more than a few peers like the marquess. Entitled, arrogant, thinking they are above the law. Many have gotten away with lawless acts for centuries. It is past time they were held accountable."

Placing her teacup on the saucer, Abbie turned her attention to her meal. She glanced upward. The sooner she finished eating, the sooner she could return to Garrett. A stab of pain lodged in her heart. He had to recover. He *must*. For she had not come all this way and exposed her vulnerable heart only to lose him.

It was not easy to admit, but her heart was still in a susceptible state, their rekindled love and passion balanced precariously on the edge of a cliff. It would not take much to fall either way, into darkness and despair, or a future and happiness. And it worried her. Greatly.

Chapter 18

"I believe the fever will break later tonight, or should I say early this morning?" Dr. Faraday murmured.

Glancing at the mantel clock, it was already close to one. The Wollstonecraft men had yet to return from their quest. "Doctor, why don't you rest? I will call you if it comes to a crisis."

"I am rather fatigued. Three hours, mind. No more. Then you must do the same. Promise me."

Abbie had grown to like and admire the young doctor. His unwavering care and competency proved the earl had not been mistaken in laying his trust with Faraday. "I promise."

"Good. I'll be in the next room. Continue with the cold compresses." The doctor departed, leaving the bedroom door slightly ajar.

They had ceased using the ice and tarps the previous afternoon, as Garrett's skin had started to turn blue. Dipping the flannel in the basin and wringing out the excess water, Abbie then laid the cloth on Garrett's perspiring forehead. At the moment he lay quiet, but earlier, he thrashed about yelling about wolves and snow. He was naked except for a pair of drawers, so Abbie swiped the cloth gently across his muscular chest. "Oh, Garrett. You are obstinate enough to fight this. Fight, my love."

He murmured in response, but she could not make out the words.

At half past one, Abbie heard commotion below stairs. Oliver, Julian, and Riordan strode into the room and stood at the foot of Garrett's massive bed.

"How is he?" Oliver asked worriedly.

"Calmer than earlier. Dr. Faraday predicts the crisis will come within hours. He believes the fever will break."

"Thank God," Julian murmured.

"What happened? Were you able to locate this man of Sutherhorne's?" Abbie asked. "Where is Jonas?"

Riordan frowned. "We escorted Jonas home before returning here. Locate Sutherhorne's man? Not exactly. We started at the inn in Sevenoaks, then branched out to the guest houses. Once completed, we expanded our search to surrounding towns and villages. Only one place acknowledged the possibility of a man of Delaney's description. He may have stayed there last week, for two nights. Of course, he did not use the name of Delaney. This is hardly solid proof."

"We can only surmise the marquess did not stay overnight. He is not easy to miss, with his fancy carriage and entourage. A carriage traveling at a swift clip could make London from here in an hour and thirty minutes. Even less." Julian crossed his arms. "We assume that is how he and his man communicated."

"What's the next step?" Abbie could plainly observe the frustrated expressions on the Wollstonecraft men's faces.

"Confronting the marquess will get us nowhere. I have a better solution: We appeal to Prince Albert directly. While prosecution remains unlikely, we may be able to persuade his Royal Highness to agree to banishment. A forfeiture of money and properties not entailed along with a guarantee that if he leaves Great Britain, and never returns, his oldest son will inherit the title. It has been done before with peers who think themselves above the law."

"But we need solid evidence," Julian said.

"You have it. Me." They all looked in the direction of the doorway where Sabrina stood, wearing her silk wrapper, her golden hair in a braid lying across her shoulder.

Riordan's look softened, the love clearly showing through, and it made Abbie's heart ache. "My darling, we agreed."

"This situation has moved far beyond any potential stress or embarrassment. We can no longer sweep it under the carpet. We are speaking of attempted murder." Sabrina moved to Riordan's side. "I'm not sure that the prince will allow me an audience, but I will tell everything, either in person or in a written account. How my father colluded with Sutherhorne to kidnap and sell me—more than once. If I remember the accounts in the papers, the prince is a tireless anti-slavery advocate. This will anger him, I am sure. For isn't what they tried to do a form of slavery?"

Oliver nodded. "You are correct, Sabrina. It will anger him. Counter it with this attempt on Garrett's life, and we could find success. Do you think your father would agree to a written affidavit stating Sutherhorne's part in your kidnapping?"

Sabrina snorted. "Only if it will benefit him. I know my wretched father well. He will no doubt ask for you to clear his debt and his name, ensure there will be no repercussions from his statement."

"Perhaps we will be able to come to a sort of pact. It will bear thinking about. Are you sure you wish to do this, Sabrina?"

Riordan's wife nodded, a determined look on her face. "In hindsight, we should have gone to the prince as soon as it happened. I appreciate you all trying to protect me, but it's well past time I stood up to these evil men, and truly place this all behind me. I have a future. And well..." Her hand trailed across her stomach. "Forgive me, Riordan, for making this announcement public, but I believe I am expecting."

Riordan cupped her cheeks, his eyes glistening. "My dearest love." He kissed her deeply, oblivious to anyone else in the room.

Abbie was not used to such a public display, and she blushed in response. Though why was a puzzle, considering her wild relationship with Garrett. Expecting? Hadn't they been married only last month? *Oh. Right.* The marriage started out as a convenient arrangement earlier in the autumn. Obviously, it had moved beyond such before their winter wedding here at the hall. When Riordan broke the kiss, the men closed ranks, congratulating them.

"I am not completely sure," Sabrina demurred. "I should consult with Dr. Faraday in the morning."

"Then we shall wake him this minute," Riordan cried happily.

Before, they had spoken in hushed tones, but with this happy announcement, the voices had grown louder, which caused Garrett to stir. Regardless, Abbie rushed to Sabrina, pulling her into a warm embrace. "I am very happy for you."

"Thank you, Abbie. And Riordan, allow the poor man to sleep. The doctor and your uncle."

Everyone laughed.

"No!" Garrett cried out.

The laughter ceased and all eyes turned to him. He was struggling to sit upright, but could not accomplish it. Abbie rushed to his side, but he thrust her away, still surprisingly strong considering his weakened and feverish condition. She almost lost her balance and fell to the floor. His eyes were glassy, his look wild. "Get away from me, far away. I don't want you near me, not ever again. I want you out of my life," Garrett snarled, his voice full of venom. "The curse. It exists. It is real and will consume us all. I want you gone!"

Abbie's blood ran cold. He still believed in it. All his talk about putting the miserable curse behind him had been wishful thinking. Call it what it truly was: lies. This hurt as much as it had fourteen years past. Perhaps more. She had placed her faith, hope, and worst of all, her heart in his hands, and he ruined it. *Again.* Abbie turned and left. Once in the hall, she broke into a run until she reached her room.

She was about to close the door, but Julian stopped her. "Abbie, don't listen to him. He is still in a fevered state. He's out of his head and doesn't know what he is saying."

Stepping away from the door, she clasped her hands in front of her to keep them from shaking. "People often speak truth in fevered states. How they truly feel deep down." Should she be discussing this with Garrett's brother? Abbie buried her face in her hands. "This will never work, Julian. Your brother is stubborn and will never embrace love and life fully. He is damaged inside, and my love cannot fix him."

Julian clasped her arms. "It is difficult to completely erase years of belief in a few short weeks. Yes, he's damaged inside. We all are, in various ways. We've been touched by tragedy on many levels. It has affected Garrett more than any of us realized."

Abbie frowned, but met his earnest and sympathetic gaze. "I understand, believe me, I do. He told me of his childhood losses and how he'd been affected by them. But most people put tragedy behind them and move forward with living. I mourned my husband, I still do, but I am ready and willing to take another chance at life. Can you say the same? Will you acknowledge your feelings for Alberta? Or will you stay cloistered away in this hall with the rest of the men?"

Julian's arms dropped to his sides, his expression grew chilly. She may have gone too far. "My feelings for Alberta are not your affair."

She glared at him. "Then my feelings for Garrett are none of yours."

They stared at each other as if they were adversaries on a battlefield. Who would yield first?

"Touché. Well struck," Julian said as a brief smile quirked at the corner of his mouth. "I shouldn't interfere, but I ask you to please stay and fight for Garrett. I know that I'm asking you to sacrifice much here."

Abbie exhaled. "That is one of the reasons I came here, to fight for our love. To see if it still existed. It does, but I'm weary from the constant conflict, Julian. He hurt me, wounded me deeply all those years ago. I refuse to even give him the chance to wreak more damage. We are leaving."

Julian's eyebrow arched. "Abbie…"

"We were going to depart this week at any rate. Garrett is fully aware of our plans, and I aim to stick to them. When the fever breaks, we will return to Standon. Though I must hire a carriage…"

"If you insist on leaving, allow me to make the arrangements. Garrett will never forgive me if I do not see to yours and Megan's safety. Use one of our coaches, and I'll send along Samuel, one of our grooms, to act as protector. He's an ex-soldier and a formidable presence. You have a spare room at your residence?"

Abbie nodded.

"Excellent. He will stay with you until this situation is resolved. We're not sure what Sutherhorne is up to, so we cannot take the chance that he will seek you out to exact revenge on Garrett. There's no doubt why he or his man fired in your direction." Julian exhaled. "We can better protect you if you stay here, but I understand why you feel compelled to leave. Garrett is not perfect. None of the Wollstonecraft men are."

"I love him for that very reason. And he loves me despite my flaws." Abbie paused. "I will see Garrett before I depart. I promise. I will tell him everything I've told you, and more besides. He will have to make a choice. It's a life with our daughter—or the curse. I will not accept any middle ground." She gave Julian a warm smile. "Thank you for listening. I did not mean to pull any of you into this situation."

Julian took her hand and kissed it. "You are family. The Wollstonecrafts look out for one another. Support each other. We may not give our hearts easily, but when we do, we love fiercely. Remember that."

A lump of emotion wedged in her throat. If she replied, she would burst into noisy sobs. Abbie nodded instead. Julian departed, closing the door softly behind him. Bringing her hand to her heart, it formed a fist. Her heart ached. Had Garrett broken it once again? Perhaps not, but there was a fissure. In the final analysis, if he ultimately chose the curse over her, she knew that the break would be permanent.

* * * *

Garrett emerged from his fevered ice fog. It took several minutes for his vision to focus, and he had hoped it would be filled with images of Abbie. The few times he had drifted in and out of this delirious haze, Abbie had been next to him, speaking in hushed, comforting tones and wiping his brow. Where was she?

He glanced about the room. It was dim except for the gas light hissing overhead. With the curtains closed, he couldn't tell if it were morning or night. His father, brother, and nephew stood at the foot of the bed. Next to them was a stranger whom he'd remembered from his dreams.

"Welcome back, Garrett," the stranger said. "I am Dr. Bastian Faraday. You were shot in the shoulder and sustained damage to your subclavian artery. Dr. Phillips and I repaired it. Then you developed a fever. It has been five days since the incident."

Well, that brought him up-to-date. "Thank...you." His father had spoken highly of the young doctor in the past. He met his father's relieved gaze. "Where...Abbie?"

His father's relieved gaze turned to one of sadness, and trepidation rolled through Garrett. "I will fetch her directly. First, allow me to give you a brief summary of what has happened." His father gave a stunning narrative, one Garrett struggled to keep up with. The consequence was that there was proof that Sutherhorne was behind the shooting. The despicable wretch. His father stated that they had a plan, but the details would wait until tomorrow.

Riordan patted Garrett's leg. "Rest, Uncle. We'll talk later."

Riordan, Dr. Faraday, and his father departed. Julian stepped closer. "Listen to what Abbie has to say. Open your heart, Brother. This may be your last chance at happiness."

What in hell did that mean? Damn it, he couldn't get his throat to work to ask. The words Julian spoke were somber in tone. Garrett's apprehension only increased when his father opened the door and Abbie walked through. The look on her face was determined, but guarded.

"I will leave you both," his father stated, closing the door with a soft snick as he and Julian departed.

Abbie stood beside his bed, her hands clasped in front of her. The fact that she did not touch him filled him with dread. What was going on? Something must have happened, but what? He gazed at her questioningly, his heartbeat pounding in his ears.

"I'm glad the fever broke. During the worst of it, you said: 'Get away from me, far away. I don't want you near me, not ever again. The curse exists and will consume us all. I want you gone!' Do you remember saying it?" Her voice was tight, the tone showing annoyance.

Damn it all to hell. He struggled to recall. It had been a dream, hadn't it? He shook his head.

Abbie frowned. "I cannot put myself through this again. I thought that in coming here I had placed most of the past behind me, but it seems I have not." A gasping sob left her throat. "I am torn. Completely miserable. You are the only man I have ever loved, and also the only one to break my heart."

He tried to sit up, to open his mouth and vehemently deny everything, but all that came out was a dry croak.

"Allow me to finish. Megan and I are leaving later today. It was the original plan, and I will follow through on it. Under the circumstances, I believe it wise. Julian is making the arrangements. Samuel Jenkins will be accompanying us and staying with us in Standon until this situation with Sutherhorne is resolved. Recover, and think about what you want. For a choice is before you: me or the curse." Abbie dashed away a lone tear. "I have done all I can with regards to this relationship. Years past, you hurled cruel words at me to hasten my departure, all because of this curse. It has happened again. If you decide the curse is more important than our love, then I never want to see you again."

The declaration sliced him. He was stunned. Even if he could get his throat to work, he could not have found the words. He closed his eyes. The words she'd spoken on one of the nights she'd come to his room played in his mind: *Not if you insist on placing the curse between us as a shield. If you cannot commit to me or love me with your entire heart and soul, then I do not want you at all. I won't settle for any less. Elwyn taught me that much.*

Both of them were vulnerable; this alliance had always stood on shaky ground. His blasted demon—the curse—reared its ugly head when he was most susceptible and Abbie had witnessed it.

"I will never deny you your daughter," Abbie continued, her voice quaking with emotion. "If she wishes, she may visit you during the summers, as you did with your grandparents in Scotland." She stepped closer and laid her hand on top of his. "Believe me when I say that I, too, need time to think. For I have *not* put the past behind me. That is clear to me now. And the fact that I do not fully trust you scares me witless."

Garrett moved to place his hand on top of hers but she pulled it away, causing his heart to squeeze with sorrow. "Abbie. Don't...leave me," he croaked, his throat raw and scratchy.

She closed her eyes, and a couple of tears escaped from under her lids. "Goodbye, Garrett. Get well." She turned and scurried from the room.

He lay dumbfounded, staring at the ceiling. Devastated. Alone. Her words reverberated in his heart and soul. Despite his desolation, a ray of hope emerged. Abbie had said: "You should do what you should have done years ago, but only if you can let the past go and reject the curse wholeheartedly." Those words were as clear as glass, for she referred to what she had said one of the nights she'd visited his room: *You didn't love*

me enough to ride in and claim me. I cursed you, for how could you do
such a thing to us? Deliver such a mortal blow to our love?

He would recover. And come to terms with this damned curse. He would
have to declare his love and commitment to Abbie, swear he'd placed the
curse behind him. It would right the wrong of years past, and also prove
that he truly wanted a fresh start. Tears ran in steady rivulets from the
corner of his eyes, dampening the pillow.

Or life would not be worth living.

Chapter 19

"Megan, please stop fussing. Gather your belongings. We will return to Alberta's and pack the remainder of our personal effects. Julian has assured me the carriage will be ready to depart later this afternoon." Julian had also related they would be making an overnight stop halfway through the journey, all arrangements made by the family. She could hardly refuse.

Megan glowered; her lips formed a pout. She would be next to impossible on the trip to Standon. "I do not understand, why the haste? There is something you are not telling me," Megan demanded.

Abbie closed her eyes, striving to hold her temper. "Sit, Megan. Truly, my relationship with Garrett is private, but I'll relate some of what has transpired. There is this curse—"

Megan sat on the edge of the bed. "Curse?"

"It is said that every man born through this particular bloodline of Wollstonecrafts suffers tragedies. Women in the family, either born or wedded into it, do not live long, no matter how many times the man remarried. You are aware that your grandfather lost three wives and a daughter. Your uncle lost his wife. This all happened when Garrett was a small boy. It had an impact on him." Abbie's brows furrowed in annoyance. "This curse has hovered over us like a dark, thunderous cloud from the moment Garrett and I met."

Megan's lips parted in shock. "Truly? A curse? He believes it? Do you?"

"Me? Of course not, but I cannot dismiss the impact it's had. All the men believe in it, to a certain extent. Garrett more than any of them. He vowed never to love or marry."

Understanding dawned on Megan's face. "Ah. The cause of the hurtful words he spoke of when we were out riding."

"Yes. Despite his recent oath to put the curse behind him, he hasn't. At least, not fully. This shooting…"

"But why? We weren't shot," Megan said, her brows furrowed.

"Garrett believes we were placed in danger because we were with him." Abbie paused, since speaking about this caused her heart to ache afresh. "We are returning home as planned. It is left to Garrett to decide what is more important to him. And I have told him to make a choice, once and for all. I ask we please not speak about this anymore. I never should have come here." Her voice shook on the last sentence.

"But I am very glad you did." They whirled about to see Oliver standing in the doorway. "Forgive my interruption, and my overhearing what you said. May I come in?"

Abbie nodded. Lord, she was not in the mood for more discussion on this subject, and certainly not with Garrett's father.

"I wanted to say what a breath of fresh air you and Megan have been. My joy at finding both of you knows no bounds. Regardless of what may happen, I wish us to stay in touch. Megan may come for visits whenever she pleases. Both of you always have a home here, and a family who cares for you very much."

Blast it all, why did these men have to be so generous and charming? "Thank you."

"To have the family expand at last is gratifying indeed. Bastian has confirmed that Sabrina is indeed with child." Oliver beamed.

"How wonderful!" Megan clapped her hands together with delight.

"I'm pleased for the family. Rest assured I will never keep Megan from you all," Abbie said.

"I cannot persuade you to stay?" he asked.

"No."

"Then I will not press you on the matter."

Thank God.

"What about the puppy?" Megan asked.

"As soon as your mother informed me of your considerate proposal, I made inquires. It appears that there is a sheep farmer in Sussex who has a half-grown collie who is not adjusting well to herding. They have no need for a pet, so I made an offer to buy him. Not exactly a puppy as such, but I believe he would be grateful for a loving home."

Megan's lower lip quivered. "You will give him to Garrett? Tell him the puppy's name is Laddie?"

Another stab of pain radiated from Abbie's heart. Megan was coming to care for Garrett. Oh, what had she done? To bring her daughter here, introduce her to her father and his family, only to take her away?

"I will," Oliver replied. "I will say he is a gift from you, Megan. He will be touched. I won't tell him of it until I have the puppy in my possession. It will be a surprise."

Megan stood and rushed to Oliver's arms. He was as surprised as Abbie by the unexpected show of affection. "Thank you, Grandpapa," she whispered.

Oliver met Abbie's gaze, and his eyes glistened with emotion. Abbie's own eyes filled with tears. "My dear girl. You are entirely welcome." He hugged her tight, closing his eyes, no doubt basking in the fact that Megan had called him Grandpapa.

"The puppy can keep him company while he recovers," Megan murmured.

Oliver smoothed Megan's hair. "Yes."

"May I see my...my...Garrett, before we leave?" Megan asked.

"Let us see him, by all means." Oliver took Megan's hand and led her from the room. Abbie waited several moments, then silently followed Oliver and Megan. Standing outside the door, she had a clear view of Garrett's room, but remained hidden. Eavesdropping was not a prudent thing to do, but she wished to see their interaction.

"I've come to say goodbye," Megan said softly. "I am so very glad the fever broke."

Abbie couldn't see Garrett's face, but he took Megan's hand and squeezed it. "Look...after...your mother," he said, his voice weak and raspy.

Hot tears gathered at the corners of Abbie's eyes at Garrett's emotionally spoken words.

"You will come and see us, as soon as you are recovered?" Megan asked hopefully.

"Yes."

"Promise?"

"I...promise."

"Megan rode for help after you were shot," Oliver interjected.

Garrett kissed Megan's hand. "My brave...girl."

A few tears trailed down Abbie's cheeks. Megan was finally warming to her father and it touched her heart.

"Please get well. Please. Goodbye." With a warm smile, Megan patted Garrett's hand before releasing it.

Abbie quickly made her way to her room before Megan and Oliver saw her hovering outside the door. Once inside, she covered her face with her hands. This was all too much. Unfortunately, she had the distinct feeling that Garrett would scurry behind the wall of the family curse and stay there, adamant in the belief he was doing "the right thing" in order to protect her and Megan. Blast his stubborn and beautiful hide! Yet the sadness in his eyes when she laid her ultimatum before him relayed that there may be a glimmer of hope. That, and his promise to visit after he recovered.

Oh, come and claim me as you should have years past. Come to me and tell me you love me. That you can't live without me.

If he didn't, Abbie understood her life going forward would be a bitter and bleak place. And it filled her with an aching pain that cut her in two.

* * * *

To hell with a long recovery. Garrett had no patience for lingering about in his sickbed, brooding over what nonsense he'd spouted while caught in a fever nightmare. By the next afternoon he was sitting upright in a chair taking a light meal. Dr. Faraday had placed his wounded arm in a proper sling, so he had to adjust to using only his right arm for most tasks. It proved to be difficult, considering he was left-handed.

By early that evening, he was perambulating about his room with assistance from Gordon, the tallest and strongest of the young footmen. The young man would act as valet until Garrett decided he was no longer needed. He asked Gordon not to shave him. He came out of his fevered state sporting heavy whiskers. He found he liked the look and decided to grow out the beard, but keep it neat and closely cropped.

Meanwhile, Garrett was determined to make it downstairs for breakfast the following day. His family had brought him up to speed on current events and on the plan to request an audience with Prince Albert, and Garrett was going to make damned sure that he stood with the rest of the family when they did.

His father had already sent a messenger to Buckingham Palace, where the royal couple was currently in residence. The note stated that there was a matter of personal importance concerning a member of the peerage, and that they also wished to discuss education reforms, a particular and favorite cause of the prince's. They didn't mention Sutherhorne by name in case word of their meeting were to make its way to the man. Riordan would make the presentation on education.

Gordon brought out black trousers, a white shirt, and a gray waistcoat. With his assistance, Garrett dressed, and, leaning on the young man, made it to the main dining room for breakfast. Weak as a bloody kitten, he pushed forward, even though cold perspiration covered his forehead. Once seated, Gordon placed coddled eggs, slices of bacon, and toast before him. The rest of the family took their seats, except Sabrina—she was taking a tray in her room. He still couldn't wrap his head around the news that Riordan would soon be a father. Good God, out of his head for five days and the world had turned upside-down. Garrett frowned. But nothing was more upsetting than Abbie and Megan departing. It left a gaping wound more painful than his blasted shoulder.

He ate as much as he could, even managed to cut his bacon with one hand and actually feed himself. The conversation stayed away from the personal and he was grateful, and he made an effort to join in. "Riordan, the board doesn't mind you having another absence so soon after the last one?"

"A family emergency, they could hardly say no. Besides, I left my schoolroom in competent hands. Factor in that I may be making a presentation before the prince about the successes in Carrbury and how the board endorsed it will more than excuse my frequent absences." Riordan took a sip of tea, then smiled. "Sabrina and I will return to Carrbury directly after seeing the prince, and I doubt we will leave again until the end of the school term. Then we will return here and settle in for the birth."

"Again, my congratulations," Garrett murmured. He had all sincere hopes everything would go well.

"I know what you're thinking, Uncle. Nothing will happen. The curse will not interfere in my life. I refuse to allow it," Riordan said firmly. "And it has made me remember something of some import recently. Regardless of what you may think, the curse did give me pause once I developed feelings for Sabrina. Then I recalled that at age fourteen Aidan and I explored various dusty nooks in the attic. We found a locked trunk. Thinking that it might hold treasure, we broke into it. We found nothing but ledgers and other correspondence. Disappointed, Aidan left, but I stayed to read what was in those ancient papers."

Everyone was riveted by the story. Riordan continued, "The Earl of Carnstone, circa early 1700s, sought out a Scottish sorceress. He begged her to remove the curse, as he had recently lost his second wife to illness. The supposed enchantress claimed that only a love bond by all the males of the family alive during a lunar year would break the curse."

Garrett could not believe this. "And you only thought to mention it now?"

"What did a love curse mean to a lad of fourteen? I had completely forgotten about the papers in the attic, until a few months ago," Riordan replied. "It isn't real, more of a plot from a fantasy novel."

"What if it *is* real? Da, you thought you'd found true love with my mother, but she died regardless." Garrett pointed to Julian. "By the time Julian met and married Fiona, I was born. Too young to form a love bond within a lunar year. Hence the curse was not broken. I sound mad, but perhaps this has merit."

His family stared at him as if he were a patient at Bedlam. Frankly, he was tired of being thought of as the crackbrained member of the clan.

"Uncle, the time has come for us to dismiss the curse once and for all. Even if you believe it has some merit—and I agree there is proof it does—you cannot allow it to rule your life. If we all believed in it as fervently as you, none of us would have ever married. Grandfather married three times. Father married. I am married. Love means taking a chance."

Garrett frowned at his nephew, his cheeks flushing with growing annoyance, but Riordan continued on. "For argument's sake, let's say this is true. If all of us accept love here at the table, it will come down to Aidan to break the curse before November. Highly unlikely, considering his state." A look of sadness haunted Riordan's features.

"I agree with Riordan," Julian said. "Everything he said."

"Riordan, could you find these papers again?" Oliver asked.

"I'll go to the attic right now."

"I'll come with you, Son," Julian stated.

"Good. In the meantime, Garrett, come with me to the nearby sitting room. I wish to have a private conversation."

Bloody hell. Garrett stood, and Gordon rushed forward to take his arm. Being a blasted invalid was tedious. Once settled in the sitting room, his father closed the door. "Am I to be lectured, Da?"

"Not as such. But I wanted to relay to you, in private, about Abbie. She never left your side. In fact, she fought off Phillips when he'd mentioned amputation. She applied pressure on your wound for over two hours before Bastian arrived. Then she assisted with the procedure to repair the artery. Barely took a break to eat or sleep. Until..."

He was aware of some of it as he'd drifted in and out of consciousness. Started to believe most of it was a dream. "Until I blathered on nonsensically about the curse. I can hardly be held responsible for maniacal mutterings while caught in a fever nightmare."

His father sat across from him. "Perhaps, but it affected Abbie regardless. Hell, the curse has affected all of us. When Gordon arrived at Riordan's to inform us of the shooting. God above, I was desolate. Inconsolable. But Mary Tuttle was there for me. I hope"—his voice softened—"that she always will be. I am in love. I will *not* deny it. Not for any curse. Life is short, and how much time do I have left? Whatever remains, I aim to live life to the fullest, and love with my full heart. Can you say the same?"

His father's emotional words cut clear to his soul. A ball of emotion lodged in his throat, making replying difficult. "I love Abbie," he whispered. "I dismissed what we had because of the curse, relegated the past to a summer dalliance and nothing more. But I was deluding myself. She never left my mind or my heart. Not in all these years. I've been a damned fool." Garrett shook his head sadly. "We have love and passion, but not trust. How can we have a future if she will not trust me?"

"You haven't given her much reason. I think Abbie understands you were caught in a nightmare state, but it is patently obvious the curse haunts you still. I see a strong, courageous woman who deep down is vulnerable as far as you're concerned. And you're vulnerable as well." His father smiled. "Trust is something you build together, with open communication. You must forego blaming the other. Share your feelings. Be a reliable and steady presence. If you do all this, the trust will build more rapidly."

"I've made a muck of this, haven't I?"

"No. And yes. But it can be repaired, *if* you accept love and reject the curse. I know that it scarred you, Son. It has scarred us all. Here is the fork in the road. Choose the right path. Abbie came all this way to see if love still existed. Now it is your turn to make the journey."

He nodded. "Thank you, Da. I needed to hear this. I will heed what you've said."

A knock sounded at the door. "Come in," Oliver called out.

Dr. Faraday entered the room, wearing his long cloak and hat. "Forgive me for interrupting. I am about to take my leave and wished to say goodbye."

Oliver took his hand and shook it warmly. "I cannot begin to thank you for all you have done. Be sure and send me a bill."

"There will be no bill, my lord. I owe you for my career. Besides, once word spreads about London that I have saved the life of the son of the Earl of Carnstone, it will garner me more rich patients, and a rise in my standing."

Oliver laughed.

Garrett stood, and the doctor came to stand before him and held out his hand. "Your recovery is going well, and it is payment enough to see you thriving. Next you are in London, be sure to call on me. Your father has the address. We will share a meal and come to know each other better."

Garrett clasped his hand and shook it. "I will. I look forward to our next meeting. Thank you, Bastian, for your competent and compassionate care. Your patients are lucky indeed."

Bastian gave him a broad smile. "Take care, Garrett, and I hope that all works out the way you wish." He nodded toward Oliver. "My lord."

Ah. It was obviously not lost on the doctor how quickly Abbie had made an exit. Bastian turned and departed, and Garrett slowly lowered himself into his chair. Hell, he still ached all over, but his heart pained him the worst. *Abbie, how could you leave me?* The answer was patently obvious. When it came to their hearts, both were wary. Be damned if he would blame her for any of this. How to convince her that he truly wished to place the curse behind him? About time he did.

"I have a gift for you, from Megan." His father opened the door, talking in a low voice to one of the footmen. Moments later, his father emerged from the hallway holding a leash with a gangly collie at the other end. The dog's tongue lolled as a canine smile spread across his furry face. He was rambunctious and pulling on the leash. "Meet Laddie."

He stared at the dog, incredulous, then at his father. "Mine?"

"All Megan's idea." His father released the leash and the half-grown puppy ran toward him with an adorably awkward gait.

Garrett petted him. Damn it all, he was touched, completely choked up. "Laddie," he whispered. The puppy woofed, then licked his hand. The beautiful collie possessed a longish, multicolored coat of gold and brown on top of white. "How on earth…"

"Found him in Sussex. A farmer was displeased with his herding skills—or lack thereof. It was fate. He will make a fine pet and a loyal companion."

He would, Garrett could tell. He scratched Laddie's ears and the puppy whimpered dolefully as if grateful for the contact. *Megan's idea.* His daughter thought enough of him to suggest it. He leaned down and nuzzled the puppy's soft neck as he blinked away the few tears welling in his eyes.

Accept love. Forego the curse.

Clinging to the past had done nothing but cause heartache and a lingering loneliness.

Well, he and Abbie had one thing going for them: they both preferred to talk things out and be honest. At least, since they'd reacquainted. None of this grand misunderstanding and sulking in silence bollocks. There was still much to discuss. First, to see that justice be done and ensure Sutherhorne receives it.

* * * *

Abbie wrapped her wool cloak about her as she stared out across the expanse of her small parcel of land. She'd been home for two days and the aching in her heart had not abated. All the way home and the night spent in the inn, she nearly turned back and headed to Wollstonecraft Hall, because a part of her longed to stay and fight. She also realized that she'd done all she could to prove not only did the love still exist, but the curse held no weight.

Garrett had admitted he may have been wrong to allow it to rule his life. He'd pledged to put it behind him, but in the end he had not. The words he'd shouted with such vehemence during his fevered state had struck her as if they were slices from a sharp blade. Logically, she understood he was hallucinating, but it had been convincing enough to have her lay an ultimatum before him. Perhaps he would stubbornly cling to the curse. As it stood now, her thin thread of trust had been shattered, along with her heart. Could both be repaired?

She never should have entered into another physical relationship with the obstinate man. It proved that she had no self-control where Garrett was concerned. All her talk of courting came to nothing in the end. They had managed a couple of days of candy, flowers, and carriage rides before it had imploded.

Megan returned to school in Little Hadham. She'd been subdued on the journey home, offering support but obviously affected by the intense drama they had been swept up in and the turbulent emotions that accompanied it. Megan had grown up a little these past few weeks. She'd stated in a firm voice that she would respect whatever decision Abbie came to. Abbie was indeed thankful for Megan's quiet strength, as it bolstered and supported her own.

Now she had returned to her lonely life. Truly, she had no close friends, except for Alberta. And from what she surmised of Garrett, neither did he. Outside of their families, it was as if the both of them, after their painful, youthful affair, had retreated and isolated themselves. Was she not doing the exact same thing once again? *Withdraw and lick my wounds.*

Sighing forlornly, she glanced up at the sky as snow flurries started to fall. The overcast sky matched her melancholy mood. She returned her gaze to the building across the way.

Samuel Jenkins, the Wollstonecraft groom that had accompanied them home, stood in the makeshift stables attending the horses. Abbie could see him from her small porch. When Elwyn passed, she sold the horses and carriage, and since Megan was away at school most of the week, she boarded her daughter's mare at a nearby farm.

In the two years since, the stables had fallen into disorder. The young man asked if he could make repairs, since it would give him something to do while they awaited word that Sutherhorne had been dealt with. Abbie approved it, along with the purchase of needed materials and oats and hay for the two horses. She would have to explain why a young man was staying with her. Lie? Claim he was a distant relative? She might, considering this was a small borough and people talked. Hated lying, but it would have to be done. Samuel had mentioned that he'd received curious looks in the village.

Perhaps she should head to the clinic and resume her volunteer duties—and her previous life. God, her heart ached with a lonely yearning. Even if Garrett rode up, claimed to love her, and vowed to place the curse behind him, how could she ever believe him? Should she even try? Yes, she would hear him out. Then she would have to decide if she were willing to take another chance on love. For Abbie did love him, she had never stopped. The trust was a more difficult hurdle, but one she was willing to make. If he met her terms.

Was Garrett recovering? Blast, she could not stop thinking about him. Worrying about him. Nor could she stop longing to be held in his arms once again. How impetuous of her to travel to Kent. Reckless even, for all those raw and hurtful memories ached afresh. There would be no packing them away now. Not ever.

Get well, my love, and please...come to me.

Chapter 20

Four days later, the men set off for London. Prince Albert had agreed to see the family the following day, February 4. After much discussion they'd agreed to bring Jonas, since he'd heard and seen Sutherhorne and could offer definitive proof to the prince.

Sitting in the carriage with Jonas, Garrett stared out the window at the overcast sky. Next to him, on the cushioned seat, Laddie slept peacefully. Garrett could not bear to be parted from him; man and dog had already formed a close bond. Absently, he scratched the puppy's ears and Laddie whined with contentment.

Despite having Laddie with him, Garrett's mood was as gray and cold as the weather. He was damned tempted to ride with all haste to Standon and beg Abbie to give him another chance. Forgive his insane mutterings. But his sluggish recovery hampered his plans. As it was, he could not ride his horse and had to travel in the carriage like a damned invalid. He was uncomfortable, still weak, and it merely fueled his sour mood. He tried to organize his thoughts and decide what he was going to say to Abbie when they did meet, but could not concentrate.

Giving his closely cropped beard a few strokes, he turned his attention to Riordan's revelations of finding the ancient papers in the attic. For all his declarations and vows to Abbie to place the curse behind him, it had been there still, as always. Mocking him, maliciously sneering at him, denying him love and happiness.

It was damned sobering to discover that *he* was the one causing the impediments by using the curse as a protective shield to guard his emotions. All these years. Why? Well past time to accept the truth: he was terrified of being hurt and experiencing loss and heartache. The irony? He'd experienced them anyway, the day that he'd turned away from Abbie. Strange how childhood traumas played such an important role in how one is shaped into an adult. He had carried this fear since the age of ten.

And the curse? Through the years, Garrett had wondered if the hall itself was cursed. It had been originally owned by a baronet during the medieval period, the curse may have originated with him. When the seventeenth century Earl of Carnstone bought the crumbling hall, perhaps the curse transferred to the family. After all, part of the original building still stood, the timber framed front entrance and hall, with the Georgian and Gothic wings added years later.

Regardless, it no longer mattered how the curse could be broken. If only it hadn't taken so long for him to comprehend it. Whether it was true love as rumored for decades, even centuries, or what the papers revealed: *all the men living had to form a love bond during a twelve month period.* Did. Not. Matter. Almost succumbing to his injury had put things in their proper perspective, along with the recent conversation with his father. Life was indeed too short. He had made enough mistakes.

How to persuade Abbie to trust him would be difficult enough. Convincing her that he would lay the curse aside would be even more daunting. Damn it, he had to try. He *must.* Lost in his thoughts, he had not heard Jonas. "Sorry?"

"How do I address the prince?" Jonas asked.

"'Your Highness' is appropriate, but speak only if he addresses you first."

"Wait until I tell Meg I met Prince Albert," Jonas beamed.

The young man truly loved Megan. Considering Jonas's liabilities, most men would discourage the association. But he would not, for Garrett did not have the heart to deny what lay between them since he'd rejected the love between him and Abbie all those years ago. Young love—a first love—was not to be dismissed so cavalierly, a lesson hard earned.

"Jonas, you had mentioned an occupation, to provide for Megan when you marry. Would you be interested in learning about horse breeding? To train as a groom, to be more specific. I will pay you a salary. If you work hard and apply yourself, as I know that you are able, you may become head groom one day."

Jonas's eyes sparkled merrily. "*When* we marry, Garrett? Not *if?* Truly?"

"A few years from now, of course. If you and Megan feel the same, I will not stand in your way."

"Then, yes, I would like to learn all about horses. I love animals."

Garrett smiled. His gray mood lifted at the happy enthusiasm displayed by Jonas. "The exact reason I thought that this would be a good fit. We will begin next month and discuss salary once we return from London." "Thank you, Garrett." Jonas reached under the seat and brought out a box. Opening it, he asked, "Bert packed me a lunch, would you like a sandwich? It's my favorite, egg and ham."

Garrett accepted the brown paper-wrapped object. "Thank you."

As he slowly nibbled on the wedge, his thoughts turned to Abbie once again. He needed her. Ached for her. Loved her more than life. More than any damned curse. And Abbie needed to hear it, understand it, and ultimately...believe it.

Once they had arrived at the London townhouse, the servants saw them all properly settled. Garrett joined his father, brother, nephew, and Jonas for a hearty dinner before retiring to his room. Thankfully he'd slept, and was well rested when they gathered the next morning to depart for the palace.

One of Prince Albert's many secretaries and two guards greeted them. They were shown into what appeared to be a library-study and instructed to sit at the table and await the prince. The dark wood walls were covered with bookcases stuffed with hundreds of books; an ornate walnut desk sat in the corner. More than thirty minutes had passed, and Garrett was losing his patience. He exchanged glances with his father, who had already warned him to hold his quick temper in check.

When the prince made his entrance, they all stood and bowed. George Edward Anson, private secretary to Prince Albert, made the introductions.

The prince sat at the head of the table and they took their seats. "Carnstone, what is this concerning?"

"It is a matter of delicacy, Your Highness, concerning Brendan Whiddon, Marquess of Sutherhorne."

"Indeed?"

"Your Highness," his father continued, "we have come seeking justice for multiple incidents directed at my family, including the injury incurred by my younger son, Garrett. A near fatal gunshot wound."

The prince gave him a cursory glance, taking in his sling, his expression neutral. His father started his narrative, beginning with Sabrina being sold to Sutherhorne after she had been married to Riordan. His father stuck to the facts and refrained from embellishment. "I have Baron Durning's signed statement corroborating the kidnapping." He slid the paper to Anson, who glanced at it before passing it on to the prince. "I also have a written statement from Riordan's wife."

The room was silent as the prince read the papers. Baron Durning had made outrageous demands for his testimonial, but Julian had made it plain that the Wollstonecrafts would not be blackmailed. The baron had been offered full payment of his outstanding debt, along with the agreement never to contact Sabrina again. But this would only take place if Sutherhorne was banished. Julian had suggested Durning leave England, promising there might be a small stipend if he agrees. The baron had grudgingly agreed to consider it.

Prince Albert looked up from the papers. "This is most disturbing, my lord."

"It is, Your Highness. There is more." His father explained about the shooting and what Jonas had overheard and observed.

Prince Albert turned his penetrating gaze to Jonas. "Is this true, young man?"

Jonas was visibly nervous. "It is true, Your Highness. It was a thin, older man with a white beard; I would know him anywhere."

"Anson, summon Sutherhorne at once. His presence is required immediately. I will brook no excuse for his absence."

"Yes, Your Highness."

Anson departed, and the prince frowned, the first show of emotion. "What is it you wish from me, my lord?"

"As I said, we require justice for these multiple incidents. To avoid public humiliation and censure, I thought it prudent to keep this private and not involve the law. In the past, peers have been banished for similar or even lesser offences. It may be best for all concerned, Your Highness, if Sutherhorne is expelled."

"That is for me to decide." The prince stood and the rest of the table followed suit. "Remain here until the marquess arrives." He departed.

"Will he inform the Queen of this?" Julian asked as they took their seats again.

"He may, after the fact; he is one of her closest advisors. Queen Victoria abhors this type of behavior in the peerage. We are saving the prince from embarrassment, since he and Sutherhorne are friends of a sort," Oliver replied.

Servants entered, carrying trays of fresh fruit and a pot of tea. More than thirty minutes later, as they sipped their tea, Sutherhorne was shown into the room. The older man startled when he noticed the Wollstonecrafts sitting around the table.

"What is the meaning of this..."

The door opened, and the prince entered followed by his secretary. After the bows, the men sat.

"You will remain standing, Sutherhorne," the prince stated in a flat tone as the marquess moved toward an empty chair.

Sutherhorne actually looked worried. *Good.*

"There is a law, not used since 1820, the Bill of Attainder. What it states, in essence, Sutherhorne, is that I have the authority to strip you of all lands, money, and title. Your son and his son will never be marquess. Complete and utter ruin. Public shaming. By God, I am tempted to recommend it to the Queen." The prince frowned, clearly annoyed. "Charges have been laid before me. Shocking charges. I require the complete truth. Did you shoot Garrett Wollstonecraft?"

Sutherhorne cleared his throat. "Outrageous and insulting. I never—"

The prince lifted his hand to silence the marquess. "This young man, sitting next to the earl, is a witness. He heard what you said to your man. Described you perfectly. This is the man you observed in the woods, Mr. Eaton?"

"Yes, Prince—I mean, Your Highness. It is him," Jonas answered, his tone firm and resolute.

Sutherhorne sputtered. "Your Highness, you would take the word of the village idiot over me? Your trusted friend and advisor—"

"How do you know enough about this young man to call him such a disparaging name, unless you have been to Kent recently?" Oliver accused.

Sutherhorne pulled out a lace handkerchief and wiped his brow. "It was an accident, Your Highness. I only meant to scare Wollstonecraft and his party by firing shots overhead. It was a response to an insult. The beast had manhandled me, you see."

Garrett had to use all his self-control to keep himself from vaulting out of his chair and pummeling the sniveling marquess into a bloody pulp. Yes, he could batter the bastard easily with only one arm. Abbie and Megan could have been harmed—*killed*—all because this puffed-up, privileged peer took insult. He gritted his teeth as his blood boiled.

"I care not for your petty squabbles. Your response was excessive, and beneath your dignity as an aristocrat. As a peer of the realm. And what of having Riordan Wollstonecraft's wife kidnapped?" The prince demanded, no longer keeping his anger tethered. "Do you deny it?"

Sutherhorne looked down. "No, Your Highness. But she was to be my bride before—"

"Enough. I have heard *enough*. Tempted as I am to invoke the Bill of Attainder, I will give you a singular option. If you agree to leave these shores and never return in your lifetime, your son can inherit all entailed property and money, along with the title. You are to have no further contact with anyone in the peerage or at the palace." The prince paused. "However, all nonentailed lands and money *will* become the property of the crown. It will be used to further education reform and assist in the Irish potato famine relief. Meanwhile, until arrangements can be made for your transport to a remote locality, you will remain here as a guest and under guard."

Sutherhorne gulped deeply. "As you wish, Your Highness."

"Is this suitable, my lord?" the prince asked the earl.

What could his father say? It is exactly what they had hoped for, though Garrett wished they were still in the era of Henry VIII, where a stretch on the rack would be welcome and well deserved.

Oliver stood and bowed. "It is, Your Highness, and thank you."

Two Grenadier Guards entered the room, resplendent in their red uniforms. They marched toward Sutherhorne, intent on escorting him to a part of the palace where he would be kept under surveillance.

"Wait. I wish a private word with Garrett Wollstonecraft," the marquess cried.

What? Everyone looked to Garrett and he gave a quick nod in response. Might as well hear what the villain had to say. One of the guards escorted Sutherhorne to the corner of the large room and Garrett followed.

"Speak, and make it quick," Garrett snapped.

"I had Delaney travel to Standon to find out what he could about your woman and the girl."

Garrett lunged for the marquess, but the guard halted him.

"Stop fretting; no harm will come to them. While there, however, he saw your nephew in a wheeled chair outside of a private clinic. You see, your wretched, drug-addled relative sold himself at a particularly debauched party I had attended in December. I bought him...for Delaney's personal pleasure." A cruel smile curved about the marquess's mouth, as if he were savoring this shocking reveal. "I believe Colm Delaney covets your nephew, for some strange inexplicable reason. I tell you this because I have no control over the man. Any action he takes is not at my urging. Fair warning: Delaney is rather a brute, and dangerous when denied what he most desires."

Rage tore through Garrett at this revelation and his heart ached in empathy for his wayward nephew. Now he knew how Aidan had sustained the violation injuries. Damn this man to a fiery hell.

The smile widened. "Such a murderous look on your face. It is quite amusing. A parting shot: I have seen to it that this gossip makes the rounds, although I did not reveal your nephew's current location. Your family will be humiliated. Perhaps ruined. 'Destroy the young heir.' I can only hope my plan comes to fruition." He raised his chin in the air and sniffed, "Guards, I am ready."

The guards escorted Sutherhorne from the room as Garrett clenched his fist, his cheeks flushing red-hot with fury.

"Alas, there is no time to discuss the education reforms, but Mr. Riordan Wollstonecraft, I expect a complete accounting of all your achievements and successes. Send it to Anson, and we will meet again later in the spring." The prince gave Riordan a genuine, but brief smile.

"I look forward to it, Your Highness," Riordan replied.

With leave-taking bows, the prince departed, his private secretary following closely behind.

Jesus. Did Aidan even know what he had been doing? Did he remember any of it? *Delaney is rather a brute.* Garrett glanced at his family, who gave him quizzical looks. They would want an accounting of what Sutherhorne had said to him. How could he lie, especially if the gossip was spreading throughout London? Peers liked nothing more than to crow over salacious tittle-tattle. Damn Sutherhorne to hell. The morally bankrupt marquess would probably live out his days in sunny Spain. How was that punishment?

He must head to Standon immediately and warn Aidan. If Aidan would even see him. But what caused his heart to skip several beats was the fact that the bully knew of Abbie and Megan and where they lived. *Stop fretting, no harm will come to them,* Sutherhorne had said. As if he could trust what the putrid marquess claimed. Garrett soon found himself surrounded by his family.

"What did the despicable miscreant want?" Riordan asked.

Hell, what to reveal. They were in London. The gossip could reach their ears while he traveled to Standon. They should be prepared. Obviously the story that Aidan was in Italy recovering from a chest infection would soon be questioned and parsed over by society.

Hang it, they were alone in the room; might as well tell all. But Jonas should not hear this, for it was private family business and would be difficult to explain. "Jonas, wait for us in the hallway, if you please."

"All right, Garrett."

Once the young man stepped outside and closed the door, Garrett relayed what Sutherhorne said, word for word. Julian and Oliver blanched, while Riordan sprinted toward the door. "I will kill the old reprobate!" he yelled. Julian and Oliver grabbed his arms, halting his action. Tears trailed down his cheeks, his face grim and sorrowful. "It is not true. Sutherhorne made up this scandalous story to discredit the family."

"It is possible he fabricated the entire story. However, Dr. Bevan did tell me that those gripped by an opium addiction will sink to unknown depths in order to obtain the narcotic. When I found him, Aidan was living in squalid conditions with dubious company." Garrett would not mention the injuries, not until he heard Aidan's side of the tale. If Aidan would even see him. To hell with it—he would insist that his nephew give him an audience.

"Blast the gossip, we can weather the storm, but what has Aidan gone through?" Julian whispered.

"Perhaps one day he will tell us. I believe it prudent that I leave for Standon immediately. Alone." The men all protested, speaking over each other, but Garrett firmly shook his head. "We cannot swoop in on Aidan like a convocation of white-tailed eagles. But if I go alone, he may see me." Garrett patted his coat pocket. "I have all your letters and I will leave them with the doctor, or with Aidan himself. Besides, I also need to talk to Abbie. It is private, and if she refuses my suit, I'd rather be alone for the trip home."

"Son, while I am glad you are allowing love into your heart at last, you have not fully recovered. Even now you are pale and perspiring," Oliver stated.

"Then I will make one concession. I will take Jonas with me. He will be a strong arm to lean on. Plus I will have Laddie to keep me company."

"Allow me to go instead," Riordan urged.

"You must return to Sabrina and to your occupation." He gave Riordan a sympathetic look. "He is your twin brother. I understand the need to be there for him. Trust me to stand in your stead."

Riordan nodded, but his devastated expression tore at Garrett's heart. "If you will permit, I will leave with Jonas in the carriage right away. You came on your own horses and have transportation home. One day soon, when the country is rife with railway tracks and steam engines, getting about will be a damned sight quicker." Garrett tried to lighten the mood, but the brooding men of his family were having none of it. "I cannot believe that you are allowing my plan. I thought you would all insist on coming with me."

"Believe it or not, Brother, we trust your judgment. Riordan told me more than once that you are the rugged stone on which our family's foundation is built. The mortar that holds us together. Never was it as true as here in this moment." Julian clapped him on the shoulder while Riordan and Oliver nodded in agreement.

Emboldened by the touching words, Garrett would do all he could to protect those he loved. Now to head to Standon with all haste.

Chapter 21

Abbie ultimately decided to return to her volunteer duties at the sanatorium. *Enough feeling sorry for myself.* Besides Aidan, there were three other men in residence from various walks of life. She had thought to tell Gethin and Cristyn about Garrett's proposal for training new physicians to treat addiction, but thought it best that it be left to him to reveal. Besides, the doctor and his daughter had no clue of her connection to the Wollstonecrafts—or Megan's. As far as they were concerned, she'd gone to Kent to visit an old friend. They knew of Aidan and Garrett by the name of Black. It was not for her to divulge their true identity.

She had toiled most of the morning in the kitchen with a new employee. Thanks to Garrett's generous contribution, Gethin had hired a woman to do the cleaning and cooking. Mrs. Williams already had a pot of beef stew bubbling on the stove. When the kind woman had offered her some for lunch, Abbie had politely refused, stating that she would head home for a light luncheon and return afterwards to assist with afternoon tea.

Stepping outside the rear entrance, Abbie slipped on her gloves. When she had arrived home, she should have returned to volunteering right away. The work kept her mind busy, and kept her from dwelling on her sadness. Taking a deep breath of cold air and exhaling, she headed for her small house about a half a mile away.

Not far from the sanatorium, Abbie observed a large man partially hidden by a cluster of pine trees. Never seen him before; who could he be? He watched her intently, and a shiver of warning curled about her spine. Though she was not able to make out his features, what she could observe worried her. The arrogant way he stood with legs apart, the scowl on his face. Abbie looked away from him and hurried along the lane. Slowing, she chanced a glance. Thankfully he did not follow her, but instead turned his attention to the sanatorium. Perhaps she was being too apprehensive. Regardless, she picked up her pace toward her home.

"Samuel, I will be fine. There is no need to accompany me."

The young man held Abbie's arm while taking in their surroundings with a wary and suspicious eye. "Mr. Garrett and the lordships would have my guts for garters if anything happened to you, Mrs. Hughes, begging your pardon. I should've come with you this morning. Especially since you told me at lunch of the strange man lurking about the clinic."

"No doubt my wild imagination, nothing more."

"Still, after you're settled, I'll reconnoiter the property and the woods surrounding it."

Once they arrived at the sanatorium, Abbie introduced Samuel as her cousin, who had come to stay for a short visit, and to do odd jobs for her. She despised lying, but everyone accepted her fabrication. Gethin even asked if Samuel would like to earn extra money and take on a couple of repair jobs for him. He agreed, then ducked out to inspect the grounds.

With her duties completed in the kitchen, Cristyn asked, "Would you deliver a cup of tea and a bowl of stew to Aidan Black? I have another patient to see to."

"Of course." Abbie had not seen Aidan since the first week of January. She wanted to see if there had been any improvement.

Entering the room, her heart squeezed with compassion at the sight of Garrett's nephew. In truth, there was not much improvement at all. Aidan sat in a wheeled chair, a wool blanket spread across his lap and another gathered about his thin shoulders. His hair had been cut, though it was still longer than the current fashion. Though his color had improved slightly. The sickly gray shade was now more of an alabaster white. "Good afternoon, Mr. Black."

He did not reply, but stared at her as she placed the tray on the small table before him. Aidan regarded her shrewdly. "Have we met?"

"I was here the first few days of your stay."

"No, that's not it. We have met before. Did we have an affair?" His intense gaze moved over her. "You look my type."

"From what I've heard, any woman drawing breath is your type."

"Abigail Wharton. I'd recognize that tart tongue anywhere. The years have been kind; you are still lovely." Aidan didn't smile, nor did he act particularly thrilled to renew the acquaintance. His tone was disinterested, but he flirted nonetheless. He was still a rake, even in faltering health.

"I didn't think you would remember me, since you were all of twelve when last we met." She poured him a mug of tea. "Milk? Sugar?"

"No. Just give me the blasted cup. God knows what strange herbs are in this, as my Welsh keepers will not give me a straight answer. As for the damned stew, I'm not hungry."

"You must eat," Abbie replied, in a kind but firm tone.

"If you knew how weary I am of hearing that statement. I will eat it shortly, if I must. I take it you haven't revealed my real name?"

"It is not for me to expose your secret." She passed him the mug, then pulled up a chair.

"I'm not in the mood for conversation. Allow me to drink this swill in peace."

"I have just returned from an extended visit in Kent."

Aidan sipped his tea, grimacing as he did. "I don't really care."

It was obvious from the bored expression on his face, and the equally bored tone of his voice, that he truly did not care. No use revealing any current events, such as Megan's existence or Garrett being shot. Abbie had volunteered here long enough to understand that the patients needed to be kept in a tranquil environment to hasten along their recovery. Shocking reveals would not be prudent. "It is obvious you do not care about much of anything, else you would not be here."

"How astute," Aidan snorted sarcastically.

"My late husband started this sanatorium. His dear friend, Gethin, is carrying on his work along with, Cristyn, his daughter. She is a lovely young woman, eager to help others. Compassionate. From what I've observed, she has given you particular attention."

Aidan glared at her over the rim of his mug, one eyebrow arching. "I am hardly in any condition to notice a pretty girl. What do you want, Abigail? Trying to play matchmaker? This from the woman who broke my uncle's heart." He scoffed and continued to sip his tea.

Well. Aidan was certainly nothing like Riordan. Twins they may be, but their personalities could not be more dissimilar. His younger brother was a serious young man committed to making the world a better place. Aidan? Out for his own pleasures. Yet she could see the pain in his eyes. The stark loneliness. "And how do you know of Garrett's broken heart?" she asked in a soft voice.

"I may have been 'all of twelve,' but I was observant enough. I also heard the two of you in the hayloft one night. You were not particularly quiet, considering that you were meeting in secret." He snorted. "Quite shocking to my young sensibilities."

Abbie's cheeks flushed hot with embarrassment.

"How did I know of his broken heart? Garrett was miserable after you left. He refused to talk about it or you. Swore me to complete secrecy."

As she was about to speak, the door burst open and the imposing man Abbie had seen on her way home for luncheon stepped into the room. He closed the door behind him. He was well over six feet in height, though not as tall as Garrett. But he was broader, if it were possible. The stranger was a lurking brute of a man with a strange countenance. A few scars, a crooked nose, yet a cruel handsomeness skulked beneath the well-worn features. It was hard to ascertain his age. Late thirties? Early forties? When the man's gaze landed on Aidan, his eyes took on a fiery heat.

"Who are you, sir?" Abbie demanded. Goodness, this man exuded an aura of danger. She stood. Should she scream for Gethin? Was Samuel still looking about the property?

"Leave us. I've come to talk to Aidan." His voice was rough, gravelly, and demanding. He also had a slight accent. Irish? Scottish? Hard to tell.

"I do not know this man," Aidan replied, looking away.

"You know me," the man barked. "Intimately."

Aidan swung his gaze to him and his eyes widened in recognition. He dropped the mug and the remaining tea splashed across the wood floor. "No. You belong in my nightmares. You are not real."

"Oh, aye. I'm real enough." The man shifted his gaze toward Aidan. "We need to talk. About what happened between us at that damned house party."

Aidan visibly paled, becoming almost ghost-like in appearance. "I don't wish to discuss it."

"I had to see for myself you're all right. That it wasn't because of me that you're here."

Abbie looked back and forth between the two men. The conversation had her riveted. And curious.

"Do not flatter yourself," Aidan replied in a disinterested tone. "I have nothing to say to you."

"Missus, get out. Aidan and me need privacy to talk," Delaney barked, giving her a cursory but menacing glace.

"I will not," Abbie replied defiantly. "He wants you to go, and I would suggest, sir, you do exactly that."

He slipped a knife with a jagged blade from his coat pocket. "I didn't come here to hurt anyone, but I will, if pushed and provoked."

Abbie gasped at the sight of the blade. A thought struck her. Was this Delaney, the Marquess of Sutherhorne's 'bullyboy,' as Riordan had called him? What did he mean about a house party? What had happened between the two men? "Your name is Delaney, isn't it? Haven't you done enough to this family? You shot at my daughter and me. Injured Garrett. How *dare* you come here and threaten a sick man?"

"I didn't shoot at anyone. It was the bloody marquess and his quest for revenge. Nothing to do with me. I'm just his hired muscle." He looked Abbie over. "Mrs. Hughes. I recognize you now. I thought that you were still in Kent. No matter, I—"

The door gave way from its hinges, and Samuel entered, with Garrett right on his heels. Hovering in the doorway was a shocked Gethin and Cristyn.

Abbie's breath seized at seeing Garrett. He was not fully recovered, judging by the sling and his pale and drawn features. Before she could muster another thought, Delaney lifted Aidan from his wheeled chair, as if he weighed nothing at all, and held him close, one large arm across Aidan's chest. The tip of the knife touched Aidan's throat.

"Mrs. Hughes, come stand next to us," Delaney barked. "Now."

Abbie looked to Garrett and Samuel, unsure of what to do.

"Delaney, drop the knife," Garrett urged.

"I think not. Come here, missus, or blood will be spilled," Delaney demanded.

Abbie, with shaking legs, stumbled over and stood next to Delaney and Aidan. Delaney nuzzled Aidan's neck as he stood behind him, as a lover might do. How shocking!

"I only came here to talk to Aidan. Nothing more. This is being blown out of all proportion. I don't want to hurt anyone. I didn't shoot at you and missus and the girl. That was all Sutherhorne."

"I know. The marquess admitted it to Prince Albert. Your employer is about to be banished from the country," Garrett stated, his voice dripping with anger. "So there is no need to carry out any further retribution. Not hurt anyone? You say that with a knife at my nephew's neck?"

Delaney snorted, but he pulled the knife away from Aidan and kept it at his side. "I'm not here to exact revenge. To hell with Sutherhorne and his feckin' stupid plans." He rubbed his nose against Aidan's neck and whispered in his ear, low enough only Abbie could hear, "Remember me now? Come away with me, let me nurse you back to health. Give you whatever you need. I promise I won't hurt you." Delaney's voice dropped another octave. "Not ever."

"You were a means to an end," Aidan murmured. "It meant nothing. Leave me alone."

A pained look crossed Delaney's features, as if Aidan's words hurt. Grunting, he released Aidan, who slumped to the floor. With a swift move,

Delaney brought Abbie against him, holding her tight. He still held the knife menacingly, but did not threaten her with it. "I'll be leaving. The missus here will allow me to get to my horse. Do not follow us, or I will be forced to use violence. Christ almighty, I just wanted to feckin' talk to..."

Abbie wriggled, trying to escape, but he held her with an iron grip. In turning her head, she saw Delaney glance at Aidan, still lying on the floor. Concern knotted the man's brows and he seemed to hesitate. But his moment of disquietude passed, and he pulled Abbie with him as he backed up toward the door. "Be gone!" he bellowed to Gethin and Cristyn. They scurried away. "Hear me. Neither you nor your man will follow me. If you chase me, I'll cut her." He pressed the tip of the blade against her side to emphasize his point. "Allow me to leave, and no one will be hurt, now, or in the future. I *will* let Mrs. Hughes go."

"You miserable bastard. Hear this: if you have any contact with any member of my family or anyone I care about ever again, it will be me cutting *you*." Abbie had never seen Garrett this dangerous and intimidating.

Before Abbie knew it, she and Delaney were moving toward the rear entrance. Then they were outside, the cold air causing her breath to catch. The man was swift; his long-legged stride pulled her along toward the thickest part of the woods. She struggled, even kicked at his leg, but it was futile. Delaney was as strong as an ox, and he carried her under his arm as if she were a wrapped package. Her feet were not even touching the ground.

Through the cluster of pines, Abbie spotted a horse tethered to a large tree. Good Lord, the horse was as much of a beast as the man who held her. The horse, which must be a dray crossbreed, had to be seventeen hands tall. Delaney pushed her away and vaulted onto the back of the animal. He slipped his knife in his pocket, then gathered up the reins. "You're free to go, missus." He stared at her, and his expression turned melancholy. "Look after Aidan. Tell him...I'll see him soon."

"Leave Aidan alone. He's suffered enough," she cried, still shaking from the cold and from fright. Her hands were turning red and numb.

Garrett's deep voice carried through the winter air. He was frantically calling her name.

"Go to your man. Do it, or I'll run you down. This horse will trample you good and proper." The words were plainly spoken, but this time there was no menace behind the threat.

Abbie lifted her wool skirt and broke into a run. Delaney may well run her down regardless. She chanced a glance, but the man had already disappeared into the forest, the booming sound of horses' hooves growing fainter.

"Abbie!"

Ascertaining the direction of Garrett's worried voice, she ran toward the sound, tears streaming from her eyes. A leafless branch scraped against her cheek, but she kept going. Abbie emerged from the thickest part of the forest to find Garrett running toward her. Her heart leapt at the sight of him. "Garrett!"

They met, and with his free arm, Garrett pulled her against him, lifting her from the ground and hugging her fiercely. "Damn it all, if anything had happened to you," he rasped huskily while laying multiple kisses along her neck.

Abbie felt safe. Warm. Protected. Despite it all, regardless of everything that stood in their way, all the complications, the curse, and whatever else, all that mattered was being in his arms.

He lowered her, then frowned, his gloved finger brushing across her cheek. Blood was on the tip. "He hurt you."

"No, it was a tree branch. He didn't hurt me."

"Samuel is fetching the horses. Not sure I can ride, but I'll hunt the bastard down and I will—"

Abbie clutched Garrett's arm. "Let him go. It is not worth your health or your safety. I truly believe he only wished to talk to Aidan. Besides, he had nothing to do with the shooting."

Garrett's mouth dropped open. "The brute threatened you and Aidan, held a knife on you both! He deserves a sound thrashing, if nothing else."

"I agree. But you're not fully recovered, and I will not allow you to be injured further. Nor will I allow you to send Samuel after the man. He could well handle himself, but...I do not wish to see him harmed."

Garrett slipped his right arm about her waist and together they slowly walked toward the sanatorium. "I am sorry you were pulled into this never-ending drama."

"There...there is...or was...something between Aidan and Delaney."

"Yes. As you've heard, Sutherhorne has been banished. But he did fire off a final volley. Gossip about Aidan is making its way about London, concerning his behavior at one of those debauched affairs certain peers like to attend. I will tell you more later. You are shivering, and the cut on your cheek needs attention."

"Why did you come to Standon? Because of Aidan?"

"In part." Samuel rode up, holding the reins to the other horse. Garrett halted the young man. "I imagine he is long gone, Samuel."

"Shouldn't we try, sir?"

"We live to fight another day. Return the horses to Mrs. Hughes's residence. We will follow you there directly."

Samuel touched his forelock, turned, and trotted away.

As soon as the young man was out of earshot, Garrett said, "I came to see you, Abbie, as soon as I well enough to withstand the trip. We need to talk." Garrett pulled her close and nuzzled her neck, causing much needed warmth to roll through her once again.

The clinic came into view, and Abbie breathed a sigh of relief. "Yes. But not today. I am utterly exhausted. Where are you staying?"

Garrett looked disappointed, but after this latest drama, she could not fully engage in an emotional conversation and give it her full attention.

"The George Inn. Jonas is there, along with Laddie. We came straight from London and the meeting with Prince Albert."

"Jonas? And Laddie, how wonderful. Well, Megan will be happy. She returns from school the day after tomorrow. Will you still be here then?"

"That is entirely up to you," he murmured sensually. "Jonas was the concession my family allowed for me to travel here, for you are correct, my love: I am not fully recovered. And the puppy? He is my constant companion. The loveable imp hasn't left my side since I was gifted with him."

Gethin rushed toward them from the rear entrance. "Thank God, you are both safe. I will send for the parish constable at once."

"The man, Delaney, has vanished, and our family would prefer if this incident was kept quiet. If you would inform your staff, and ensure their discretion, it would be greatly appreciated."

"Your family name is not Black then, I take it?" Gethin remarked.

"No, Doctor. Between you and me, it is Wollstonecraft, and I, and my father, the Earl of Carnstone, and the rest of my family, would prefer we kept it between us. To everyone else, including your daughter, the name is Black. Agreed?"

Gethin escorted them to a private room. "Agreed. Allow me to treat your cut, Abigail." Both men helped her to take a seat.

"May I see Aidan?" Garrett asked.

Gethin reached for a bottle of antiseptic from the nearby shelf. "Ah. He fell unconscious briefly when Delaney released him. When he woke, he immediately became agitated, so I gave him a liberal dose of laudanum. He will be sleeping soon enough. Also, he asked that he be left alone the rest of the day. I must defer to my patient."

"I must talk to him, Doctor, at some point. It is important, and to do with what happened today," Garrett said, his voice firm.

"Then come by tomorrow morning, and I will convince him to give you a brief audience." Gethin blotted her cheek with a clean cloth soaked with the antiseptic. "It is fortuitous, your arrival. I was about to post my first report to you. Come to my office later, and we will discuss it. I also wish to know of this man and what he wanted with my patient." Gethin placed a small plaster on her cut. "As for you, my dear, I recommend rest. Are you injured anywhere else?"

Abbie shook her head. "No, he did not harm me. I did this running through the forest." She looked between the two men. "Delaney asked me to look after Aidan, and said he would see him soon. Strange as it may sound, I believe he cares for Aidan in some inexplicable way." She placed her hand at her forehead. "Perhaps I should head home. My head is pounding."

"I will escort you," Garrett stated in a firm voice. He would accept no argument, it seemed.

Gethin held out an envelope to Garrett. "Headache powder. Add it to a hot cup of tea."

Once they collected her cloak and gloves, Garrett gently took her arm, and escorted her outside. A carriage stood by the entrance. They remained quiet during the short journey, but his intense and heated gaze never left her, which made her tingle all over.

Garrett entered her house, filling it with his masculine presence. "Where is your bedroom?"

"Down this hall, first door to the left."

Again he took her arm, and slowly led her to the door. Abbie wasn't certain who was leaning on whom. With tender and deliberate care, he assisted her with the removal of her coat, then her wool skirt and blouse. Every brush of his fingers caused her skin to heat. Lastly, he loosened her stays, then laid her on the bed, pulling the quilt over her. Leaning down, he kissed her on the forehead, then a soft kiss on the lips. "Rest. Before I leave, I will fetch you that cup of tea. Samuel will be nearby, and will send for me if needs must. After I speak with Aidan tomorrow, I will come straight here." He smoothed her forehead with the tips of his fingers. "I love you, Abbie. Never doubt it. Never forget it."

"Oh, Garrett," she swallowed down a sob. "You came for me."

"Always. You'll not be rid of me so easily, my dearest love. Not ever again. In fact, I will stay with you this afternoon as long as you wish. Unless you want to be alone."

Hot tears burned at the corner of her eyes. "I would like for you to stay awhile. And hold me, nothing else."

Garrett kissed her softly on the lips again, causing her heartbeat to speed up. "We will leave the serious conversation until tomorrow. Let me fetch your tea and I will hold you close to my heart as long as you wish."

He gave her such a heated look, her breath caught. "For the rest of our lives. Hell, forever."

Garrett departed, leaving his enticing scent in his wake. She inhaled, then the sob she had held in escaped. As did the tears. Not only from what had happened at the sanatorium, but the fact that Garrett had come to her. Would he claim that he was leaving the curse behind him? Could she believe him? All she knew was that in a moment of pure terror, leaving aside their daughter for the moment—she had wanted Garrett. Most desperately. To hold her. To tell her in his deep but soft voice that all would be well. She yearned for him to protect and love her. To claim nothing else mattered to him—but *her*. Not the curse, not any outside influences or dramas. Not the past, or recriminations and mistakes on either side.

Now Abbie just had to find the courage to do the same.

Chapter 22

After making Abbie her tea, Garrett stayed with her for close to two hours until she fell asleep in his arms. His meeting with Dr. Bevan had been frank and rather emotional, as he'd revealed Aidan's connection to Delaney. At least, what he knew of it. The doctor had not acted surprised, relaying that he'd heard similar stories from various patients through the years. He told of one man who had prostituted his daughter in order to procure opium. The man had been a respected doctor at a London hospital.

How disappointing to learn that Aidan's recovery was not progressing as quickly as the doctor had hoped. His nephew's attitude hampered most of his recuperation. But the doctor remained positive that Aidan would recover.

He had returned to the George Inn sick at heart, but Jonas and Laddie's happy greetings helped elevate the gloom. Over dinner, he'd decided not to mention to Jonas about Aidan being in Standon, or the drama-filled episode of the afternoon. Nor would he mention it to Megan. He'd rather that they be introduced when Aidan was fully recovered. Deep down, Garrett believed his nephew would come through this. Damn it, he *must.*

After a fitful sleep, Garrett rose early and shared breakfast with Jonas. He'd informed him that he would be speaking to Abbie, and had asked the young man to stay in the room at the inn until he returned. Jonas held up a book, one Megan had given him. *The Old Curiosity Shop* by Charles Dickens.

At the last minute, Garrett decided to take Laddie with him to visit Aidan. "Perhaps, Doctor, you are not keen having a rambunctious canine on the premises," Garrett said as he pulled gently on Laddie's leash.

Gethin patted Laddie on the head. "It may prove to be therapeutic. I heartily approve." He straightened and met Garrett's gaze. "Aidan has agreed to see you, but only for five minutes. I am to keep a rigorous timing of the visit. I will extend it a couple of minutes beyond, but no more. I hold firm to the belief that family should not be involved at this stage of recovery." Dr. Bevan led him to Aidan's room and opened the door.

Garrett entered, and the energetic Laddie lurched forward and pulled on the leash, tongue lolling, eager to greet someone new. Aidan, dreadfully thin and pale, sat at the front of the room in the wheeled chair, covered in blankets. Yesterday, he hadn't had much of a chance to observe his nephew's appearance. It still was a shock to see.

Aidan gave a cursory glance at the dog, then looked away. "If you have come to warn me about Delaney, you're too late."

"Yes, I've been late regarding many things." Garrett let the leash drop, then reached into the inside pocket of his greatcoat, pulling out a small stack of envelopes. He set them on the table by Aidan's bed. "Here are letters from your father, grandfather, and brother. Some of the recent news is in these dispatches. Read at your leisure."

Laddie loped toward Aidan, woofing softly. With his wet nose, the puppy nudged at Aidan's hand, no doubt hoping to be petted or have his ears scratched. But Aidan ignored the gesture.

"The Marquess of Sutherhorne—you may remember his name mentioned yesterday—is responsible for a number of incidents that have occurred toward our family." Aidan's indifferent gaze slid to the sling on Garrett's left arm. "This peer was a guest at a party in December. One he claims you attended. He bought you for his man Delaney's pleasure. The man here in this room yesterday. Is this true?" Garrett took a step closer. Laddie had given up trying to encourage Aidan to pet him and instead sat at his feet. "Did you sell yourself for money in order to acquire opium?"

"It appears so," Aidan answered in a flat tone.

"Did Delaney force himself on you?" Garrett's voice was soft, but his insides tumbled with apprehension.

"I do not remember much of the incident. But I was a willing participant. I wanted and needed the opium desperately enough to debase myself. The episode is merely part of many that haunt my disturbed dreams."

Jesus. Garrett took a deep breath and exhaled. "Well, Sutherhorne is spreading this gossip about London. I thought you should be aware. I doubt it will reach here; no one knows that you are a Wollstonecraft anyhow— except Dr. Bevan. I swore him to secrecy yesterday."

"After how low I've sunk? I hardly think that gossip will affect me."

"No, but it will affect your family. Not that you gave us any thought as you made your steep decline into debauchery."

Aidan met his gaze. "No, Uncle, I didn't. Not once. Doesn't bode well for my soul, does it?"

"I am sorry," Garrett rasped.

"For what?"

"For not reaching out to you, offering help and support. We failed you. And I am heartily sorry for blaming you just now for your decline and the gossip. You do not deserve my censure."

Aidan exhaled a shuddering breath. "I've failed myself, Uncle. I do deserve your censure. And I believe your five minutes is up." His nephew pulled the blanket tighter about his shoulders.

"Yesterday, Delaney's parting words to Abbie were for her to take care of you. And to tell you he will see you soon. She believes it is not a threat as such, but I would like to leave Samuel here in Standon in case the brute makes another appearance." Garrett had already written a letter to Edwin Seward last night to begin an investigation into Colm Delaney. The way things were going, he may have to place Edwin on permanent retainer.

Aidan shook his head. "No. I don't want a guard. It is my mess. Leave it be." Regardless of Aidan's pronouncement to "leave it be," Garrett would post the letter anyway.

"What did he want of you?" Garett asked.

"He never got a chance to explain. Whatever it was, it has made me realize just how low I've sunk. To discover that my nightmares are actual events…it also made me realize I don't want to live like this anymore. I intend to recover, but it is something I must work through. Alone."

"I understand. If you don't mind, I would like Laddie to stay here with you while I see Abbie. Much has happened. I want her in my life. I love her, I always have." Aidan did not react, nor did he reply. Garrett continued. "Aidan, I have learned so much these past months. How important it is to allow love into my life. To not wallow in fear, as I had with the curse. As a result, I denied my love for Abbie, I broke both our hearts. I aim to make it up to her. Beg her for forgiveness. Make her understand that I have finally left my insecurities behind and am ready to embrace all life has to offer." Garrett paused, and his heart squeezed with sorrow as he stared at Aidan. "It is a lesson worth learning. I heartily recommend it. I don't like that we've drifted apart. Your family loves you—I love you—and we want nothing more than for you to be returned to us hale and hearty. Allow us to assist you in your recovery—when you are ready." Garrett smiled warmly. "You are loved, Aidan. Treasured. Not all is lost."

His nephew looked away, but not before Garrett observed that his eyes were moist. Garrett stepped outside the room, then hesitated. Peeking around the door, he watched as Laddie whimpered and laid his head on Aidan's leg, staring up at him mournfully. His nephew leaned down, and with great effort, pulled the gangly puppy into his lap. Laddie licked his face, happy to be acknowledged at last. With a gasping sob, Aidan embraced Laddie, burying his face in the dog's furry neck, his shoulders heaving. Garrett quietly closed the door, his heart squeezing with compassion. *Not all is lost. Thank God.* It would be a long road to travel, but Aidan had the right of it; he must do most of it alone. He climbed into the carriage and banged on the ceiling. Now to go to Abbie and lay his heart and soul bare.

She greeted him at the door, still looking weary, but beautiful despite it. "Ask your coachman to come in and join Samuel in the kitchen."

"Jacob, climb down, lad, and come here," Garrett said.

The young man tethered the reins to the post, then stood before Garrett. "Mrs. Hughes will show you to the kitchen." He slipped several shillings into Jacob's hand. "Go with Samuel and enjoy a hearty breakfast at the George Inn, then join Jonas Eaton in room three until I come for you. Relax in front of the fire. Read a book. Order an ale—only one mind—and a lunch. If there is not enough coin here, have the innkeeper add any charges to my bill. I wish for privacy with Mrs. Hughes. Understand?"

Jacob touched his forelock. "Thank you, Mr. Garrett. Leave the carriage here, or take it to the inn?"

"Take it to the inn."

Abbie arched an eyebrow at him, but turned and explained to Jacob how to find the kitchen. Would not be difficult, considering how small the place is. Once Garrett heard the carriage depart, he followed her to the parlor. Abbie silently assisted him in removing his greatcoat.

"You have a beard," she murmured softly. "I didn't have a chance to mention it yesterday."

Garrett scratched his chin. "The beginnings of one. Do you like it?"

"It becomes you."

They sat on her settee, at opposite ends. The awkwardness between them was plain, despite his declarations of love yesterday and her asking him to stay and hold her. Abbie sat ramrod straight, her hands tightly clasped on her lap. As if she was steeling herself for disappointment. Garrett would do everything in his power to ensure that did not happen.

"I love you, Abigail Wharton Hughes. From nearly the first moment that we met all those years past. It has been intense, agonizing, haunting, and heartbreaking." He slid a little closer and, in taking her hand, laced his fingers through hers. "And I would not change or alter it but for one thing: I should have told you all this during our summer of love. It is a tragic regret I will carry the rest of my life. A youthful mistake of epic proportions. Yet the one I made while lying in my sick bed nearly equals it." He kissed her hand and released it. "I was out of my head with fever, and having horrible nightmares of a large wolf hunting me, eager to rip my throat. I came to realize the wolf represented the curse. It is why I yelled at you, I imagine. I was trying to protect you from the wolf. The curse. After my proclamation of doing my upmost to place the curse behind me, it must have been a slice to your heart."

Tears welled in her eyes as she nodded. "And then I departed. Again, I did not stay and fight. For all my brave talk, it turns out I'm a coward after all."

"Perhaps it is best you returned here, for you needed time to think, as did I. A coward? No. Not in my eyes. Not ever. You came to Kent to face me. You stayed at my side when I was shot, and kept me alive through sheer courage...and love. Unfortunately, my injury has hampered me from 'riding in and claiming you,' but I am here, nonetheless, missing you terribly. Loving you desperately. Anxious and eager for us to share the rest of our lives."

At his heartfelt confession, her look softened. Encouraged, Garrett moved closer to her on the settee. "As for the blasted curse, Riordan revealed a shocking revelation. Papers he found in the attic, a way for the curse to be broken. I found as he explained that I did not care how it could be broken, not anymore. All that mattered—was you. What Riordan said is true. 'Love means taking a chance.' I want to take that chance with you."

Abbie's lower lip quivered. "And when the next crisis arises, will you withdraw and push me away? For my heart cannot take it. I do not know if I am able to...to..." She sighed, her hand waving in frustration, as if she searched for the right words.

"May I finish for you?" he asked, remembering her request that he not interrupt her, for he respected Abbie far too much to do it again.

She nodded.

"Trust me?" he supplied.

"Yes, that's it."

"Without trust, how can there be love? But I firmly believe we can build the trust between us. Sage advice from my father: trust is something you build together with open communication. Forego blaming the other. Share your feelings. Be a reliable and steady presence." He cupped her cheeks. "Please, allow me to prove my worth. To prove to you I am worthy of your love *and* your trust." With the tips of his fingers, Garrett caressed her flushed cheeks. "You are the air that I breathe, the marrow of my bones.

My very heart and soul." His voice shook as his eyes burned. "Forgive the stubborn man, the foolish boy, and love me. Please."

A ragged sob escaped her throat as a tear trickled down her cheek. Abbie embraced him tight, careful of his sling. He nuzzled her neck, allowing her alluring wildflower scent to fill his senses. "I will court you as you wish, do whatever it takes for you to trust me. And love me."

"I already love you, stubborn and foolish as you were—and are. The trust will come, I know it. It has already started. No more blame. No more recriminations of the past. We will look to the future." She kissed him hungrily, and he returned it as the heat sizzled between them as it always had. Abbie ended the kiss slowly, then gazed at him, the love shimmering in her beautiful brown eyes. "I love you, Garrett Wollstonecraft. My Scottish warrior. My dearest heart. Let us not be parted again. Ever."

"Not ever," he whispered.

And he meant it. His heart beat at a furious pace. He was alive. He was loved. Never again would he take any of it for granted.

Epilogue

Scotland
April 1845

Since Garrett and Abbie's reconciliation in February, he had indeed courted her. He stayed in Standon with Abbie for three weeks. After the first week, he'd sent Jonas, Jacob, and Samuel home in the carriage and instructed Samuel to return with more clothes and other items. He'd brought her flowers and chocolate when he could procure them, and took her on carriage drives and shopping expeditions to the nearby town of Stevenage.

He'd kept his room at the inn for propriety's sake, but on the nights Megan was away at school he was in Abbie's bed. No doubt his attentions on Mrs. Hughes had been noted and speculated about by the villagers, but Garrett was beyond caring what others thought.

He had tried to see Aidan during his three-week stay in Standon, but his nephew had refused, though Dr. Bevan had kept him up-to-date on his progress. The gossip about Aidan made the rounds in London, and when his father and grandfather returned to parliament at the end of February, they'd refused to comment on it. All that it appeared to do was enhance Aidan's reputation as a notorious rake. Many young ladies were anxious to make his acquaintance in hopes that they would be the one woman to tame him. His absence from London had fanned the excited flames of speculation.

March arrived, and Garrett, Abbie, and Megan made the trip from Standon to Wollstonecraft Hall. Megan was officially removed from school with the agreement that a tutor would be hired once they had completed their journey to Scotland. Abbie and Megan had stayed at the hall. Garrett decided to hell with proprieties for once and all. Late at night, he and Abbie met at the hunter's hut, loving each other with a fierceness that never ceased to surprise him. An upcoming marriage had been implied, expected, but no solid plans were put in place. Abbie and Garrett were enjoying getting to know one another. Building the trust. Deepening the love.

Since the end of March, Abbie, Garrett, Megan, and of course, Laddie, had been traveling in Scotland. Upon their arrival, Garrett had met with his grandfather's barrister and been told that he'd not only been willed the house outside of Edinburgh, but a share in the Mackinnon liquor business along with a generous settlement.

Then came the burial, a sad and solemn occasion, and many of his grandfather's friends and neighbors gave tribute to an honorable man. Alec Mackinnon had been buried next to his beloved wife, and Garrett was touched his mother's name, Moira, had been etched in remembrance on the tombstone even though she was laid to rest in the cemetery at Wollstonecraft Hall.

They had decided to stay at his grandfather's house instead of at an inn, and Abbie suggested that he use it for yearly summer sojourns. He could not think of a better solution. Garrett would keep on his grandfather's small but loyal staff to handle the maintenance. One night, over a hearty dinner, Megan had suggested the house be rented to people for short stays, with the proceeds going to his 'physicians training to treat addiction cause'. His grandfather's housekeeper had agreed wholeheartedly.

With the last week of April drawing near, they'd reluctantly decided to end their trip to Scotland with promises of returning late in the summer. As the carriage headed south, Garrett gazed out the window at the turbulent sky above. Abbie was curled up next to him, reading, and Megan sat opposite, also reading, with Laddie curled up next to her. Laddie was hardly a puppy any longer, but fit into their little family as if he had always belonged there.

Garrett clenched his fist, grateful that his arm had healed fully, and for the fact he had not lost any mobility. In the interim, he and Dr. Bastian Faraday had become good friends. They had visited him on the way to Scotland, and would again on the way home. Abbie especially had grown fond of Bastian, grateful not only for his intervention in Garrett's treatment, but for his good-natured personality, innate intelligence, and gentle humor.

The carriage pulled up in front of a small inn. "Where are we?" Abbie asked while yawning.

"Gretna Green. We will stop for a meal, and allow the horses and Samuel to rest. As well as ourselves. We should stretch our legs," Garrett replied.

Once they entered the inn, the man behind the counter called out, "Are ye here for a weddin'? For ye are a lad and lassie in love, I'll be bound. 'Tis plain. The smithy next door 'tis the best place for a genuine anvil weddin'." The ruddy-faced man smiled broadly.

Garrett faced Abbie, taking her hand and kissing it. "Marry me, my love?"

Her eyes widened. "Here, in Scotland? Can we? Should we?"

He kissed her hand again, then caught her gaze, giving her a smoldering look. "Absolutely."

Megan clasped her hands together excitedly. "Oh, yes, Mama. How romantic!"

Abbie laughed. "Then yes, I will marry you."

They hurried next door to the blacksmith shop. A wedding was just concluding. As the young couple left the building, the smithy waved them forward. How impulsive to marry like this, but it stayed within the parameters of their turbulent and passionate relationship.

After introductions, the brawny smithy, Mr. Campbell, nodded with approval. "So ye wish ta wed? We need two witnesses."

"Our daughter, Megan, will act as one. My coachman and assistant groom will serve as well," Garrett replied. "Megan, be a dear and fetch Samuel." Laddie woofed, making his presence known. "And unofficially, Laddie will act as one."

As Megan hurried away, Mr. Campbell's heavy eyebrows raised at the "our daughter" statement, but wisely let it pass. "A Scotch collie is always welcome at any of my weddin's. Do ye have a ring?" Garrett shook his head. "Ye can purchase one here." He slapped a wooden box on the table and opened it. There were a number of plain gold bands along with more antiquated designs.

"Oh, I like this one," Abbie said, pointing to a gold ring fashioned into a key unlocking a heart.

"'Tis a luverly choice. Made of the finest gold. Now, stand before the anvil. Ah, here be the witnesses." Mr. Campbell fussily arranged them in a semi-circle. "'Tis too bloody bad the heather 'tisn't bloomin' as yet, begging yer pardon, ladies." Mr. Campbell blushed at his curse. "But these posies 'twill do." Mr. Campbell handed Abbie a bouquet of bluebells and white wood anemones, early spring wildflowers they had seen in abundance during their travels. Abbie's eyes twinkled with amusement. "There now. Are ye unmarried persons?" Mr. Campbell asked, his tone serious.

"Yes," they answered simultaneously.

"Do ye take this man to be yer husband?" Mr. Campbell intoned.

Abbie's gaze softened. "I do. Most happily."

"Do ye take this woman to be yer wife?"

"I do. Most gratefully."

"I like ye both." Mr. Campbell beamed. "Now place the ring on her finger."

As Garrett did, Mr. Campbell picked up a length of gold ribbon and loosely tied it about their wrists. "I hereby declare ye are married and joined in God. 'Twill be twenty-two pounds all total. For the ring, posies, and certificate."

Garrett and Abbie laughed. "Well worth it, my good man. And the certificate?" Garrett asked.

"'Twill be drawn up directly. Ye can fetch it after ye consummate the marriage, begging yer pardon, young lassie," he bowed slightly at Megan who smiled in response.

"We will be taking a meal at the inn, then will obtain the certificate before we continue on our journey. I imagine we will be about an hour," Garrett replied.

Mr. Campbell frowned. "Ye shouldn't remove the ribbon 'til the union 'tis consummated, as it 'twill bring a curse upon ye…"

Garrett and Abbie groaned as Megan giggled.

Kissing Abbie's hand, Garrett stated, "I no longer hold much weight in curses. I only believe in never-ending love. But rest assured we will follow your suggestion as best as we are able." Garrett managed to reach in his pocket and pull out a small roll of pound notes. "Keep the change, my good man." He turned to Abbie and said softly, "We are married, my love." He kissed her deeply as Megan and Samuel applauded and Laddie woofed happily.

For most of the journey, they had kept the ribbon on except when taking a meal or using the necessary. Once checked into their room at the inn, it was difficult to remove their clothing with their wrists bound. They managed it, laughing as they did. Garrett and Abbie tumbled to the bed, and he raised their joined wrists above their heads as he thrust into her. Abbie moaned, clutching his rear with her free hand. "Stay inside me. No more American rubber contraptions or withdrawal. I want to feel all of you."

"I will make proper, languorous love to you later, but for now, I need this." Garrett pumped in and out of her, moving faster as his passion built. The crescendo hit them both at nearly the same instant. Married. Abbie was truly his. Forever. Breathing hard, he removed the ribbon and pulled her into his arms. "It may not have been a society wedding, but I would not change it for the world."

Abbie lay across his chest, and playfully nibbled on his lower lip. "Neither would I." She then gazed into his eyes. "I love the way that you are looking at me. You had the exact expression on your face years ago, the one evening we'd met in the shed."

"In what way?" Garrett asked, kissing the tip of her nose.

"As if there was no one in the entire world but the two of us. It was as if you wanted nothing else but to possess me." Abbie paused, and sadness glittered in her eyes. "You savored the love and desire, then, the look was gone. As if you had placed the emotions in a dusty attic. To be forgotten."

"It is true what you say. For a brief moment, I knew that it was love. Then I immediately dismissed it and refused to acknowledge it. And we have suffered for it ever since."

"We will suffer no more, my dearest," Abbie whispered. They kissed, and when they broke apart, Abbie curled up in his arms.

After many minutes passed, Garrett said, "I believe we will have a proper winter wedding. Remember? The one you'd spoke of all those years ago. The one you longed for."

"Oh, I do remember. How surprising to find you recall it."

"I recall everything that you've ever said to me." Garrett caressed her arm as he spoke. "Every kiss. Every touch. Every time we joined as one." Abbie's eyes glistened with emotion at his words. "A small ceremony at Wollstonecraft Hall, you wearing a white cape with silk snowflakes..." Abbie kissed him fiercely. Already he was becoming aroused again. It would be a long, passionate night.

Abbie ended the kiss, then held up the gold ribbon. "At least we will manage to keep the curse from our door." He smiled in response. "Speaking of curses, I meant to ask, what did Riordan discover about breaking the Wollstonecraft curse?"

"When he was a young lad, he'd discovered ancient papers belonging to the sixteenth century Earl of Carnstone. The man sought out a Scottish sorceress and begged her to break the curse. Her response was that it could only be broken when all the men living formed a love bond within a lunar year, any twelve-month period, I imagine."

"How fascinating. So, you and Riordan have found love, and if your father and brother accept their growing feelings toward Alberta and Mary Tuttle, that would leave..."

"Aidan."

Both remained quiet for several moments, lost in their thoughts.

"I believe Cristyn Bevan has feelings for Aidan," Abbie stated.

"Truly? What makes you believe that?"

"I've observed their interactions, before leaving Standon in January, and again recently." Abbie played with his chest hair, twirling it about the tip of her finger as she spoke. "I've never seen Cristyn give such focused attention to any other patient before. But it was more the way she spoke to him, gazed longingly at him. It's hard to describe. I thought when I first met Bastian that Cristyn would be a good match for him, considering their mutual interest in the medical field." She shrugged. "Fate has other plans, for I caught Aidan staring at Cristyn with a stark yearning. Perhaps nothing will come of it."

Fascinating. Could Aidan find it deep within himself to forego his vices and disreputable past and accept love? It remained to be seen.

However, his and Abbie's story was not over, nor was it for the rest of the men of Wollstonecraft Hall. Garrett had his soul mate, the lady of his heart. Hell, he always had her, though he'd stupidly denied it for years. All because of the curse. Well, curse be damned.

Now if only the remaining men of his family could embrace love. As he pulled Abbie closer, he silently wished for all of them to find love and discover true happiness.

If anyone deserved and needed to be loved, it was Aidan.

Author's Note

Obviously the Wollstonecraft men are fictitious, but the progressive causes they supported were not. The 1840s were the beginning of many changes for the decades that followed: reforms to improve the quality of life for all, especially for women, children, and the poor.

As for addiction, it was the generally accepted opinion during the Victorian era that it was merely a bad habit or a moral flaw, not a disease. Treatment was nonexistent, and since drugs like opium were legal, not considered a crime. The treatment that I describe in this story did not come into use until the early twentieth century, after World War I.

In Great Britain, it wasn't until the Pharmacy Act of 1868 that it was finally acknowledged that these drugs were dangerous and needed to be dispensed by qualified pharmacists and druggists. Opium addiction, and deaths therefrom, declined immediately, but it wasn't until the Rolleston Act of 1926 that the dispensing of opium and its derivates was placed in the hands of medical doctors.

Meet the Author

Karyn Gerrard, born and raised in the Maritime Provinces of Eastern Canada, now makes her home in a small town in Northwestern Ontario. When she's not cheering on the Red Sox or travelling in the summer with her teacher husband, she writes, reads romance, and drinks copious amounts of Earl Grey tea.

Even at a young age, Karyn's storytelling skills were apparent, thrilling her fellow Girl Guides with off-the-cuff horror stories around the campfire. A multi-published author, she loves to write sensual historicals and contemporaries. Tortured heroes are an absolute must.

As long as she can avoid being hit by a runaway moose in her wilderness paradise, she assumes everything is golden. Karyn's been happily married for a long time to her own hero. His encouragement and loving support keeps her moving forward.

To learn more about Karyn and her books, visit www.karyngerrard.com.